# Christmas time and *juletid*

## Traditions from the United States and Norway with songs, food, decorations, and stories for the season

Written and edited by
Christine Anderson
Theresa Appelö Bakken
Noel Wannebo Bruzzichesi

Illustrations by
Rosemary Antel

Music by
Paul Allen and Darrel Eide

Leikarringen of Leif Erikson Lodge No. 1
Sons of Norway
1997
Seattle, Washington

Published in the United States
by Leikarringen of Leif Erikson Lodge No. 1
2245 NW 57th
Seattle WA 98107

This book is intended to be an informational resource and should be used as a general guide and not an ultimate
source of Norwegian or American cookery, music, or folk culture. Every effort has been made to make this book as
factual as possible. The editors, illustrators, musicians, and publishers have neither responsibility nor liability to any
person or entity with respect to any loss or damage caused, or alleged to be caused, directly or indirectly by the
information in this book. Any person not wishing to be bound by the above may return this book to the publisher for
a full refund.

Library of Congress Catalog Card Number: 97-092750

ISBN 0-9661699-0-5

First edition

# Table of Contents

# Foreword / *Forord*

## *Leikarringen of Leif Erikson Lodge No. 1*

*Leikarringen of Leif Erikson Lodge No. 1* is sponsored by Leif Erikson Lodge No. 1, Sons of Norway. The purpose of our group is to learn and perform the song dances and folk dances of Norway. It is composed primarily of Norwegian and Scandinavian descendants. We are the only Nordic dance group in the Seattle area specializing in the traditional songs and dances of Norway.

*Leikarringen of Leif Erikson Lodge No. 1* had its first meeting on August 31, 1959, at the home of Lila Granaas. It was her birthday and to celebrate she invited other Norwegian immigrants including Mary Viken. Mary, our founder, wanted to start a group for performing Norwegian dances in the Seattle community. Our group was officially chartered on February 19, 1960. Over the years *Leikarringen* has had its ups and downs and ins and outs.

The idea for this book came many years ago when *Leikarringen* visited Norse Home, a retirement and nursing care facility in Seattle, for our annual singing of Christmas carols. We carried around many songs in a disorganized fashion. We were constantly shuffling papers: Was it on the green set, in the small book, or the one with the picture? We were never known as the best singers, but we always had a lot of fun singing until the residents finally decided they would rather see us perform Norwegian folkdancing. They wanted us to leave the Christmas caroling to the better trained choral groups.

Oh well! We had all this information and there still wasn't a book out there with all of our favorite tunes from the United States and Norway. We thought why not put together a book with our favorite stories, decorations, songs, and recipes to help celebrate the holidays of the Norwegian-American in the Pacific Northwest. Now, almost ten years later, here it is.

## Thank yous

We thank the Sons of Norway Foundation for providing the original grant money allowing us to buy software programs for the music portion of this book. Many people have kindly lent us information and books to help us succeed in this venture. They are Marian Berg, Jan Alfred Andersson (a visiting folkdancer from Norway who danced with our group for two years), Jody Haug, Pastor Wesley Howell, Jane Mjolnes, Linda Finney, Daniel Griffin, Carol Ollestad, Bergljot Ringset Roswick, Sissel Feroy, Debbie Mazur, Pastor Maynard Atik, Thomas Stang, Julie Svendsen Schmidt, Alf Knudsen, Jan Olav Langseth, Ed Egerdahl and the Scandinavian Language Institute, Ballard First Lutheran Church, Our Redeemer's Lutheran Church, Norwegian Information Service, Royal Norwegian Consulate General, Seattle Public Library, Margaret Anderson and the Leif Erikson Lodge Library, and the University of Washington Libraries. Marshall Nelson assisted us with copyright information. Jill-Michelle Cosart, Arne Thogersen, and Ed Egerdahl helped identify the suitable words in English and Norwegian for how to play the music. Thanks to Pastor Dennis Andersen, who was able to identify the English versions of some Norwegian songs. We also thank the Lutheran Brotherhood for kindly donating the *Carols and Hymns for Christmas* for our use during the years prior to publication of this book.

A very special thanks goes to our contact in Norway, Terryanne Baker Reinert, who supplied us with favorite Norwegian songs and Norwegian versions to popular American songs. Leif Dramstad of Norsk Musikforlag A/S in Norway also provided help and information about the Norwegian artists and their music.

Paul Allen, organist from Our Redeemer's Lutheran Church and now at Bothell United Methodist Church, reviewed the music before publishing and wrote harmonizations. Darrel Eide spent his summer also writing harmonizations for some pieces. Valerie Shields, organist for Phinney Ridge Lutheran Church; Sherry Bruce, the choir director for Our Redeemer's Lutheran Church; and Rosemary Antel have all assisted in selecting appropriate harmonizations, made suggestions to improve the contents, and reviewed the music. Trygve Bakken spent hours and hours inputting the data into our music program. Larry Reinert assisted in the computer data entry of the music in its early stages.

Many thanks to our ancestors and families for keeping these traditions alive and giving us the freedom to start new ones. It would be interesting to see if the Christmas season will change radically in the next several hundred years or if the traditions will continue as many of them have now for thousands of years.

To my co-editors, Noel Wannebo Bruzzichesi and Theresa Appelö Bakken, thank you for being such great friends and working on this book with me. Noel did the interviewing for the personal stories found throughout the book, collected recipes, and tested recipes. Theresa checked factoids, summarized information, tested recipes, filled in on any aspects for the book she could, and provided moral support throughout all the work. Rosemary Antel illustrated the book in between her own art projects. Stop in and see her watercolor flowers when you have time.

*Med hjertelig tusen takk*, with a hearty thousand thanks, to my parents Donald and Elaine Anderson for their continuous support of this project and many more.

To *Leikarringen*, thanks for working on all those pancake breakfasts to get the book published!

*Christine Anderson*, editor

# Acknowledgments

This book would not be possible without the permission of the authors, composers, publishers, and copyright owners of the songs and stories included in this volume. It has taken years to find information about many of the pieces used and every effort was made to trace copyright owners. Thank you to the following people for their time, patience, and permission:

Karen Merrick at Augsburg Fortress in Minnesota
Arve Brunvoll in Norway
Per Hognestad in Norway
Per Lønning, Bishop of Bergen, Norway
Jan Olav Lohne at Concordia Noteforlag in Oslo, Norway
Pamela Burgdorf at Concordia Publishing House in Missouri
First United Methodist Church in Seattle, Washington
Anne Lømo at Gyldendal in Oslo, Norway
Zoraya Mendez at G. Schirmer and Music Sales Corporation in New York
Mona-Lisa Ahlstrand at Gehrmans Musikförlag in Sweden
Anniken Lange at H. Aschehoug & Co. in Norway
A. Damsgaard and Unni Boretti at Musikk-Husets Forlag A/S in Norway
Don Parker-Burgard at the National Council of the Churches of Christ in the USA
       in New York
Janet Rasmussen, author of *New lands, new lives: Scandinavian immigrants to the Pacific
       Northwest*
Ragnar Grøm at Norges Kirkesangforbund in Norway
Leif A. Dramstad at Norsk Musikforlag A/S
Lloyd Hustvedt at the Norwegian-American Historical Association in Minnesota
Brian Hill at Oxford University Press in New York
Michael Marks at St. Nicholas Music Inc. in New York
Aaron VanderWeele at The Salvation Army in New York
Michael Sevig at Scandisk Music in Minnesota
Liv Dahl at the Sons of Norway in Minnesota
David C. Olsen at Warner Bros. Publications U. S. Inc. in Florida
Odd Steenburg at Warner/Chappell Music Norway A/S in Oslo, Norway

If any rights have been overlooked or unintentionally infringed, *Leikarringen of Leif Erikson Lodge No. 1* requests that these be pointed out so that due acknowledgment may be made and corrected in subsequent printings.

## Donations

We thank the following individuals and organizations for their significant monetary donations in the publication of *Christmas time and juletid*:

Cascade Lodge No. 87, Sons of Norway
Don Anderson Company
Leif Erikson Lodge No. 1, Sons of Norway
Leikarringen of Leif Erikson Lodge No. 1 Pancake Breakfasts
Sons of Norway Foundation
The Nordic Heritage Museum
The Norwegian Ladies Chorus
Anonymous

# A little about Christmas time and *juletid*

The word Christmas comes from Christ mass or a festival mass in the Christian church celebrating the birth of Christ. Christmas time or *juletid* are the days before and after December 25. Some time in the fourth century this date was picked to be the birthday of Jesus Christ. While the exact date of Christ's birth is not known, this time of year had many non-Christian winter celebrations representing the coming of the light into the world in the northern hemisphere and that light also represented Christ's coming into the world. As pagan and Christian rites intermingled and cultures joined together, traditions were adapted through the centuries, making each generation's celebrations unique. While some traditions may remain unchanged through time, it is now difficult to separate the various traditions from their origins.

*Jul* has come to mean Christmas in Norway. The actual origin of the word is subject to debate. It may be from an old Norse word *hjul* meaning wheel. In pagan times, anything with wheels, such as a wagon or a spinning wheel, was given a rest during this time of the year. To let a wheel turn against the sun, which was considered holy, was a sacrilege. It meant whoever turned the wheel wanted the sun "wheel" to move faster and cause the light to go away.

It may also be named after the head of all the gods, *Jolnir* known as Odin in Norse mythology. He was the god of the dead, who died in battle, and the ruler of the home of dead, called *Valhall*. This palace was located in *Åsgard*, home of the gods. Each year a sacrificial feast was held to honor these dead and appease any restless spirits, wandering the earth, who were believed to come back to haunt the living at the time of the winter solstice.

The Viking *jól* was also celebrated with great feasts throughout northern Europe during the winter solstice to promote the fertility of the land, ensure plentiful harvests, and increase fertility in man and animals. Odin, according to mythology, gave intoxicating drink to humanity. *Jól* was a time to sacrifice to Odin by drinking his gift since it was a product of the land and harvest. It is possible these feasts were brought together, as the winter solstice marked both the end of the dark time that signified death and the return of the sun with the new light signifying fertility and a new beginning.

The first recorded Christmas celebration in the United States was in 1608 in the colony of Jamestown, Virginia. Captain John Smith wrote in his journal, *"... the extreame wind, raine, frost, and snowe, caused us to keepe Christmas amongst the Salvages, where wee were never more merrie, nor fedde on more plentie of good oysters, fish, flesh, wild foule and good bread nor never had better fires in England then in the drie warme smokie houses of Kecoughtan."* [1]

---

[1]Kecoughtan was a hunting town near the mouth of the James River and south of Jamestown. From: *The Complete works of Captain John Smith (1580–1631)*, Edited by Philip L. Barbour. Chapel Hill, NC: The Institute of Early American History and Culture, Williamsburg, Virginia, by The University of North Carolina Press, 1986. Vol. 1, page 245.

There are many cultures influencing Christmas customs and traditions in the United States. In this book, we highlight Norwegian traditions and the traditions of the Pacific Northwest as represented by some of the 3.5 million people in the United States who claim Norwegian ancestry and have woven other ethnic backgrounds into their celebrations.

Since where and how the traditions included here have been lost through the centuries, perhaps, by reading this book, you will begin or reestablish new traditions. We hope you enjoy using it as much as we enjoyed putting it together. You too can start a tradition of, "It wouldn't be Christmas time without ..."

# Christmas words in English and *Norsk*

American words and Norwegian words may be used interchangeably throughout the book. Included here is a helpful list of words.

| *Norsk* | **American** |
| --- | --- |
| *annen juledag* | day after Christmas, December 26 |
| *gledelig jul* | Merry Christmas |
| *god jul* | Merry Christmas |
| *granbar* | spruce |
| *holde jul* | keep Christmas |
| *julaften* | Christmas Eve, December 24 |
| *julebakst* | Christmas baking |
| *juleblomster* | Christmas flowers |
| *julebord* | Christmas table |
| *julebrennevin* | liquor bought or made for Christmas |
| *julebukker* | Christmas billygoats, but now refers to a group of people who wear masks and costumes going door to door from December 27–31. |
| *juledag* | Christmas Day, December 25 |
| *juleevangelium* | Christmas gospel |
| *juleferie* | Christmas holidays or vacation |
| *julegater* | Christmas streets |
| *julegaver* | Christmas presents |
| *julegleden* | Christmas begonia |
| *julegris* | pig fattened especially for the Christmas holidays |
| *julegrøt* | rich Christmas pudding usually eaten Christmas eve |
| *julehelgen* | The Christmas season |
| *julekake* | Christmas bread with various dried and candied fruits |
| *julekaktus* | Christmas cactus |
| *julekort* | Christmas card |
| *julekurver* | Christmas baskets in a heart shape |
| *julekveld* | Christmas Eve, December 24 |
| *julelys* | Christmas candle |
| *julemat* | Christmas food |
| *julemerke* | Christmas seal |
| *julemiddag* | Christmas dinner |
| *julenatt* | night before Christmas |
| *julenek* | sheaf of grain for the birds on a pole or the peak of a roof |
| *julenisse* | Christmas elf |
| *juleøl* | Christmas beer or ale |

| Norsk | American |
|---|---|
| julepresang | Christmas present |
| julesang | Christmas song |
| julesanger | Christmas carols |
| julestemning | Christmas spirit or cheer |
| julestjerne | Christmas star |
| julestjernen | the poinsettia |
| julestri | preparation before Christmas |
| juletid | Christmas time |
| juletre | Christmas tree |
| juletrefest | after Christmas celebration |
| juletrelys | Christmas tree light or candle |
| juletrepynt | Christmas tree decorations |
| juleved | wood chopped especially for Christmas |
| juleveke | Christmas week |
| kongerøkelse | incense of kings |
| lille julaften | Little Christmas Eve, December 23 |
| småkaker | cookies |
| svibel | hyacinth |
| trettendagen | Epiphany, Twelfth Day, January 6 |
| tulipaner | tulips |

# The calendar stick / *Primstaven*

Society was once governed more by the seasons and weather signs when determining the best time to plant, harvest, fish, or prepare for special days such as Christmas. Today we may not realize it, but some of the days are still observed even though we no longer know the special name of the day or what it represents. By September we begin complaining about how early the Christmas decorations are in stores, but long ago preparations for the holidays began early in the fall, too.

Centuries ago, instead of having a calendar or almanac produced on expensive parchment made from the skin of a sheep or goat, people in Norway counted the days on a wooden calendar stick called a *primstav*. The name may come from the Latin word *Prima*, short for *Primatio Lunae* or new moon. This long, flat stick or board had a notch cut for each day of the year with special carvings or marks representing the holidays. These carvings tell a story and a picture was worth a thousand words even then. During the Middle Ages it became essential to have readily identifiable pictorial information for counting the days because life began to revolve around important feast days, *ting* meetings and fairs, in addition to the everyday farming duties of planting and harvesting. When Christianity came to Norway in the 900s, 37 additional holidays were to be observed. Strict penalties and fines were imposed for not observing a Catholic Mass day.

A *primstav* is carved on both sides. One side represents summer and starts on April 14. The other side represents winter, starting on October 14. Beginning with the summer side, the symbols on the stick show when to start winter preparations in the late summer months. The oral tradition or interpretation behind each symbol varied from the northern to the southern parts of Norway because the weather and climate varied between the different districts. The west coast was governed by its fishing and boating traditions while the eastern districts were governed by the planting and harvesting of crops. Some districts even had their own saints. *Red letter* days of the calendar were painted red as they marked an important saint's day or other commemorative day when the church used red as the color during a service. These symbols are noted in the description of the significant days leading up to, through, and at the end of the Christmas season.

**September 14**

*Krossmesse om høsten* or Holy Cross Day in the Fall is a red letter day in the church even today. It represents the Holy Cross being discovered between AD 325 and 347 and the dedication of the basilica at the site of the Holy Sepulcher near Jerusalem. The Holy Cross was erected again on this day in Jerusalem in AD 628 after being recaptured from the Persians. In Norway any grains planted were harvested by this date and fences were removed so livestock could roam freely. The summer farm in the mountains was left behind as autumn began. School sessions have started throughout the United States. The symbol is a large cross.

## September 21

*Mattismesse om høsten* or Saint Matthew's Mass in the Fall commemorates the Evangelist Matthew, who was a tax collector before following Jesus. It is also a red letter day. Cutting and gathering leafy twigs for winter fodder were part of the day's activities. Any corn ripening after this day was not fit for humans and was left for the animals. The symbol is an ear of corn.

## September 29

*Mikkelsmesse* or Michaelmas is in memory of Saint Michael the Archangel's victory over the devil. It is considered one of the great feast days and has been celebrated since the first century. Because leaves start falling now, it is also known as Leafshaking Day. It was the last dry weather for harvesting any food crops to be used during the winter. Hunting season for some animals started just as it does today. All the cows, sheep, and goats were brought home from the mountains because snow was expected. Northerly winds arriving on this day meant good luck. The symbol may be a scale representing Saint Michael seeing the souls being weighed in Heaven or a *lyster* (leister), a fishing spear with three barbed prongs.

## October 14

*Vinterdagen* or Winter Day was the beginning of winter in Norway and thus it was the first day on the winter side of the *primstav*. It is also a day commemorating Pope Calixtus, or Saint Callistus, a former slave who was martyred around AD 222 after being Pope of the Church of Rome in the years AD 217 to 222. Nice weather meant a good winter. Horses were decorated with sleigh bells. The slaughtering month started and in the very old days the winter sacrificing. Farmers in the Midwestern States start their winter preparations with the slaughtering of sheep. In the Pacific Northwest, the hunting season for geese begins. The symbol is a glove or mitten showing winter clothes need to be taken out and repaired.

## October 21

*Jomfrudagen* or Virgin Day is in commemoration of Saint Ursula, a British princess. She escaped from Britain to avoid the invading Saxons only to be massacred by the Huns, with 11 virgin handmaidens near Cologne in the third or fourth century AD. As time went by, the story was embellished to 11,000 maidens. In Norway boats were laid up for winter. The symbol is a ship on land.

## October 28

*Simonsmesse* or Saint Simon's Day is a red letter day in memory of the Apostle Simon, the patron saint of curriers and pit sawyers, and Saint Jude, the patron saint of desperate cases. Both saints lived during the first century and traveled to Persia where they were martyred. The first snowfall was expected, along with the first traditional sleigh ride. Newlyweds in West Norway went from farm to farm gathering food, grain, wool, and other necessities from neighbors. The threshing started on this day so the symbol is a flail. A flail has a long wooden handle with a shorter, free-swinging stick attached to its end to beat the grain away from the plant.

## November 1

*Allehelgensdag* or *helgemesse* is All Saints' Day or Hallowmas. It is a day commemorating all the saints and martyrs who have died over the centuries. Celebrated in the Eastern Orthodox Church since the first century and in the Roman Catholic Church since the ninth century, it is now a day to also remember friends and relatives who passed on during the previous year. In the United States it is the day after Halloween or All Hallow's Eve celebrated on October 31 when the spirits of the dead are said to wander the earth. Now children dress in costumes and go door to door "trick or treating." In Norway a flood could be expected, but if it did not arrive, winter would be delayed and the flood wouldn't come until the spring. The symbol is a church building, sometimes carved as a ship.

## November 11

*Mortensdag* or *Mortensmesse* is known as Saint Martin's Mass or Martinmas. Saint Martin was born of pagan parents around AD 316 and became Bishop of Tours, France, around AD 371. He died in AD 397. When church dignitaries came to make him the Bishop, he tried to hide in the goose pen as he was very shy. The geese betrayed him by honking loudly. He then had the geese killed. This may be why his sign on the *primstav* is a goose. Geese are traditionally served at mealtime and any animals not being kept through winter were slaughtered on this day, too. The breast bone of the goose served on *Mortensmesse* was used to predict the winter weather. If this bone had white speckles, it meant snow. If it had brown speckles, it would be a cold winter with little snow. The winter would be very severe if the day was clear. If it rained, it would stay wet until the New Year. This is Veterans' Day in the United States and commemorates the World War I armistice in 1918.

## November 23

*Klemetsmesse* or Saint Clement's Mass is in memory of Clement of Rome, a Bishop who died around AD 102. He is considered the seafarer's patron saint. Unfortunately, in Norway his name was interpreted as *klemme*, which means "to pinch," in Norwegian so parents started limiting gifts to their children as they believed their children would then appreciate Christmas more. The symbol is an anchor representing Saint Clement drowning with an anchor around his neck.

## November 25

*Karimesse* or *Katarinasmesse* or Saint Catherine's Day is in memory of the martyr Catherine of Alexandria. In AD 307 she was condemned to death by torture on a machine invented for the event. It had four wheels armed with points and saws that turned in opposite directions. The day is also known as *Kari med rokken* or Kari with the spinning wheel. The main event of the day was spinning wicks for Christmas candles made from local hemp or linen and, in later years, cotton. Candles were made from cow or sheep tallow, the hard fat from the slaughtered animals. If the weather was clear, the Christmas candles would be beautiful. In Telemark the day was known as *Kari vaskar* or Kari the washer because clothes, sheets, and blankets were always washed in preparation for the many guests expected at Christmas. As Catherine is the patron saint of millers, grinders, spinners, and wheelwrights, the symbol is a spinning wheel.

## November 30

*Andreasmesse* or Saint Andrew's Day is a red letter day in memory of the Apostle Andrew who lived during the first century. He was a fisherman before following Jesus so it is also known as *Anders fiskersdag* or Andrew the Fisherman's Day. As he is considered the patron saint of fishermen and fishmongers, people started their Christmas fishing on this day. The night before was known as *Andreasnatta* or Saint Andrew's night when, it was believed, young men and women dreamed of their future spouse. In western Norway it was the main day for mating sheep. Newly cut wood, sometimes from seven types of trees, was set out to dry for the next year. The wood shed was filled from floor to ceiling so the *julebukk* could not hide on the top of the pile. The symbol is an oblique cross.

## December 4

*Barbromesse* or Saint Barbara's Mass is in memory of Saint Barbara, who was tortured by non-Christians and beheaded in AD 236 by her father because of her faith. She is the patron saint of those who fear a violent death and is the protector of the dying. The spinning and knitting were started for Christmas. In those olden days under the Julian calendar, the sun went away on *Barbrodagen* and started returning on *Lussinatt*, December 13, the longest night of the year or the winter solstice. Now winter solstice occurs around December 22 because the Gregorian calendar was adopted in the 1700s. The symbol is a tower representing the palace tower where Barbara was imprisoned by her father. It is believed she added a third opening to the tower to honor the Trinity.

## December 6

*Nilsmesse* is Saint Nicholas' Mass day. He was a Bishop of Myra, an area in what is now Turkey, who died around AD 342 and was made a saint for his zeal in saving souls. Nicholas is also the patron saint of children and sailors. *Nils Skinnekar*, or Nils the Leatherman, came to repair shoes for Christmas. After December 6 it was bad luck for ships to leave the harbor. In other cultures, this is the Saint Nick or Saint Nicholas who put coal or good things in the shoes or stockings of youngsters. He is thought to be the person upon whom our present day Santa Claus is based. The symbol is a serpent biting its own tail, symbolizing the continuity of time or it may be interpreted as a bishop's crook.

## December 8

*Annadagen* or Saint Anna's Day is also called *Maria unnfangelse*, or the Conception of Mary, in memory of the Virgin Mary's mother, Anna. In some parts of Norway this was a day to wash clothes as it was believed the linen would be whiter if washed on *Maria unnfangelse*. If a woman were pregnant, now was the day to pray for a healthy child. In some areas it is called Fishing Day. The symbol is a fishing net.

## December 13

All preparations for Christmas were to be finished by December 13 as it was traditionally the beginning of the festival season. Because this day was also known as *solsnudagen* or the sun turning day, any work involving circular or rotating movement was forbidden for the next twelve days, including baking, grinding flour, spinning, and painting. It was believed on this night one could see the water in the rivers turn to wine.

During the common European winter solstice celebration of *Kalendae*, people believed the dead came back in a fury to haunt the living. Each district in Norway has a tale to tell about terrifying experiences with *julereia, Åsgårdsreia* or *oskoreia* who came as ghostly riders on horseback to unprepared households. These frightening visitors may have been ancestors returning home or even Odin upon his eight-legged horse, *Sleipner*.

*Lussi* was another one of these evil spirits and on this longest night of the year she would take revenge on any careless household. *Lussinatt* or Lussi's night, unlike the festival of *Sankta Lucia* in Sweden, was a night of terror. If a household was not prepared, she was said to tear down the chimney of the house and destroy what else she could. From this day on throughout the holidays, children were kept indoors at night to prevent them from being taken away by the spirits of the night.

To prepare for these unwanted visitors, a farmer would take a pot of tar and a brush outside as darkness fell. Then he would paint a cross over the doors and stalls of all farm buildings to ward off the evil ones. Steel was believed to have special qualities so it was put in the wall over the farm house doors and over the stalls where the animals were kept. In the United States, putting a horseshoe over the door with the tips up is still a symbol of good luck and may be based on the very old beliefs about steel.

Now the good Saint Lucy or *Sankta Lucia* is gradually becoming part of a tradition in Norway and *Lussinatt* has diminished. The legend about *Sankta Lucia* varies, but it is generally believed she was martyred in the year AD 304 because of her beliefs. When her mother was miraculously healed, Lucy became a Christian, refused to marry a pagan noble, and gave away her dowry to the poor. Because it was forbidden to be a Christian, Lucy was condemned to be burned at the stake. She was smeared with pitch, resin, and oil, but the fire wouldn't start and the flames did not burn her. She died by a dagger piercing her throat. Two hundred years later, *Lucia* was canonized by the Catholic Church. The symbol is a blazing bonfire which represents Lucy being burned at the stake and the light coming into the world again with the longer days.

As a celebration of light, it is customary for the eldest daughter in the family to portray *Sankta Lucia*. She dresses in a long white gown, representing her innocence, and tied with a red sash for her martyrdom. A crown, symbolizing a halo for holiness, is made of candles and greens to adorn her head. Early in the morning she serves saffron buns in traditional shapes with hot coffee to her parents and others in the home. A burning candle is also on the tray. The *Lucia* bride has, as attendants, maids and star boys who are usually the other children in the family.

The days and the symbols from December 21 through the January 20 are described in more detail in the following chapters.

# Advent / *Advent*

Advent is the season in the Church calendar prior to Christmas which is celebrated throughout Norway, the United States, and elsewhere in the world as a time to prepare for the birth of the Christ child. It gives us a small taste of the celebration to come. Advent is the beginning of the Church year and a time of waiting, expectation, and preparation. The word Advent comes from a Latin word *adventus,* which means arrival or coming near.

## Advent wreath / *Advent krans*

The Advent wreath traditionally is made in a circle with no beginning or end and evergreen boughs representing life and growth. This wreath is a primary part of the season in Norway and the United States.

Four blue or purple candles adorn the Advent wreath in Norway. The first candle is lit on the first Sunday in Advent and on each Sunday thereafter until the four candles are glowing, signifying the end of advent. The candles represent hope, caring, joy, and love. In the United States an additional fifth candle is placed in the center of the wreath. It is often a white candle which symbolizes the day of Jesus' birth and is lit on Christmas Eve or Christmas Day.

Variations on Advent wreaths are left to each household's imagination. Sometimes it is a ring of greens tied with four red ribbons joined at the top and hung from the ceiling. The candles are evenly spaced between each ribbon. *As drying greens pose a serious fire hazard, keep a watchful eye on the wreath when the candles are lit.* Other ideas include a wood log made with four holes drilled into the log. Be sure to place foil or a brass holder in the hole so if the candle burns down to the wood, the log will not start to burn. Crystal wreaths may be purchased to add a sparkle to the table. Wooden wreaths may be made in various shapes for an interesting Advent wreath. The candles should be at least 10" in length or longer so they will last the whole season.

Christmas is a special time for family togetherness. During these busy days a small ceremony of lighting candles in the Advent wreath, along with some songs, may add to your Christmas peace. Included here are some verses to say as you light the candles. They were written by the staff of the First United Methodist Church in Seattle and used with its permission.

When lighting the first Advent candle, the following is spoken, "Today we light the first Advent candle to proclaim the coming of the light of God into our darkness. We remember that with the coming of this light there is *hope.*"

The second Sunday in Advent represents love. As the candles are lit, the following is said, "We light again the candle of *hope* and now a second candle to proclaim the coming of the light of God into our darkness. With the coming of this light there is *love*."

The third Sunday in Advent is for caring. When lighting the candles say, "We light the candles of *hope* and *love,* plus this third candle, to proclaim the coming of the light of God into our darkness. With the coming of this light, there is *caring*."

On the final Sunday of Advent the fourth candle is lit. "Today we light three candles to symbolize *hope, love,* and *caring*. We also light the fourth candle to proclaim the coming of the light of God into our darkness. With this light there is *joy,* joy that is ours always."

# One candle we will light tonight
## *Så tenner vi ett lys i kveld / Adventslysene*

Tune: Daniel Helldén (1917-   ) (1963), harmonized by Marian Berg (1997)
Norwegian lyrics: Inger Hagerup (1905-1985) (1962)
English lyrics: Theresa Appelö Bakken (1997)

2 Two candles we will light tonight,
  two lights for hope and joy.
  They stand and shine so very bright
  for us all here to enjoy.
  Two candles we will light tonight,
  two lights for hope and joy.

3 Three candles we will light tonight,
  for caring, hope, and joy.
  They stand and shine so very bright
  for us all here to enjoy.
  Three candles we will light tonight,
  for caring, hope, and joy.

4 Four candles we will light tonight
  and let them burn down low,
  for caring, joy and hope and peace.
  But mostly for lasting peace
  upon this little round earth
  where Jesus was given birth.

2 *Så tenner vi to lys i kveld,*
  *to lys for håp og glede.*
  *De står og skinner for seg selv*
  *og oss som er til stede.*
  *Så tenner vi to lys i kveld,*
  *to lys for håp og glede.*

3 *Så tenner vi tre lys i kveld,*
  *for lengsel, håp og glede.*
  *De står og skinner for seg selv*
  *og oss som er til stede.*
  *Så tenner vi tre lys i kveld*
  *for lengsel, håp og glede.*

4 *Vi tenner fire lys i kveld*
  *og lar dem brenne ned,*
  *for lengsel, glede, håp og fred,*
  *men mest allikevel for fred*
  *på denne lille jord,*
  *hvor menneskene bor.*

# Now we light the first candle / *Nå tenner vi det første lys*

Tune: Emmy Köhler (Sweden) (1858-1925)(1898), harmonized by Paul Allen (1997)
Norwegian lyrics: Sigurd Muri (1927-   ) (1963)
English lyrics: Christine M. Anderson (1997)

1 Now we will light the first candle, all alone it must stand.
*1 Nå tenner vi det første lys, alene må det stå.*

We wait for the little child born in a faraway land.
*Vi venter på det lille barn som i en krybbe lå.*

2 Now we light the second candle,
   so we can better see.
   We wait for our God and Father,
   to send his son to be.

3 Now we will light the third candle,
   it is a holy number,
   We wait for the King of ours
   to be with us in slumber.

4 Now we will light the fourth candle,
   and the night turns to day.
   We wait now for our Savior,
   He can show us the way!

*2 Nå tenner vi det andre lys,
   da kan vi bedre se.
   Vi venter på at Gud, vår Far,
   vil gi sin sønn hit ned.*

*3 Nå tenner vi det tredje lys,
   det er et hellig tall.
   Vi venter på at Kongen vår
   Skal fødes i en stall.*

*4 Nå tenner vi det fjerde lys,
   og natten blir til dag.
   Vi venter nå på frelseren
   for alle folkeslag.*

## Advent calendar / *Advent kalender*

The Advent calendar represents the days from the first of December through the twenty-fourth of December. The calendar does not strictly follow the four Advent Sundays since the first Sunday may actually be at the end of November. In the United States, the four-day Thanksgiving holiday vacation usually precedes the first Sunday in Advent. It is an ideal time to begin preparations for the Christmas holiday.

Whether purchasing an Advent calendar with glitter and beautifully drawn pictures behind windows or making one at home, Christmas can be anticipated by children one day at a time until Christmas Eve. Under each window a different scene is found, depicting holiday preparations and festivities in Norway or the United States. Opening each day's number before children go to school or after the dinner meal is an ideal time for this special ceremony.

For a more elaborate Advent calendar than the windows, either purchase a cardboard jewelry box with 24 drawers or collect 24 small boxes. Match boxes are a good size. If using match boxes, first glue the top cover of the first match box onto the bottom of the second match box. Continue until there is a column of 12 match boxes. Repeat the process to form a second column of 12 match boxes. Then put glue on the inside of the two columns to join them together. To make the drawer pulls, glue a colorful small button, ball, or knob onto the front of each box or drawer. Each drawer or match box represents one of the 24 days from the first of December to Christmas Eve. The outside of the box is covered with construction paper, gold foil paper, silver foil paper, or other glossy papers. Decorate with stars, Christmas scenes or other drawings you like. When the drawers are completed, label them from 1 to 24. Place inside the drawers small plastic toys, candies, cookies, tree decorations, or sayings from the Christmas story.

Another idea is to make 24 small, colorful packages and hang them with ribbon on a decorated hanger. The packages may contain the same things as the boxes.

Start making a paper chain for the tree by writing a short verse each day on a piece of paper to be formed into a link. Add a link every day to the growing chain. On Christmas Eve, decorate the tree with the Advent chain. Complete directions for making chains are in the tree decorations section on page 86.

## Advent star / *Advent stjerne*

Christmas would not be complete without a shining Advent star made of paper, wood, or brass hanging in the window of every Norwegian home. As a symbol of the Star of Bethlehem showing the Wise Men the way to the Christ child, it may also be found adorning the top of the tree. In the United States the star is represented by lights put on the roof or chimney of a house, often in the shape of a star.

# Christmas cards / *Julekorter*

The first Christmas cards in the United States were sent in 1851. By 1870 this new tradition reached Norway. Postcards were used for the first Christmas cards. Christmas cards are our excuse to write to friends and relatives on an annual basis. We write to tell them how the year has gone for us, updating them on family births, deaths, weddings, divorces, vacations and whatever else has pleased or displeased us during the year.

The cards may be elaborate with gold and silver, with pictures of Mary and the Christ Child, or funny and sarcastic, depending on our holiday mood. Making cards may be something your family enjoys, but often with the holiday rush we resort to commercially printed cards. Cards with the Three Wise Men can be used until Epiphany on January 6.

During the Thanksgiving holiday weekend people start writing and sending cards. As time grows shorter, the once long and newsy card or letter becomes just a signature at the bottom of the card. Writing one Christmas letter and having it copied has gained in popularity over the years, even in Norway. Thus, one doesn't get tired of writing all the news to loved ones. With a small personal note at the end, we still know the sender remembers us fondly and the receiver has a more complete picture of our lives in the past year.

I love to keep Christmas cards for many years. To reuse beautiful cards, make them into note cards for packages. First cut the front off the card or around the saying on the inside of the card with regular scissors or use pinking shears for a more decorative edge. Cut heavy, colored construction paper slightly larger than the card to provide a colorful border. Punch two holes at the top of the card about ½" apart. Take approximately 7" of yarn, string or decorative ribbon and thread through the holes so both ends are on the front of the card. Tie a small, attractive bow on the front of the newly made card. Attach to a Christmas package or use them as Christmas cards again.

Small commercially made stamps are often used to make cards, but it is fun to carve half a raw potato or linoleum stamp into a holiday design. Stamp the design onto a nice paper, such as rice paper, or on paper you have made for your unique holiday greeting.

# Christmas food / *Julemat*

Christmas is traditionally the time of the year to serve the best food and to show off our cooking skills to family and other guests. When just about everyone lived on a farm, apples, as well as other fruits and vegetables, were harvested in the fall. They were stored in a cool basement, root cellar, storage house or *stabbur* and would still be reasonably fresh and flavorful at Christmas. Grains, also harvested in the fall, were plentiful this time of year, too.

Hospitality is as important during the holidays as it is throughout the year. It was considered a virtue and practiced by the Vikings and required by their gods. *Hávamál*, The Words of the High One, is a poem compiled in the ninth century and included in the *Elder Edda*, a collection of Icelandic poems. Odin, the High One, was known for his words of wisdom and sayings. Included in *Hávamál* is this saying, which is as important now as it was so long ago.

> *Fire is needed by the newcomer*
> *Whose knees are frozen numb;*
> *Meat and clean linen a man needs*
> *Who fared across the fells (mountains).*
>
> *Water, too, that he may wash before eating,*
> *Handcloths and a hearty welcome,*
> *Courteous words then courteous silence*
> *That he may tell his tale.*[1]

Norwegians and those of Norwegian descent continue to share the art of hospitality. Though not as elaborately prepared as in the past, the cup of coffee or tea we serve to our visitors and friends today is but a small reminder of this ancient tradition. During the Christmas season, hospitality comes to the forefront as we open our homes to share our bounty, blessings, food, and gifts with so many people, including strangers.

The ancient Norwegian tradition of a *koldtbord* or *smørgåsbord* with cold cuts, breads, and cheeses has become known in the Pacific Northwest as the buffet table. It is a favorite way to serve food at open houses during the holidays where much visiting takes place by the table or in the kitchen around all the good food.

In the Pacific Northwest, the traditions of what to eat first at the buffet table have disappeared. In Norway, one usually begins with bread, butter and herring followed by additional fish dishes, salads, and any egg dishes. Meats are then served and the meal is finished with cheeses and fruit. Of course, each time a new course is served, a new plate is taken so the flavors of the various fish and meat dishes do not mix on the plate or in one's palate.

---

[1] From the *Elder Edda: a selection*, translated from the Icelandic by Paul B. Taylor & W. H. Auden. New York: Vintage Books, 1970. Page 38.

To prepare for these holiday meals at Christmas and *jul*, sausages and head cheeses were made from the pigs slaughtered in the fall. Other meats such as lamb or mutton, game birds, and fish were dried, dressed, aged, salted, or smoked. As winter wore on into February and March, these foods become less and less plentiful so Christmas would be remembered fondly for its tasty and mouth-watering food.

Traditional menus vary according to geographical location in Norway. Cod, known in Norway as *torsk*, is dried and then soaked in lye. This fish is the infamous *lutefisk* and is generally served in the north. Dried mutton ribs called *pinnekjøtt* are cooked over birch twigs and are the traditional meal in the western portion of Norway called *Vestlandet*. In the eastern part of the country, spareribs called *ribbe* and pork sausages known as *medisterpølser* are the customary meal.

Pork, as traditional fare during Christmas, goes back to pre-Christian times when swine were sacrificed to the fertility god, Freya, during *jul*. It is believed this sacrificed pig became the main dish of the feast. Perhaps it is why a marzipan pig is usually the gift for finding the almond in the Christmas pudding. Thus, the poor pig is again sacrificed to please our own taste buds. On a Norwegian farm, a pig was selected to be the *julegris* or Christmas pig. It was fattened with the best food during its last few months of life for the Christmas or *jul* feast. All parts of this pig were used. Even the feet were pickled in a salt brine and called *syltelabber* or pickled pig's feet. Farmers were known to salute the slaughtered pig with a *skål* to all the bones in the pig's feet which number more than two dozen. With so many toasts to the pig, beer was also "sacrificed" to Frey, another fertility god. Other parts of the pig were used to make blood pudding, salted pork, ribs, and cured hams. Only the squeal remains to be repeated by the children as they squeal for joy during the holidays.

Torvald Opsal of Tacoma was born in 1910 in Vikedal, Norway. He immigrated to the Midwest and later came to Washington State as a nineteen-year-old. Here he tells us about the food and festivities in his area of Norway:

*What we got out of Christmas wasn't presents like now; it was food, good food. That's what we looked forward to. I don't remember ever having a present or giving one until the last year or two before I left. Nobody did. Christmas Eve, the guy went up to church and started ringing the bell. Everybody had the holidays off. There was no police or anything like that, so there was nothing to have open. It was quiet, peaceful.*

*Christmas Eve at our place was mostly meat, a roast, and risengrøt [rice porridge]. That was a must. I remember when we were real young, we had a big bowl, a tureen, that sat on a stand. It was cooked so fine and so nice you wouldn't know it was rice. It was floating in butter and they had this red sauce on top. That was the best stuff. We all took a spoon and ate out of that bowl. That's the custom of that time. Later on, we had our own plates. We went to church, everybody, Christmas morning. Then mother would usually leave church a little early and go home and get the food ready for the rest of us. We had meat and potatoes. We lived good.*

*Sandbakkelse and krumkake and all that [typical cookies] was kept in a big tin can, so you had it for weeks after New Year's. Of course you didn't get all you wanted; that was more or less rationed. When people came to the house, they had to have coffee and goodies. We never went anyplace and nobody ever came to us from an invitation; it was always, if they stopped by. We didn't have much of anything except we had good food. At least it tasted good to us! I never tasted lutefisk until I came here to Normanna Hall [Tacoma, Washington], and I didn't like it. Nobody had it where I came from.*[1]

Carol Ollestad was born in Seattle in the late 1950s and grew up here with first generation Norwegian traditions and language. Her mother came from Åndalsnes in Romsdal and her father came from a small town inland from Egersund in Rogaland. While her parents were Norwegian immigrants, her family didn't take long to adopt some American customs.

*We always celebrated Christmas Eve with a dinner of spareribs or pork roast, boiled potatoes, gravy, and sauerkraut, mashed rutabagas, cranberry sauce— to be in place of tyttebaer sauce unless we could get some tyttebaer from Norway— homemade rolls, peas and carrots, brussels sprouts, too. Maybe a salad on the side. We always would eat in the dining room with the table decked to the hilt and the good china. At our house we always had caramel pudding and whipped cream for dessert. We made a lot of cookies, both traditional Norwegian and American. We would sing a table grace that had a different tune for Christmas time. We always had a glass of akevitt no matter how big or how young we were. We had as many dishes as we could make authentically.*

*In my very young days, we usually had dinner at home—myself, and at that time, I had two brothers. We ate dinner and then we packed up the car and went to visit my Dad's friend and their family on Christmas Eve for awhile. We kids would get dressed up and get out into the car and wait a little bit. Mom was always lagging behind. We would visit with them for a couple of hours. We kids would, of course, be antsy to get home because we knew Santa Claus would be there when we got home. We'd visit for awhile and, sure enough, when we got home, there would be some presents for us by the fireplace. We opened our gifts and celebrated Christmas at that time.*

*The next day on Christmas morning, we usually got a package of sardines from my dad's family from Norway. That was our treat on Christmas morning—to get toast or sandwiches with hard boiled egg and sardines on them and a little bit of akevitt for breakfast. We got to eat as much chocolate as we wanted for breakfast to keep us home so we didn't go visit the American kids and spoil their Christmas.*

*When I was a teenager, we celebrated Christmas a little differently because my cousins from Norway came to this country so we did have some family at that time and they came to visit us. By that time I had another brother, too. We had the same kind of meal, and usually during*

---

[1]Used by permission from: Rasmussen, Janet E. *New land, new lives : Scandinavian immigrants to the Pacific Northwest*. Seattle, WA: Norwegian-American Historical Association and University of Washington Press, 1993. Pages 54-55.

*dessert Santa Claus knocked on the door. There would be presents at the door and we would take the presents in and we could open up one present. After that, there would be the Christmas story from the Bible, both in English and in Norwegian, and we'd sing some Christmas songs. We'd open up our presents, and usually after opening up the presents, there would be lots of coffee and cookies and cakes and candies, lots of good things to eat.*

*Our tree is always a mixture of things we made as children and other family ornaments, not a decorator tree with everything all one color scheme. My mother always made me a new dress for Christmas, too, usually out of velvet.*

In the Pacific Northwest our traditional menus depend on our varying ethnic backgrounds and the areas we came from in the United States. Since many of us are a combination of several European cultures, our traditions have been modified with each generation. Some of us have saved, in some small way, at least a part of the traditions from the districts of our Norwegian ancestors. We have chosen some of our favorite treats and memories to include here. We hope you enjoy them as much as we do. Fortunately, here in the United States we are not as tradition bound as the more homogeneous societies of Europe so each Christmas may bring a little something new.

In the United States meats for Christmas Eve or Christmas Day dinner vary, but are based more on personal preference. Main dishes include standing rib roast of beef, baked ham, turkey, or goose. What is served really depends on what you enjoy most or wish to try as something new.

Robert Haug was born in the St. Paul-Minneapolis area of Minnesota in 1924. He now lives in Ballard and is an active member of the community. Bob remembers his Norwegian-American Christmases in the following story told to Noel Wannebo Bruzzichesi.

*My father grew up in Valdres. He and my uncle and grandmother came here together in 1905 and they emigrated to North Dakota and he stayed there until he found out that farmers don't make money. Then he started a restaurant in a neighboring town where the railroad was coming through and went from there to Montana and back to North Dakota running a hotel and restaurant. My mother died in 1929 so most of my remembrances are with my father who was a good cook.*

*On Christmas Eve he used to cook the lutefisk with melted butter, boiled potatoes, boiled peas, and julekake. We had potato lefse and we used to have roast goose on Christmas, too. There was a good reason to have goose on Christmas because goose grease was a pretty valuable item back in Minnesota. We used to have so much trouble with chapped hands and it was really good for that. It wasn't really fragrant, but it didn't smell bad.*

*Then usually the youngest person who could read would distribute the gifts. The gifts themselves weren't big gifts, they were small gifts. Often times they were gifts the person had made, especially the women. In the case of my father, because he was a cabinet maker, a wood worker, he might make a special gift for someone in the house.*

*Christmas was a family time, a real fun time. With all the relatives coming to visit, the kids would get to sleep on the floor in one room. What more could you ask? The kids were up playing until 1 o'clock.*

*We generally had hazelnuts and walnuts, an assortment, and candies we bought at the store like the curly ribbon things and chocolate covered angel hair. We might make fudge. There were a lot of pies, but I can't remember any special ones. My father had an extensive garden and we used to can apples, sliced, so there was probably apple pie at Christmas. We often had wine at Christmas, sometimes homemade Concord grape wine. The kids drank it, too, a watered down version but this wasn't just for Christmas. We did occasionally have a cherry drink at Christmas, which was really Danish and we knew it was Danish. We drank a lot of coffee, too.*

# Christmas menu for the Christmas table / *Julemeny for julebordet*

We have chosen a traditional Norwegian menu and a traditional American menu so you may pick and choose the recipes you might like to try for your feast.

| **Beverages** | *Drikkevarer* |
|---|---|
| Beer | *Øl* |
| Mulled wine or cider | *Akevitt* |
| Cranberry punch | |

| **Appetizers** | *Småretter* |
|---|---|
| Carrots | *Gravlaks* |
| Celery | *Flatbrød* |
| Cheeses | *Oster* |
| Shrimp Dip | *Rullepølse* |
| Olives | |

| **Main Course** | *Hovedrett* |
|---|---|
| Goose | *Svineribbe med svisker* |

| **Vegetables and Potatoes** | *Grønnsaker og Poteter* |
|---|---|
| Wild rice, prune and apple stuffing | *Surkål* |
| Sweet potatoes | *Kålrotstappe* |
| Mashed potatoes | *Poteter* |
| Gravy | *Saus* |
| Green beans with cream of mushroom soup | |
| Creamed onions | |

| **Bread** | *Brød* |
|---|---|
| Dinner rolls | *Lefse* |
| | *Julekake* |

| **Condiments** | *Tilbehør* |
|---|---|
| Butter | *Smør* |
| Salt | *Salt* |
| Pepper | *Pepper* |
| Whole cranberry sauce | *Tyttebær* |

| **Desserts** | *Desserter* |
|---|---|
| Gingerbread cookies | *Pepperkaker* |
| Cutout sugar cookies | *Krumkaker* |
| Divinity | *Sandbakkelser* |
| Meringues | *Berlinerkranser* |
| Thumbprint cookies | *Goro* |
| Spritz | *Rosettes* |
| Pumpkin pie | *Fattigmann* |
| Pecan pie | *Kransekake* |
| Apple pie | *Riskrem med rød saus og en mandel* |

| **After the Christmas Dinner** | *Etter Julemiddag* |
|---|---|
| Coffee | *Kaffe* |
| Tea | *Te* |
| Cream | *Krem* |
| Sugar | *Sukker* |
| Cognac or brandy | *Konjakk* |

# Beverages / *Drikkevarer*

## Christmas ale or beer / *Juleøl*
## Thomas the Brewer's Day / *Tomas bryggersdag*

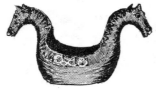*Tomasmesse* or Saint Thomas' Mass Day is celebrated on December 21 and commemorates the Apostle Thomas. It is also known as *Tomas bryggersdag* or Thomas the Brewer's Day.

The symbol on the *primstav* is two bare pine twigs. It symbolizes the mild weather called *kakelinna* or the " cake thaw " expected now. In the Pacific Northwest this type of weather is called a *chinook*. If the weather was good, according to the tradition, it would stay fine the rest of the winter.

Up until *Tomasmesse* in Norway, all the people were busy trying to complete their work for the holidays. A minimum amount of work was to be done after December 21 when the peace of Christmas traditionally started. All preparatory work, especially food preparation, including lefse making and baking, had to be completed. Even the supply of chopped wood had to be enough to last through Epiphany on January 6. It was time to enjoy the festivities, and the fruits of much labor, with family and friends in peace and harmony. Tasting the strong barley Christmas home-brewed beer known as *juleøl* was the highlight of the day.

Beer was a symbol of grain and harvest during the Viking era. *Juleøl* making began during the first full moon before *jul*. As it was important to make sacrifices to the gods, the *juleøl* would be dedicated to Odin and the fertility gods, Frey and Njord. Thus the gods were honored by those who drank the special brew.

Over a thousand years ago Harald Hårfagre, or Harald Fairhair, who ruled Norway from AD 874–932, drank *jul*. According to medieval Norwegian laws, *juleøl* was to be "blessed in grateful remembrance of Christ and Saint Mary for a good harvest and for peace" by every household. Thus the Viking tradition of drinking *jul* was inadvertently passed down through the centuries and the custom of dedicating the *juleøl* was carried on by Norwegian farms as recently as the last century. In Christian times, the symbol of the cross was used at some point during the brewing process to ensure the beer was protected from any of the evil spirits. A cross could be found on the outside of the container or placed in or on the bottom of the beer barrel.

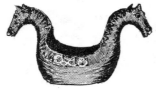*Juleøl* continues to be served from drinking horns and vessels passed from generation to generation. These elaborate horns and vessels include a bowl with two handles shaped like a Viking ship called a *kjenge*.

In Norway *juleøl* is generally sweeter, darker in color, and has an alcohol content of about 7% instead of the normal 4–5% for regular beer. It has a clean, dry, firm, malt taste.

Local breweries in Seattle have a tradition of making a dark, strong Christmas beer. Home-brewed beer is also a popular pastime in the Ballard area, but brewing at home can be somewhat challenging. If the bottles are not strong enough for the brewing process or the caps are not on tight, beer brown may be the new decorator color for the basement or kitchen wall in your living space.

Be sure to visit a store with a staff who can advise you about the proper process and the correct equipment to purchase to make your home-brewed beer before attempting to make the following recipe.

> 4¼ pounds Australian Light Extract
> ½ pound crystal malt
> ¼ chocolate malt
> ⅛ pound flaked barley
> ½ cup brown sugar
> 2¼ ounce Northern Brewer hops
> ½ cinnamon stick
> 1 teaspoon whole cloves
> 1 ounce Cascade hops for finishing
> 1 package Ale yeast
> water

Before starting the brewing process, sanitize with bleach a 10-gallon plastic container being used as the primary fermenter. Pour out bleach and rinse container well with water.

Warm Australian Light Extract for 30 minutes in a small pot of hot water. While extract is warming, add crushed grains of crystal malt, chocolate malt, and flaked barley to 1½ gallons cold water in a separate large pot. Bring to a boil. Watch for foam over. When it comes to a full boil, pour through a sieve into a large saucepan to sparge the grain. Rinse out large pot and pour the hot liquid back into it. Add the warmed extract to the large pot. Add the brown sugar. Stirring constantly to prevent scorching, return the solution to a boil. This takes about 15 minutes. Add the Northern Brewer hops and continue to boil for an additional 45 minutes. Then add the cinnamon stick and cloves. Add the Cascade finishing hops during the last 2 minutes of boil.

Add 2 gallons cold water to the primary fermenter recently sanitized. Sparge hops immediately into your fermenter. Add cold water to 5 gallon mark on container. When temperature has dropped to 70–85°F, sprinkle the yeast, which is called "pitching the yeast," over the mixture. Cover. Leave 3 days in primary fermenter and then siphon to carboy. Leave in carboy for 1–2 weeks. Take hydrometer reading before bottling, and bottle when you get a consistently low reading.

Yield: 5 gallons

## Water of life or aquavit / *Akevitt*

Each area in Europe seems to have its own version of the water of life, known in Norway as *akevitt*. Even Captain John Smith wrote about "aquavitæ" in his journals. The flavor of this strong, alcoholic beverage varies widely from country to country because of the local products used to make it. All with unique qualities, they have the same effect, a powerful burning sensation on the way to the stomach if one is not familiar with distilled spirits. *Brennevin* or hard liquor came to Norway in the 1500s.

Potatoes are the basic ingredient of *akevitt*. Originally, distilled spirits were made with grains, but potatoes soon became the most used raw material because they were plentiful and cheap. Potatoes have been in Norway for over 250 years. Caraway seeds are very pungent and aromatic and enhance the flavor of the *akevitt*. Caraway grows wild in Trøndelag near Trondheim and in central Norway near Lake Mjøsa. It is a native plant in Eurasia, probably brought to Norway by traders or brought back from trips taken by Vikings to Eurasia. These particular areas in Norway were also known for their production of potatoes, so combining it with the caraway was a natural step.

Aquavit is found throughout Scandinavia, but Norway's is slightly different from the other Nordic countries. In Norway, the Linie *akevitt* makes a "world tour in a vat" from Oslo to Australia and back. This trip takes about 14 weeks. Consumers found the trip made the flavor of the aquavit better. Also, Linie is colored with caramel while the others are generally clear.

*Akevitt* is best when accompanied by the heavy and fatty food of the Christmas season and is generally served ice cold from the freezer. The bottle is placed in a paper milk carton filled about halfway with water and put in the freezer. The water will freeze but due to the alcohol content, the aquavit will not. To serve the aquavit, peel the milk carton off, exposing the ice around the bottle. Wrap a towel around the bottle still frozen in the ice. This will prevent the ice from dripping on anything as it melts. A more attractive container than a milk carton can be used as long as a bit of ice remains on the outside of the bottle to keep the bottle cold. The heavy amber liquid is then poured into "shot" glasses which are small enough that it is impossible for the liquid to reach room temperature before it is consumed.

Some people prefer aquavit served at room temperature and they sip it slowly. Another traditional way is to drink the "shot" all at once followed by a beer chaser.

The toast or *skål* in Norway is a very important part of its culture and is traditionally given when aquavit is served. It has come down from Viking times, and it is still expected at dinner and parties today. In Viking times pledges to perform certain deeds were often made during toasts. Toasting at meal times needs practice and many people are uncomfortable giving a toast here in the United States. We hope the following instructions will help you give a successful toast.

The formal toast for the meal is done after everyone has been served wine, soup, or the first course. The guest of honor is generally seated to the left side of the host or hostess. The principle speech for the guest of honor is given after the second helping of the main course. The host requests his guests to join him in a *skål* for the guest of honor who remains seated while everyone else stands. The *takk for maten* or thanks for the food speech is done by the guest of honor and is addressed to the hostess. Toasts to everyone else are done after this.

If it is Christmas Eve, a toast may be, *"Et vel, drikk vel og trivs vel, for i kveld er det den hellige julekveld."* It means, "Eat well, drink well and thrive well, for tonight is the holy Christmas Eve." This Østfold blessing was given on Christmas Eve to ensure healthy animals, but it seems appropriate for people, too.

For a proper *skål* in a more informal setting, first find a person to toast, raise your glass, look straight into the person's eyes you are toasting and say *"skål."* The person you are toasting does the same. Then you drink your "shot" simultaneously. Lower each of your glasses to chest level and nod your head. The toast is then complete. It is the custom to never *skål* the hostess or she may become too drunk to continue the party. Often the toast is accompanied by a brief song. Our group often uses, *"og så svinger vi på seidelen igjen, hei, skål!"* In English this means, "and so we swing the beer stein again, hey *skål!*"

## Mulled wine or cider

This drink is a favorite during cold winter evenings and is especially welcome while sitting in front of a crackling fire.

3 bottles (750 milliliters each or 2.25 liters total) red, burgundy *or* Zinfandel wine
  *or*
1.89 liters apple juice *or* apple cider
⅔ cup granulated white sugar, adjust for taste as warmed (use only with the wine)
4 or 5 cinnamon sticks
2 cracked nutmeg seeds
1 tablespoon whole star anise
1 teaspoon whole allspice
1 teaspoon whole cloves
8 small pieces fresh ginger, attractively sliced
1 large tart apple, thinly sliced at a right angle to stem. Remove seeds so star shape from core
  appears when cut in this manner.
1 large orange, which is the same size as apple, halved and also thinly sliced
1 orange peel spiraled from another orange

In a 3-quart uncovered heavy gauge non-reactive Dutch oven (do not use cast iron or aluminum as wine will react with pan and cause the drink to have a metal taste), combine all the ingredients. Stir over medium to low heat for approximately 15–20 minutes. Serve in Christmas or glass mugs. May be kept warm for up to 2 hours by reducing the heat to low.

Makes approximately 16 four-ounce servings.


## Cranberry punch

1 12-ounce package of whole cranberries
3.78 liters cranberry *or* cran-raspberry juice
2 liters ginger ale
750 milliliters champagne, brut, *or* sparkling wine*
1 or 2 sliced star fruit *or* oranges

*may substitute 1 liter of ginger ale

Prior to serving the punch, make an ice mold with half the package of cranberries poured into it. Freeze until hard. Place ice which has been removed from mold into the punch bowl. Combine all liquid ingredients into the punch bowl. Decorate punch with sliced star fruit and remaining cranberries. Depending on the size of the cranberry crop, whole cranberries may only be available around Thanksgiving. Buy the cranberries then and freeze for Christmas use.

Makes approximately 54 four-ounce servings.

# Appetizers / *Småretter*

## Marinated salmon / *Gravlaks*

2–3 pounds salmon (may use two salmon filets)
¼ cup salt
¼ cup granulated white sugar
1½ teaspoons freshly ground white pepper
6 or 7 sprays fresh dill (dried dill weed may be used but it will not have
    the fresh taste or look)
¼ cup brandy *or* cognac (optional)
1 three–four pound brick or similar compact weight
1 whole lemon, sliced

    Cut salmon lengthwise along the central bone. Filet salmon, removing all bones. Discard bones. Combine salt and sugar and sprinkle evenly over both halves. Grind pepper evenly over both halves. Then chop half of the dill and spread over both filets. Sprinkle brandy or cognac evenly over filets before placing one filet on top of the other filet to reform into original salmon shape, skin side out. Put more dill under and over the salmon. Put salmon in a plastic bag or wrap tightly in plastic wrap. Place wrapped salmon on tray or in glass baking dish with the brick or weight on top of it. Refrigerate for at least 24 hours, but it is even better after 72 hours. Turn twice a day. Before serving, remove any remaining salt, sugar and dill. Skin if so desired. Slice through both filets at an angle, very thin.

    Decorate with slices of lemon. Serve plain on *flatbrød* or crackers or with the mustard sauce below.

Makes approximately 16–32 servings.


## Mustard sauce / *Sennepssaus*

1 8-ounce jar Dijon mustard
1 pint half-and-half cream
2 teaspoons granulated white sugar
1 cup fresh finely chopped dill
salt to taste
pepper to taste

    Mix mustard, half-and-half cream, and the sugar together in a small bowl. Sprinkle in dill. Add salt and pepper to taste. Serve in an attractive dish with spoon to accompany the *gravlaks*.

## Cheeses / *Oster*

Select cheeses you like to serve at Christmas time. Some suggested cheeses are Cheddar, Swiss, and Brie. They may be served sliced, cut into cubes with toothpicks inserted into the cubes, or as a brick of cheese to be sliced with an attractive cheese slicer on a crystal plate with crackers.

1 wedge Brie *or* other soft cheese, about ½ pound
1 tablespoon Dijon mustard
1 tablespoon honey (optional)
⅛ cup sliced almonds

Remove wrap from soft cheese. Place cheese on ovenproof plate which is attractive enough for serving. Drizzle mustard and honey on top of cheese. Sprinkle almonds on top. Place plate in oven at 250°F for about 12 minutes until cheese is slightly melted and bubbly. If oven is too hot, the oil from the cheese will separate out. Serve hot with crackers.

Makes approximately 6–8 servings.


## Relish tray

Raw vegetables attractively sliced on a diagonal, cut into quarters, or stuffed can be served as hors d'oeuvres while your guests await the main meal. Many of the vegetables are low in calories. Quickly blanching the vegetables prior to serving, but after cutting or slicing, helps keep the wonderful bright colors of the vegetables. Suggested vegetables are:

Carrots
Broccoli
Cauliflower
Radishes
Mushrooms (usually not blanched)
Celery (usually not blanched)
Pickles (do not blanch)
Olives (do not blanch)

To blanch the carrots, broccoli, cauliflower, and radishes, plunge small amounts of the vegetables into rapidly boiling water about 30 seconds. Do not allow the boiling water to die down. Remove the vegetables and quickly plunge them into an ice bath to prevent further cooking. This will set the colors, helps preserve nutrients, kills bacteria, and keeps the tissues of the vegetables firm so they don't looked dried out after sitting for long periods of time. Do not blanch different vegetables together as the natural color found in carrots or broccoli may change the color of white vegetables such as cauliflower.

## Shrimp dip / *Reke dyppe*

1 cup cocktail sauce
1 8-ounce bar cream cheese at room temperature
1 6-ounce / 4½-ounce dry weight canned *or* fresh shrimp *or* crab meat, drained
1 or 2 parsley sprigs (optional)
1 slice *or* wedge of lemon

Combine cocktail sauce and drained shrimp or crab meat in a small bowl. Pour mixture over bar of cream cheese which has been placed on an attractive plate. Add parsley sprigs and a slice or wedge of lemon for decoration. Serve with crackers or vegetables.

Makes approximately 6 servings.

## Rolled lamb / *Rullepolse*

This recipe requires at least four days to complete the entire process.

*Special equipment*: Sterilized needle strong enough to sew through the meat;
     heavy, white cotton thread; cheesecloth; press for rolled lamb or
     1 three–four pound brick or similar compact weight

*The brine is made first:*

4–5 cups rock salt
1 gallon water
1 medium potato

Prepare brine by combining rock salt and water in a non-reactive kettle or pot, such as stainless steel or enamel. Do not use an aluminum or iron pot. Bring brine solution to a rolling boil so salt dissolves in the water. A medium potato will float on the top of the brine solution if the solution is in the correct proportions. If potato doesn't float, add more rock salt. Remove potato from the solution and continue boiling until salt is dissolved. Remove pot from heat and allow solution to cool overnight before putting *rullepolse* in the brine.

2½–3 pounds lamb flank. (This is the weight before it is trimmed and deboned. The size of
     the meat will be about 8"–12" x 16" in length after trimming.)
1 medium onion, chopped fine
½ teaspoon ground ginger
½ teaspoon ground cloves
½ teaspoon ground pepper
1½ teaspoons salt
½ teaspoon ground allspice
1 teaspoon saltpeter (optional) This ingredient may be purchased at a pharmacy and is used
     only to preserve the red color in the meat.

33

Remove bone and trim surplus fat and tendons from lamb flank. Lay meat on a clean surface. Spread chopped onions over flank piece. Combine ginger, cloves, pepper, salt, allspice, and saltpeter and sprinkle these spices evenly over the lamb flank. Carefully roll flank so there is an even distribution of seasonings. Sew the roll together with strong thread so there are no loose ends of meat. Place roll into cooled brine solution for 3–4 days. If roll is in the solution for a longer period of time, soak roll in fresh water to get out the brine solution. Remove roll from brine and allow to drain well.

Wrap cheesecloth around roll and tie heavy cotton thread tightly around roll in an elliptical fashion with ½" spacing around roll. Place roll in a non-reactive pot such as stainless steel or enamel and cover completely with fresh water. Using a large fork, poke holes over entire roll so it won't blow up during the first 15 minutes of boiling. Bring water to a boil. Simmer roll about 2 hours until tender. Remove roll from pot.

Place roll in a press or between two cookie sheets or flat plates. Place heavy weights such as bricks on top of the cookie sheet or plate so the roll compresses. Put into the refrigerator until cool. Slice roll into as thin slices as possible. Cut so slices show off the attractive circular section of the roll. Serve with old style rye bread and enjoy.

Makes approximately 16 appetizer servings.

# Main courses / *Hovedretter*

## Lye fish / *Lutefisk*

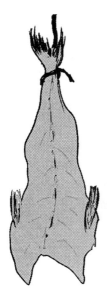

To many people in Norway, especially those in the northern part of Norway and here in the United States, *lutefisk* is a treat at Christmas time. From October to Christmas, there are *lutefisk* dinners all across the Puget Sound region at Norwegian strongholds. This can be a very good meal, but if the cooks are not too sure of what they are doing, *lutefisk* becomes the quivering, gelatinous mass of which jokes are made. Now for me, after seeing my mother's best silver spoon turn black after seconds of only touching the fish, I decided this type of codfish was best left untouched, especially by my mouth.

In our folkdancing group, *Leikarringen of Leif Erikson Lodge No. 1*, we decided to keep our codfish dried and uneaten so we haven't soaked it in the traditional lye for a Christmas dinner. Our fish looks a bit prehistoric, but it does make a very good conversation piece. The following history of our dried codfish was written by Michael Schuh, a member of our group since December 1979.

*Most folks who have been around Leikarringen for awhile have seen, or at least have heard of, The Fish. Always spoken with capital letters and frequently in reverent tones, The Fish refers to a rather dead codfish that has adorned the walls and/or cellars of several Leikarringen homes. It is one of our most cherished traditions, dating back more than twenty years.*

*While scavenging in Norway during a trip in 1972, Dick Armstrong tasted some dried fish and discovered that he liked it. Upon his return, he shopped around for some and found reasonable facsimiles in Johnsen's (now Olsen's) Scandinavian Foods on Market Street in Ballard. He bought two of these dried fish. When Doug and Ingrid Lieberg had their housewarming a year or so later, Dick gave one of the critters to the Liebergs. Several years after that, they passed it on to Margaret Lysness (now Margaret Vann) and so the tradition was born. When contacted during the research for this article, Dick said he felt that passing The Fish on with each subsequent housewarming was appropriate, as "no one should be burdened with that."*

*Not everyone who has possessed The Fish has really appreciated the honor and sacred trust its possession implies. Sissel Feroy, for example, kept it in her basement, "so the cat won't eat it." John Anderson, on the other hand, suspended The Fish from the center of his living room ceiling.*

*The Fish is passed on to another member of Leikarringen only when the member has a housewarming party for a house that he or she has recently purchased. No particular ceremony has been established, but Sissel paraphrased the Ballard High School cheer when she bequeathed The Fish to Beth Sankey:*

*"Lutefisk, lutefisk,*
*Lefse, lefse,*
*Now it's yours*
*Ja, sure, ya betcha!"*

*Should The Fish ever pass into your life, treat it with the same loving respect that you would bestow on any other treasure. While no one seriously believes that The Fish brings good luck or fortune, neither is anyone really certain that it will not bring bad luck. Don't, for example, place The Fish in a moist or humid area. It is doubtful that it would come back to life, but its aroma might. As Doug said, "May the stench be with you." And no matter how desperate your personal financial plight might become or how hungry you might get, DO NOT nibble on The Fish! The other members of Leikarringen might forgive you, but your stomach might not.*

*Traditionally The Fish is passed on, for the most part, on Halloween—it is already dressed for the occasion. Another traditional day is on May 17, Norwegian Constitution Day. Thank goodness the celebration in Seattle lasts all day and we guests only have to be around The Fish a short time as it is passed on to its new home. Sometime after being given to Rosemary Antel on May 17, 1993, our original fish became home to something unidentified and was discarded. On November 11, 1995, a new fish was passed to Carol Ollestad. At her newly built home, the fish resides in an odor proof box until it is passed on to a new home owner.*

## Pork ribs with prunes / *Svineribbe med svisker*

4 pounds pork ribs *or* 1 pound of pork ribs per person
1 cup all-purpose flour
1 teaspoon salt
½ teaspoon pepper
ground ginger to taste

Mix flour, salt, pepper, and ginger in a pie plate or in a bowl large enough for the ribs. Roll ribs in flour mixture. Fry ribs in greased frying pan until brown. Transfer ribs with fat side up to a broiler pan and bake uncovered in oven at 375°F for 30–45 minutes until tender and done.

1 cup pitted prunes
1 cup water

Put water and pitted prunes into a 1-quart saucepan and bring water to a boil. Cover and simmer 10 minutes. Remove prunes from water and drain well.

Serve the pork ribs together with the prunes on the same serving platter.

Makes approximately 4 servings.

## The Christmas goose / *Julegåsa*

The Christmas goose has been a tradition in Europe since the Middle Ages. In the Pacific Northwest the tradition has waned in favor of other meats. Many Canada geese travel through here during the winter so they may soon succeed at being more than the brunt of a Stan Boreson song. Hunting season for small game birds is generally from September through Christmas in both Norway and the Northwest. Autumn is the best time for hunting these types of birds as they have feasted on the autumn harvest of wild herbs and ripe, luscious berries. October 14 is opening day of hunting season for geese in the Northwest.

Our recipe for goose follows a Scandinavian tradition of a tart stuffing, baked separately, for traditionally sweet meat. Goose is found in the freezer section of the meat department at most grocery stores.

12–14 pound goose (allow 1 pound of meat per serving)
1 medium-sized onion
½ lemon
pieces of celery
4 tablespoons of drippings should be saved, after cooking, for stuffing and gravy

Leave the goose in its original plastic bag while thawing in refrigerator for 2 days. Place a large paper bag under the goose to prevent blood from dripping on refrigerator racks. Keep refrigerated until ready to roast.

Remove giblets, neck, and fat from body cavity of goose. Also remove all fat lumps from neck. Rinse goose with cold running water. Drain or pat dry with paper towels inside and outside of the goose. Prick skin of goose with a fork at regular intervals in thigh and lower breast areas. Place an onion which has been cut in half, ½ lemon, and some cut pieces of celery in the body cavity. These will draw out any off flavors as the goose cooks.

With breast side down, fasten the neck skin to the back with skewers. Tie legs together or tuck into the loose skin of cavity or sew closed with heavy thread. Place goose breast side down on a rack in a large roasting pan. Roast at 400°F for 1 hour then turn goose over so breast is up. Be sure to protect your hands. Roast for an additional 2–2½ hours at 325°F. Place meat thermometer in the breast of the goose, avoiding the bone. Every 30 minutes, siphon or ladle off fat at the bottom of the pan. When thermometer reaches 185°F, remove goose from oven. To test for doneness, pierce a thigh. If the juice runs a clear yellow, the goose is done.

Take goose out of the roasting pan, remove skewers and ties, and discard onion, lemon, and celery. Allow it to rest for about 20 minutes before carving. As carving a goose is messy, carving it in the kitchen and presenting cut pieces on a serving platter, instead of carving it at the table, is usually the best alternative.

Total cooking time is 3–3½ hours.

Serves 8–10 people.

## Wild rice, prune, and apple stuffing

6 cups water
1 teaspoon salt
1 cup wild rice*
1 cup white rice*
¾ cup pitted and soaked prunes
1–2 tablespoons butter *or* goose fat
1 diced medium-sized onion
1 cup blanched, slivered almonds
1 cored and diced medium-sized tart apple
1 teaspoon ground cinnamon
salt and pepper to taste

Since goose is fatty, the stuffing generally is baked separately.

Pour 6 cups of fresh water and 1 teaspoon of salt into a 3-quart saucepan and bring to a boil. Add rice slowly. Reduce heat and cover saucepan. Do not stir. Cook about 40 minutes or until rice is tender.

While rice is cooking, soak prunes in enough water to cover the prunes. When plump, chop into small pieces. Saute diced onion in butter or goose fat until onion is clear. Add almonds to onion mixture. Dice apple and gently mix with prunes and onion mixture into a 3-quart casserole. Add cinnamon, salt, and pepper. Then gently combine cooked wild and white rice to mixture. Bake covered for 25 minutes at 350°F.

Allow 1 cup of cooked stuffing for each pound of goose. Adjust recipe accordingly for the number of people being served.

Makes approximately 10 servings.

*If the rice being used is domestic packaged rice, it should not be rinsed before using. Rinsing removes nutrients in the starchy coating.

*If using imported rice, such as basmati or jasmine, rinse them before cooking. Also rinse any rice purchased from open store bins.

# Vegetables and potatoes / *Grønnsaker og poteter*

## Sweet and sour cabbage / *Surkål*

1 large head white *or* green cabbage, about 2½ pounds
2 tablespoons all-purpose flour
1 teaspoon salt
1–2 cups water
2 tablespoons butter *or* pork drippings
2 tablespoons caraway seed (may use less if desired)
¼ cup apple cider vinegar (add more if desired)
¼ cup granulated white sugar

Cut cabbage into quarters and remove the core. Finely chop or thinly slice cabbage. Layer cabbage in a non-reactive saucepan large enough for all ingredients. Sprinkle flour and salt between each layer. Add water and cook covered about 30 minutes on low heat. Stir periodically. While cabbage is cooking, melt butter in a small saucepan. Pour melted butter over cabbage mixture and continue to simmer mixture for an additional 30 minutes. Add the caraway seed, vinegar (adjust for personal taste), and sugar. Return to a boil and simmer uncovered over low heat until cabbage is tender and liquid is gone, about another 30 minutes. Be careful not to overcook. Stir well after removing from heat. More caraway may be added, if desired.

Makes 4-5 servings. Allow ½ pound of uncooked cabbage per person.

## Mashed rutabagas / *Kålrotstappe*

3 cups water *or* enough water to cover the rutabagas while cooking
pinch of salt
4 medium-sized rutabagas, about 2 pounds
¼ cup butter
¼ cup all-purpose flour
1¾ cups milk
white pepper to taste
salt to taste

In a 3-quart saucepan, bring water to a boil with a pinch of salt. While water comes to a boil, wash, peel, cut, and remove any bad spots from the rutabagas. Drop cut rutabagas into boiling water. Cover and cook until tender and easily pierced with a fork, about 20–30 minutes. Drain water from pan. Mash rutabagas in pan lightly with an electric mixer, potato masher, or fork then place pan over low heat again for about 5 minutes to dry and fluff the rutabagas. Be careful not to let rutabagas burn. Add butter, flour, and milk to hot mashed rutabagas. Mix thoroughly until smooth. Serve with a sprig or two of parsley.

Makes approximately 8 servings.

## Potatoes / *Poteter*

4 cups water *or* enough water to cover the potatoes while cooking
pinch of salt
12 small new potatoes
parsley *or* chives

In a 3-quart saucepan, bring water to a boil with a pinch of salt. While water comes to a boil, wash potatoes well and remove any bad spots or roots. Leave skin on the potato or use a potato peeler to remove a small strip around middle of each potato. Drop potatoes into boiling water. Cover and cook until tender and easily pierced with a fork, about 20–30 minutes. Drain water from pan, leaving potatoes in pan. Place pan with potatoes back on the burner with low heat for 1 or 2 minutes while sprinkling parsley or chives over potatoes. This will help remove some of the water in the potatoes. Be careful not to let potatoes burn. The potatoes may be served with the skins on or with the skins removed.

Makes approximately 4–6 servings.


## Mashed potatoes / *Potetstappe*

3–4 cups water
pinch of salt
6 medium-sized potatoes, about 3 pounds
3 tablespoons butter
salt to taste
pepper to taste
⅓ cup of hot milk *or* cream

In a 2-quart saucepan, bring water to a boil with a pinch of salt. While water comes to a boil, wash, peel, cut, and remove any bad spots from potatoes. Drop cut potatoes into boiling water. Cover and cook until tender and easily pierced with a fork, about 20–30 minutes. Drain water from pan. Lightly mash potatoes in the pan with a potato masher or fork then place pan over low heat for about 5 minutes to dry and fluff the potatoes. Add butter, salt to taste, and hot milk or cream to potatoes. Remove pan from heat and beat potatoes until creamy with an electric mixer or potato masher. Serve potatoes while hot with gravy or butter.

If a sweeter version of mashed potatoes is desired, use the recipe for potato bannock or *lefse* without adding the flour.

Makes 6 servings.

## Gravy / *Saus*

Gravy or sauces are usually made from the drippings of the meat or poultry roasted for the meal. Make the gravy in the pan used to cook the meat. Remove the meat or poultry from the pan and set the meat aside on an appropriate platter for carving.

2 tablespoons drippings
1–2 tablespoons all-purpose flour
1 cup liquid, such as milk *or* cream for a non-clear gravy. If a clearer gravy is desired, use
     stock, white or red wine, beer, *or* pan juice which has had the fat removed
salt to taste
pepper to taste
herbs or spices to taste

Pour off all but 2 tablespoons of hot drippings from the cooking pan. Place pan on burner at low heat. Blend in flour gradually and stir with a fork or wire whisk until mixture is smooth. Continue to heat and stir constantly while adding liquid to prevent lumpy gravy. Season to taste with salt, pepper, or other spices and herbs. Serve in a gravy boat or small pitcher.

Makes 1 cup. Adjust recipe to make additional servings.


## Sweet potato, yams or candied yams with marshmallows

At least one generation of Americans has grown fond of the sweet potato with golden brown, oozing marshmallows on top. I must confess for many years it was the only way my mother could get me to eat this vegetable, which was supposed to be good for us.

Preheat oven to 350°F.

4 sweet potatoes or 4 yams *or* 2 31-ounce cans of candied yams
½ teaspoon nutmeg
1 teaspoon cinnamon
½ teaspoon salt (optional)
⅓ cup firmly packed brown sugar (do not use with candied yams)
⅓ cup granulated white sugar (do not use with candied yams)
1 teaspoon vanilla
½ cup melted butter (1 stick)
1 egg, beaten
16 large marshmallows
¼ cup pecans (halved *or* chopped)

Wash, peel, remove bad spots, and cut sweet potatoes *or* yams into approximately 2" pieces. Place into a lightly greased 1½-quart casserole dish or 9" x 13" cake pan. Mix nutmeg, cinnamon, salt, brown sugar, granulated sugar, vanilla, melted butter and beaten egg in a separate dish. If desired, chop pecans and add to this mixture. Pour mixture over the sweet potatoes or yams. Bake uncovered at 350°F for 60 minutes. Remove from oven and cover with marshmallows and pecan halves if not used before. Bake another 15 minutes or until marshmallows are golden brown.

For a creamy version, after washing the sweet potatoes or yams, lightly rub their surfaces with some vegetable oil. Pierce the sweet potatoes or yams several times with a fork to allow the steam to escape. Bake for 75 minutes at 375°F until tender. Remove potatoes from oven and peel. Lower oven temperature to 350°F. Mash the sweet potatoes with an electric mixer or potato masher. A blender may also be used for an even creamier texture. While beating, add all ingredients except the marshmallows and pecans. The pecans may be added now, though, if they are chopped. Pour mixture into a lightly greased 2-quart casserole dish. Cover mixture with marshmallows and pecan halves. Bake uncovered in 350°F oven for 15 minutes or until marshmallows are golden brown.

Makes 8 servings.

## Green beans with cream of mushroom soup

This holiday casserole has been a favorite of Americans for over 40 years. Originally created in the Campbell Soup Kitchens, it has been modified over the years with a variety of ingredients.

Preheat oven to 350°F.

1 10¾-ounce can condensed cream of mushroom *or* cream of chicken soup
½ cup whole milk
pepper to taste
4 cups frozen *or* canned and drained French cut style green beans
½ cup slivered almonds (optional)
½ cup grated cheddar cheese (optional)
½ teaspoon soy sauce (optional)
1 2.8-ounce can fried onions

Blend soup, milk, pepper, and selected optional ingredients until smooth in the greased 1½-quart casserole dish you will be serving the green beans. Add green beans to mixture. Bake 25 minutes at 350°F then stir mixture until well blended. Sprinkle onion rings on top of mixture. Continue to bake for an additional 5 minutes until onion rings are crisp, warm, and golden.

Makes 6–8 servings.

## Creamed onions

1 cup water
pinch of salt
1 10-ounce bag of white pearl onions *or* 1 14½-ounce can whole onions
2 tablespoons butter
1½ to 2 tablespoons all-purpose flour
1 teaspoon dry mustard
1 cup whole milk

In a 2-quart saucepan, bring water to a boil with a pinch of salt. Add onions to water, cover pan, and continue to boil until onions are tender about 30 minutes. Remove pan from heat, drain and peel onions. Return peeled onions to saucepan. (If using canned onions, heat onions in own juice until boiling. Drain and return to saucepan.)

While onions are cooking, melt butter at low heat in a small saucepan. Slowly blend flour and dry mustard with butter for 3–5 minutes over the low heat. Stir the milk in slowly to prevent the mixture from becoming lumpy. Continue to stir until creamy. Pour white sauce over drained onions and heat combined ingredients for 1 minute. Serve hot.

Makes 4 servings.


## Whole cranberry sauce

1 cup granulated white sugar
1 cup water
1 12-ounce package of whole cranberries

Put sugar and water into a 2-quart saucepan. Stir so sugar dissolves in the water. Bring solution to a boil. Meanwhile wash and pick over cranberries, removing any berries of poor quality. Add cranberries to boiling solution and bring to a boil again. Cover saucepan and reduce heat. Simmer and occasionally stir the berries for about 10 minutes or until the skins burst. Remove from heat. Cool to room temperature and then refrigerate. Serve cold.

Makes about 2¼ cups or about 18 servings.

# The Christmas baking / *Julebaksten*

Baking plays a big role in holiday preparations in both Norway and the Pacific Northwest. The baking starts about twenty days before Christmas in Norway. Here it is about the same although our baking may start a little closer to Christmas. We often make a party of it by sharing recipes and kitchens.

Traditionally, at least, seven different kinds of cookies and cakes were baked in every home in Norway. We can be thankful the old tradition of serving twenty different varieties, representing all the days of the Christmas season from December 25 through January 13, was reduced to fourteen and now to the more popular seven varieties. In the Pacific Northwest we don't have a set number of cookies to make. Most of us are more specialized and make only a few of our favorite cookies. We are most inclined to branch out with some of our favorites, such as sugar cookies, frosted and decorated in various colors, and cookies from other ethnic backgrounds. Norwegian goodies include *fattigmann, hjortetakk, goro, rosettes, sandbakkelser, krumkaker, pepperkaker,* and *berlinerkranser.*

After all the baking was done in Norway, the house would be cleaned from top to bottom by scouring the walls and floors, the furniture would be polished, the silver polished, and all the sheets would be washed for the many guests expected during the holidays. We continue something similar and call it "holiday panic cleaning" in the United States.

All the recipes have been tested several times. As we tested them, we discovered it is best to use fresh dairy products and brand name products. For example, the lesser quality butter products may affect the results, causing the dough to be more fatty than usual and the cookies to spread more during baking. Also for the best results, do not substitute margarine for butter. Most of the cookie doughs require chilling, so plan ahead. We have tried to balance out the egg yolks and the egg whites so nothing is wasted.

As another helpful hint, flour gets compacted when stored so it is recommended to at least "fluff" the flour before measuring. Do this by putting a measuring cup in the bag, filling it and pouring the contents back into the bag several times or using your fingers to stir up the flour a few times. Few people now sift or "fluff" flour which causes an additional 3–4 tablespoons of flour to be added to a recipe which means special cookies taste as if they have too much flour.

# Breads / *Brød*

## Potato bannock / *Potet lefse*

*Special equipment:* Ricer; griddle or electric lefse griddle; lefse rolling pin if available; thin lefse turner

3–4 cups water
pinch of salt
6 medium-sized russet potatoes (yield is 5 cups hot riced potatoes), about 3 pounds
2 tablespoons granulated sugar
1 teaspoon salt
2 tablespoons melted butter
⅔–¾ cup of half-and-half cream
1½–2 cups of flour depending on amount of water in potatoes

This favorite was once made of leftover mashed potatoes so it basically follows that recipe. In a 2-quart saucepan, bring water to a boil with a pinch of salt. While water comes to a boil, wash, peel (peels may be left on to provide better flavor), cut, and remove any bad spots from potatoes. Drop cut potatoes into boiling water. Cover and cook until tender and easily pierced with a fork, about 20–30 minutes. Drain water from pan. Peel potatoes now if cooked in their skins and place back into saucepan. Lightly mash potatoes in the pan with a potato masher or fork then place pan over low heat for about 5 minutes to dry and fluff the potatoes. Remove potatoes to a bowl. Place hot potatoes into ricer and rice into saucepan or other clean bowl. To 5 cups of riced potatoes, add sugar, salt, melted butter, and cream. Refrigerate overnight.

After completely cool, add 1½–1¾ cups flour so it makes a nice soft dough. Roll potato mixture into 2 balls of equal size, then roll into 2 logs about 2½" in diameter. Cut logs into ¾" slices. Keep slices in refrigerator while rolling out a slice at a time. Using some of the reserve flour, lightly sprinkle rolling surface, roll each piece out as thin as possible with lightly floured lefse rolling pin. Bake on an ungreased griddle until there are light brown spots. Turn with lefse turner. Bake on other side until light brown spots appear. Remove with lefse turner. When cool, store and refrigerate or freeze in an airtight container until ready to use. Allow enough time to cook entire batch of dough because once the flour has been added to the riced potato mixture it does not hold up well.

To serve, spread liberally with softened butter. If lefse is served as a dessert, add sugar and cinnamon to butter mixture. There are many ways of cutting lefse attractively. Fold outside edges into the middle forming a rectangle. Slice at an angle. Another method is to put 2 buttered lefse together and cut the lefse into 12 triangular pieces. Roll each piece from large end toward smaller end. The lefse may also be served in just the triangular pieces.

Makes 20 whole lefse or approximately 40 servings of three 2-inch pieces.

## Christmas bread / *Julekake*

This sweet bread flavored with cardamom and filled with raisins and citron has always been very popular in Norway and is usually the last of the baking to be done. The breads may be shaped into round loaves or into geometric designs and crosses to symbolically bless the eater and ward off evil spirits.

2 packages dry yeast
½ cup lukewarm water
3 cups whole milk, scalded and cooled
½ cup butter
1 cup granulated white sugar
2 eggs, beaten
2 teaspoons salt
½ cup chopped citron
2 cups raisins
½ cup candied cherries, chopped *or* 1 cup mixed candied fruits, if desired
½ teaspoon freshly crushed cardamom seed
10–11 cups all-purpose flour

Dissolve yeast in water with a little sugar in a small bowl. Scald milk in a 1-quart saucepan, remove from heat and pour over butter in a large bowl. When milk is lukewarm, add yeast, sugar, salt, and about half the flour. Stir well for 10 minutes with wooden spoon. Add eggs, one at a time, beating well after each addition. Add candied fruit, cardamom, and enough flour to make a light dough. Knead 10 minutes and place in greased bowl to rise until light, for approximately 45 minutes. Shape into 4 loaves or braids. Place in buttered pans to rise for about an hour or until light. Brush with beaten egg yolk and milk. Sprinkle with pearl sugar, if desired. Bake in a preheated oven at 350°F about 35–45 minutes, depending on size and shape of loaf. Cool on racks. May be glazed with powdered sugar icing.

Makes 4 loaves.

# Desserts / *Desserter*

## Spice cookies / *Pepperkaker*

*Special equipment:* Holiday cookie cutters in heart or pig shape

Preheat oven to 350°F.

⅔ cup butter at room temperature
¾ cup packed light brown sugar
3 tablespoons water
2 tablespoons dark molasses
1 teaspoon grated fresh lemon peel
2 cups all-purpose flour
1 tablespoon ground cinnamon
1½ teaspoons ground cloves
1 teaspoon ground ginger
1 teaspoon freshly crushed cardamom
1 teaspoon baking soda
Sliced blanched almonds (optional)

Cream butter and brown sugar in a large bowl. Add water, molasses, and lemon peel. Sift flour, cinnamon, cloves, ginger, cardamom, and baking soda into creamed mixture. Mix well. Shape dough into a ball. Refrigerate 30 minutes. Roll a portion of the dough as thin as possible on a lightly floured surface. Cut with floured heart-shaped or other holiday cookie cutter. Place cut dough on lightly greased cookie sheets. Decorate with a sliced almond, if desired.

Bake at 350°F until firm and medium brown for 8–10 minutes. When cool, may be decorated with piped frosting.

Makes 5–6 dozen cookies.

## Curved cookies / *Krumkaker*

*Special equipment:* Electric or regular *krumkake* iron, wooden cone for rolling *krumkaker*

1 whole egg, lightly beaten
3 egg whites
1¼ cups granulated white sugar
½ cup melted butter
½ teaspoon freshly crushed cardamom
1 cup whipping cream, lightly whipped
1¾ cups all-purpose flour

Heat *krumkake* iron while preparing mixture. Lightly beat eggs in a bowl. Beat in sugar, melted butter, cardamom, lightly whipped cream, and flour. Test to see if iron is hot enough by dripping some water onto the iron surface. If water bubbles, iron is ready. Drop mixture, a teaspoon at a time, on the hot *krumkake* iron. *Krumkaker* should be a light golden color when done. Some people prefer the darker, crispy color. Remove flat *krumkake* from iron, quickly roll into cone shape with wooden cone or *krumkake* will remain flat. If *krumkake* is lacey, add flour one teaspoon at a time until it becomes an even cookie.

When cool, store in an airtight container until ready to use. *Krumkaker* easily become soggy if exposed to air.

Makes approximately 5 dozen.


## Sand cookies / *Sandbakkelser*

*Special equipment*: *Sandbakkelser* tins

Preheat oven to 350°F.

1 cup butter
1 cup granulated white sugar
1 egg
3 cups all-purpose flour
1 teaspoon almond extract

In a bowl, cream butter and sugar until fluffy. Add egg to mixture and beat until creamy. Add almond extract and flour gradually and mix well. Chill at least 20 minutes. There are two methods to get the dough into the tins. Either roll mixture into small balls of about 1 tablespoon of dough, then press dough into tins, beginning at the bottom, until a thin layer about ⅛" thick covers the bottom and sides of the tin OR roll a portion of the dough flat to about ⅛" thick on a lightly floured surface. Find a glass or round cookie cutter about the size of the tin, if it were flat, and use that to cut out the dough. You may need to test a few glasses to see which one works best. Lift cut dough into tin and press into tin. Be sure dough is no thicker than an ⅛" on the bottom of the tin. Place tins on cookie sheet and bake for approximately 12 minutes at 350°F until light golden color. The cookie should be crisp and not doughy. Cool in tins. Remove when cold by inverting tins and tapping very gently on the bottom to release the *sandbakkelser*.

When cool, store in an airtight container until ready to use. May be served plain or filled with custard, whipped cream and jam, or ice cream.

Makes approximately 5 dozen.

# Berlin wreathes / *Berlinerkranser*

2 hard cooked egg yolks
½ cup sifted powdered sugar
1 cup butter
2 raw egg yolks
1 teaspoon vanilla *or* almond extract (optional)
2 cups all-purpose flour
1 slightly beaten egg white
⅓ cup pearl sugar, sugar crystals, crushed loaf sugar *or* crushed sugar cubes

Mash the hard cooked egg yolks in a small bowl. In a separate medium-sized bowl, cream the powdered sugar and butter until fluffy. Add mashed yolks and raw yolks one at a time into the creamed mixture, mixing well after each addition. Add extract. Sift flour gradually into mixture. Test consistency of dough by rolling a little bit between your fingers. It should not be fatty, sticky or crumbly, but just right for rolling. A little more flour may need to be added. Chill dough for about 2 hours.

Work with a small amount of dough at a time, keeping rest of dough well chilled. Break off walnut-sized pieces of dough. Roll dough to ⅜" thick round rope shape about 5" long by keeping hand parallel to the rope shape. Shape into wreath, overlapping about ½" from the ends. Press overlap down lightly to keep ends together. Place on ungreased cookie sheet. Since dough is so buttery and gets soft when worked in your hands, put rolled dough on cookie sheet into refrigerator to chill. After cooling for a few minutes, remove from refrigerator. Take chilled rolled dough and dip into egg white, then dip into the crushed sugar before being placed on the cookie sheet again. Bake 325°F for about 8–10 minutes until a light golden color. This cookie needs to be baked so it is not raw in the middle, but color should be as light as possible.

Makes approximately 4 dozen cookies.

## Wafer cookies / *Goro*

*Special equipment: Goro* iron; rolling pin with cloth cover; wax
      paper; cardboard pattern; marble slab, if available

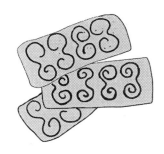

1 cup whipping cream
1 egg
1¼ cups granulated white sugar
1½ cups (3 cubes) plus 2 tablespoons butter at room temperature
3½ cups all-purpose flour
2 teaspoons cognac *or* brandy
½ teaspoon freshly crushed cardamom. Prepare by removing seeds
      from cardamom pods. Finely crush in a mortar and pestle.

Keeping dough chilled is the key to success in this recipe. If available, put marble slab in freezer until very cold. In a small chilled bowl, whip cream until firm. In a separate large bowl, beat egg and sugar until light. Add cognac or brandy and cardamom. Blend cream and egg mixture. Add 3 cups of flour into the mixture. Reserve ½ cup flour for rolling out the dough. Gradually work in butter. Completely chill dough.

While dough is chilling, cut a cardboard pattern to fit *goro* iron and also cut many pieces of wax paper which are slightly larger than the iron pattern. Sprinkle some of the reserve flour onto a pastry cloth which has been laid over the frozen marble slab or a regular bread board. Sprinkle enough flour on the pastry cloth to keep the dough from sticking to the cloth. The frozen marble slab keeps the dough from melting in your hands or while rolling out the dough. Roll out dough into very thin sheets approximately 1/16" to 3/32" thick. Handle dough as little as possible because heat from your hands will cause dough to soften. Place the *goro* iron pattern over the dough, cut the rolled dough to this size, using a sharp knife around the pattern. Place cut dough on a piece of wax paper. Put cut dough and wax paper on a plate and place immediately into the refrigerator to chill again. Keep bowl of dough in refrigerator as much as possible, especially while rolling out pieces of dough. The dough becomes difficult to handle when it gets warm. Continue to roll and cut all dough, separating each pattern with wax paper. Put in refrigerator until all dough has been rolled.

Heat *goro* iron until hot. Test if iron is hot enough by dripping some water onto the iron surface. If water bubbles, iron is ready. Remove *goro* pieces from refrigerator one at a time. Place on hot *goro* iron and bake until a light golden color, keeping it as light as possible on both sides. Be very careful to place dough squarely on iron just the way the pattern was cut. Because the dough is so buttery, once the dough is on the iron it cannot be moved.

Use a small pastry brush to clean excess cookie off iron. Fat collects in parts of the iron as well. Keep dishcloth or paper toweling close by to wipe off excess fat. Be sure not to touch hot burner with dishcloth or toweling as it may catch fire. Remove cookie from iron by using a wide spatula. Place cookie on a cutting board, cut into three smaller cookies with a sharp knife while the cookies are still warm. Trim edges, if necessary. Cookies become crisp when cooled and will break into small pieces if cut after cooling. When cool, store in an airtight container.

Makes about 33 sheets of *goro* or 8½ dozen separate cookies.

## Rose cookies / *Rosetter*

*Special equipment: Rosette* irons; candy thermometer; deep fryer or heavy gauge Dutch oven

**Hot oil will cause severe burns. Always be careful while using it.**

2 quarts of vegetable *or* peanut oil (canola oil is not recommended)
2 eggs
2 teaspoons granulated white sugar
1 cup whole milk
1 cup all-purpose flour
¼ teaspoon salt
powdered sugar (optional)

Pour vegetable oil in a 4 or 5-quart deep fryer or heavy gauge Dutch oven so it is about ½–⅔ full. Heat to 400°F by measuring heat with a candy thermometer or to about a medium high heat. While oil is heating, beat eggs slightly in a medium-sized bowl. Add sugar. Then add milk and sifted flour with salt mixed into flour. Beat until smooth or until about the consistency of heavy cream.

Place *rosette* iron in hot oil to heat form. Remove form from oil and quickly drain excess oil onto paper towels. Dip hot iron about ¾ of the way into batter, being careful not to let batter run over the top of the form; otherwise, you may not be able to remove the *rosette* without breaking it. The layer of batter should be smooth and even. If it is too thin, redip iron. Dip the coated iron into the hot oil until the *rosette* is golden brown. The oil will stop its rapid bubbling when the batter is cooked. Remove *rosette* from form with a fork and place onto absorbent paper towels or brown paper bags to drain and absorb the oil. When cool, store in an airtight container.

Some people serve the *rosetter* with the smooth side up and others serve the *rosetter* with the edges up. Whichever way you choose to serve them, if desired, sprinkle powdered sugar on that side just before serving.

Makes 6 dozen.

## Poor man's cookies / *Fattigmann*

*Special equipment:* Candy thermometer; deep fryer or heavy gauge Dutch oven

**Hot oil will cause severe burns. Always be careful while using it.**

2 quarts of vegetable *or* peanut oil (canola oil is not recommended)
6 egg yolks
½ cup granulated white sugar
¾ teaspoon freshly crushed cardamom. Prepare by removing seeds from cardamom pods.
  Finely crush in a mortar and pestle.
6 tablespoons whipping cream
2 tablespoons cognac, brandy, whiskey *or* use artificial flavoring
2–2½ cups all-purpose flour (reserve some flour for rolling the dough)
powdered sugar (optional)

  Pour vegetable oil in a 4 or 5-quart deep fryer or heavy gauge Dutch oven so it is about ½–⅔ full. Heat to 400°F by measuring heat with a candy thermometer or to about a medium-high heat. While oil is heating, beat egg yolks in a medium-sized bowl. Add sugar gradually into yolks and beat for about 5 minutes. Add cardamom, whipping cream, and flavoring. Sift 2 cups of flour gradually into the mixture. Mix or knead by hand into a soft dough. Dough should be soft, but firm enough to roll out to less than ⅛" thick on a surface lightly floured with some of the remaining flour. Cut dough into diamond shapes by first making straight 1¼" wide strips in rolled dough. Then cut 2½" diagonal strips across the previous cuts. Make ¾" slit lengthwise in center of diamond shape. Pull one end of diamond through the slit. Deep fry until light golden color. The oil will stop its rapid bubbling when the cookie is done. Remove *fattigmann* with a slotted spoon and place onto absorbent paper towels or brown paper bags to drain and absorb the oil. When cool, store in an airtight container. May sprinkle with powdered sugar just before serving.

Makes 5–6 dozen cookies.

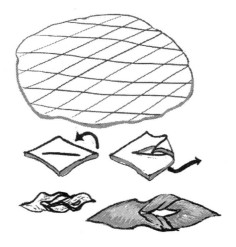

## Wreath cookie / *Kransekake*

*Special equipment: Kransekake rings*

4 egg whites, lightly beaten until frothy
2¼ cups powdered sugar
4 cups almond paste
shortening
all-purpose flour

Almond paste may be purchased in a can at most grocery stores or purchased from a bakery. A helpful hint is to buy a little more than two pounds and measure it into cups as the weight of 8 ounces=1 cup may not be accurate. If you prefer to grind your own almonds, follow the method for grinding in the recipe for marzipan.

Lightly beat egg whites until frothy in a large bowl with a heavy duty electric mixer. Gradually add powdered sugar. Break almond paste into small pieces while continuing to beat mixture. Dough will become increasingly heavy as almond paste is added. If you do not have a heavy duty mixer, you may need to knead the dough by hand; otherwise, the motor may burn out in your mixer. Dough should be firm and even.

Put bowl of dough in refrigerator for several hours or remove dough from bowl and put into a plastic bag and seal. After chilling, dough will be easier to work. While waiting for dough to cool, generously apply shortening to forms, then lightly flour. If available, a product called Baker's Joy®, which combines the shortening and flour, can be sprayed on the forms instead. Roll chilled dough to little finger thickness or about ½" or smaller by keeping palm of hand parallel to the rope shape. The top ring thickness is slightly smaller. If dough becomes sticky when rolling, sprinkle powdered sugar on rolling surface. Cut rolls to appropriate length for *kransekake* forms. Place rolls in the well-greased and floured *kransekake* forms.

Place forms on cookie sheet and bake at 325°F about 13–20 minutes until light golden. Cool cookie in form thoroughly or cookie may break when removed from forms. Remove cookie by running a knife around the edges of the form, if necessary. To clean forms, simply wipe shortening and flour from the surfaces. Washing with soap and water removes the curing done by the shortening. Store forms in container.

For an extra tall cake, bake two rings of each size. May be stored in an airtight container several weeks. Finish *kransekake* by trimming it with glaze or thinned white butter cream frosting used for the sugar cookies.

## Glaze / *Glase*

*Special equipment:* Pastry bag

1 egg white
1 cup powdered sugar
1 teaspoon vinegar

In a small bowl, slightly beat egg white. Add vinegar. Beat in powdered sugar until smooth. If you are leery of using a raw egg white, use the recipe for butter cream frosting and thin with enough milk so it can go through the pastry bag tip. Fill pastry bag with glaze or thinned frosting. Starting with largest ring, decorate rings with glaze using a V-shape or zig-zag stream of glaze. When finished with the first ring, find the next smaller ring and place on top of larger ring. The glaze holds the rings together. While it is desired not to break any rings before being served, broken rings may be pushed together and the frosting technique will hold the pieces together until serving time.

To store, place top half of rings in container and place the rest of the *kransekake* bottom rings over top so it is half as tall.

Decorate before serving with noise makers, flags, greens, or appropriately colored ribbons and flowers. If serving at a wedding, ribbons in the colors of the event can drop from the top of the *kransekake*.

To serve, break bottom rings first into bite-size pieces and place around cake. Traditionally, rings are taken from the bottom up so the *kransekake* looks whole while it is being served.

Makes about 100 servings.

## Rice cream / *Riskrem*

Usually served as dessert following the Christmas Eve meal, it is sometimes eaten as a light meal in the middle of Christmas Eve day. It is traditionally served with one blanched almond. Finding the almond in the rice cream means good luck for the new year. The person who finds the nut usually receives a prize of a marzipan pig with a red ribbon tied around its neck. The almond may also signify marriage for the finder in the new year. Often, to keep everyone guessing who found the almond, the person who found it will keep it hidden in his or her cheek until everyone is done eating the *riskrem*. To trick everyone at the table, sometimes the host or hostess will put an almond in each portion of the *riskrem* so each person will think, "I'm the lucky winner," or it may be left out entirely, leaving everyone in a mystery.

In some families the person who gets the almond is honored as the person to pass out the Christmas gifts.

3½ cups whole milk
1 cup uncooked white rice
salt to taste
½ pint whipping cream
granulated white sugar to taste
cinnamon to taste
whole blanched almond
currant juice or raspberry juice (optional)

In a double boiler, warm the milk until bubbling. If using a saucepan, be sure to keep the heat very low to prevent the mixture from scorching. Sprinkle rice into warmed milk while continually stirring the mixture. Bring to a second simmer and cover. Continue simmering for about an hour, occasionally stirring the mixture until the rice grains are cooked and the porridge has thickened and all milk is absorbed. Remove from heat and chill. In a separate chilled bowl, whip cream with a little sugar to taste. Add cream mixture to thoroughly chilled rice mixture with the one whole blanched almond. Stir thoroughly. Add the salt to taste. Serve in individual bowls and sprinkle top with sugar and cinnamon, as desired, or pour currant or raspberry juice over the top.

Makes 8 servings.

The prize marzipan pig is made from almonds ground into a paste with sugar and egg white. If you want to make your own pig or special prize from marzipan, follow the recipe below. Almond paste may also be purchased at a bakery or grocery store. The commercial marzipan pigs can be purchased at Scandinavian food shops.

## Marzipan / *Marsipan*

1 pound whole, blanched almonds or slivered almonds
1 16-ounce box powdered sugar
¼ cup of water and sherry *or* 2 egg whites, lightly beaten until frothy
food coloring, if desired

Almond paste is a heavy substance and can burn out equipment which is not made to handle heavy dough. Proceed with care.

Skins may be left on the almonds, if desired, for a darker mixture with brown specks. Blanched almonds will make a whiter dough. With a coffee grinder, grind ½ cup of almonds at a time until finely ground. Combine each batch of ground almonds in a large bowl with sugar. As weather and other things may affect this mixture, gradually add liquid of water/sherry or egg whites while mixing with fingers and hands until smooth and stiff. The entire ¼ cup of liquid may not be needed, as mixture should not become runny or gooey, just smooth. Do not handle dough too much as it will become gray.

If using a food processor, process all the almonds until finely ground and then add the sugar and water/egg whites until the mixture forms a ball. The ingredients can also be mixed with a heavy mixer if you don't like using your fingers to mix the dough.

Divide the mixture and add different food colors to it for a festive touch. Blend color in by rolling and overlapping the dough. Form into desired shapes such as fruits, berries, vegetables, flowers, *julenisser*. Shapes should be small and solid.

Traditionally the marzipan pig is left the color of the almond paste. A narrow red ribbon is tied around its neck to add a bit of color.

Almond paste is best when it is freshly made. Store in an airtight container in the refrigerator so it does not dry out. May be frozen.

## Cutout Christmas sugar cookies

*Special equipment:* Holiday cookie cutters

¾ cup softened butter
1 cup granulated white sugar
2 large eggs
1 teaspoon vanilla *or* almond extract
2 cups all-purpose flour (reserve ¼ cup for the floured
        surface)
1 teaspoon baking powder
1 teaspoon salt

Cream butter and sugar. Add eggs and beat until light and fluffy. Add extract. Beat until smooth. Combine 1¾ cups flour, baking powder, and salt. Gradually beat into butter mixture until well blended. Refrigerate until firm, approximately 2 hours.

Using part of the remaining ¼ cup flour, lightly flour rolling surface. Roll dough to ⅛" thick or thinner, if desired. Cut with your choice of Christmas cookie cutters. Place 1" apart on ungreased cookie sheets. If using egg yolk paints instead of butter cream frosting, paint the cookie dough with the egg yolk paint before baking. Bake at 350°F for 4–8 minutes. Cool baked cookies on a rack immediately after removing them from the oven.

Makes about 4 dozen cookies depending on cookie size.

## Egg yolk paints

1 egg yolk
1 teaspoon water
tint with food colors, as desired

Mix egg yolk and water. Divide mixture into small bowls or cups—shot glasses work very well—and tint with food colors as desired. If paint thickens, stir in a few drops of water. Paint cut, raw dough with Christmas designs.

Bake at 350°F for 4–8 minutes until lightly browned around edges. Cool on a rack. After cooling, cookies without egg yolk paint may be frosted.

## Butter cream frosting

6 tablespoons butter
1 1-pound box powdered sugar, sifted
¼ cup (approximate) cream, half and half, *or* milk
1½ teaspoons vanilla *or* almond extract
tint with food colors, as desired

Cream butter and about half of the sifted powdered sugar. Beat in vanilla and 2 tablespoons of the milk. Gradually add the rest of the sugar. Add enough milk to make the consistency you prefer. Add a few drops of milk if it is too thick and more powdered sugar if it is too thin. Divide frosting into separate bowls and tint with food coloring as desired. Spread or pipe frosting on the cookies or add colored sugar, candies, etc.

Frosts about 4 dozen sugar cookies or one *kransekake*.

## Gingerbread people

*Special equipment*: Gingerbread figure cookie cutter or trace patterns from page 89

Preheat oven to 350°F.

¼ cup butter
½ cup granulated white *or* brown sugar
½ cup dark molasses
3½ cups all-purpose flour
1 teaspoon baking soda
¼ teaspoon ground cloves
½ teaspoon ground cinnamon
1 teaspoon ground ginger
½ teaspoon salt
¼ cup water

Cream butter and sugar in a large bowl. Beat in molasses. In a separate bowl, sift together dry ingredients. Add sifted ingredients slowly to butter mixture. Add ¼ cup of water alternately with dry ingredients. If your mixer can't handle heavy dough, you may need to finish mixing with your hands. On lightly floured surface, roll dough about ¼" thick. Using a floured cookie cutter or pattern you have made, cut out shapes from rolled out dough. Place figures on greased cookie sheet. Add raisins, candied cherries, or sprinkles before placing cookie in oven. Bake at 350°F for 8–10 minutes depending upon thickness. If using for a tree ornament, cookie needs to be baked longer. Also, remember to make a small hole at the top of the cookie before baking for the yarn or string to hang the cookie. Cookies are done when dough springs back after pressing it with your finger.

After cookies are completely cooled, frost with white or colored icing. Gingerbread cookies are a pleasant and spicy accompaniment to the sugar cookies. If using as an ornament, thread a 7" ribbon or string through hole after cookies are cooled.

Makes about 16 figures.


## Never fail divinity

*Special equipment:* Candy thermometer

3 cups granulated white sugar
¾ cup light corn syrup
¾ cup water
3 egg whites
1 3-ounce package flavored gelatin (pink or green colors for the holidays)
1 cup chopped nuts, candied cherries, or crushed peppermint candy (optional)

Mix sugar, corn syrup, and water in a 2-quart saucepan. Cook to the boiling point, stirring constantly. Cover for about 3 minutes to allow the steam to wash down any sugar crystals. Remove lid. Reduce heat and continue cooking, stirring occasionally, until a few drops tested in cold water form a hard ball (252°F on a candy thermometer).

While syrup mixture is cooking, beat egg whites in a separate bowl until they are fluffy. Add the dry gelatin gradually, beating until the mixture holds a definite peak. Pour the syrup into the egg white mixture in a thin, thin, stream beating constantly until candy holds a shape and loses its gloss. Do not over beat as divinity will have a rough appearance when finished. Stir in optional nuts at this point. Quickly spoon out divinity, using two soup spoons or teaspoons, and drop on marble slab or wax paper. Store in an airtight container after completely cool.

Makes 5–6 dozen pieces.

## Meringues

These light, airy cookies are a pleasant change from the heavier cookies already discussed. They do not store well and pick up moisture when left sitting. Fortunately, since they are frequently the first to go at any party, soggy meringues are rarely a problem. The basic recipe is 1 egg white for every ½ cup of powdered sugar and ¼ teaspoon of vanilla for flavoring.

Preheat oven to 200°F.

6 egg whites
1½ teaspoons vanilla
⅛ teaspoon cream of tartar
1½ cups sifted powdered sugar

Egg whites should be at room temperature. For best results with meringues recipes, all utensils should be absolutely free of fat or grease, including the bowl, beaters, and any spatulas. When separating the egg yolk from the egg white, do not allow any of the yolk to mix in with the egg white as this will prevent the egg whites from getting stiff.

Beat egg whites until frothy with an electric mixer. Add vanilla and cream of tartar. Gradually add sifted powdered sugar about a tablespoon at a time. Beat until mixture forms glossy, stiff peaks in bowl. Be careful not to overbeat.

Cover cookie sheets with parchment or wax paper to spread the heat evenly. Drop the mixture onto the wax paper with a spoon or use a pastry bag with a decorative tip. Bake for about 1 hour until cookie is dry inside. Lower temperature to 175°F if meringue starts to brown too much. Cookie will be almost white. Turn off the oven and allow the cookies to gradually cool for at least 5 minutes in the oven away from any drafts. Remove from the paper when completely cool. Store in an airtight container.

Makes 4 dozen cookies.


## Thumbprint cookies

Preheat oven to 350°F.

½ cup butter
¼ cup packed light brown sugar
1 egg, separated
½ teaspoon vanilla
1 cup all-purpose flour
¼ teaspoon salt
¾ cup finely chopped nuts
jelly

Mix butter, brown sugar, egg yolk, and vanilla until creamy in a medium-sized bowl. Sift together flour and salt. Add gradually to butter mixture. Roll dough into small balls, using about 1 teaspoon of dough. Beat egg white slightly with fork. Dip balls in egg white. Roll in the nuts. Place about 1" apart on ungreased baking sheet. Press thumb gently in the center of each ball. Bake 10–12 minutes. Fill thumbprint with jelly when cookies are completely cool or wait until cookies will be served.

Makes 3 dozen cookies.

## Spritz

These are a Christmas favorite of most Norwegian-Americans. It takes some practice to get the cookie press working at its best. All the more cookies to sample!

*Special equipment:* Spritz cookie press

Preheat oven to 400°F.

1 cup butter
½ cup granulated white sugar
1 egg
½ teaspoon salt
1 teaspoon almond *or* vanilla extract
2 cups all-purpose flour

Mix butter, sugar, egg, salt, and extract until creamy in a medium-sized bowl. Sift flour into mixture gradually, 1 cup at a time. Refrigerate for 10–15 minutes. If dough gets too hard, it doesn't go through the cookie press easily. Spoon about ¼ of the dough at a time into the cookie press, force dough through the press and pattern onto an ungreased baking sheet. Bake at 400°F for 6–9 minutes until a light golden. Cool cookie sheets between uses as a warm baking sheet will cause the dough to melt and pull away from the sheet when the press is lifted.

Makes about 5 dozen cookies.

# American pies

The pie symbolizes the abundance and generosity of Americans. The fruits and berries our ancestors used sparingly and frugally are presented in mounded pies during the holidays. Pumpkin pie lends itself to the openness of a single crust, berry pies to latticework, and apple pie to a double crust with intricate designs. The fragrances of cinnamon, nutmeg, and ginger combined with pumpkin, pecan, and apple are as decadent as they are heavenly.

## Pie crust

1 egg
4 cups all-purpose flour
2 cups shortening
½ cup cold water
1 teaspoon salt
1 tablespoon apple cider vinegar
1 egg white
granulated white sugar and cinnamon (optional)

Beat egg slightly in small bowl. Mix flour and shortening with pie cutter in a medium-sized bowl. Add egg. Add cold water, salt, and vinegar. Divide dough into 4 balls. Roll each ball of dough to ⅛" thickness. Cut 3 to size of 9" pie plate with about an 1" overhang. Form pie edge as desired. Lightly beat the egg white and brush it onto each of shells to prevent the crust from getting soggy. Fill the 3 pie shells with pumpkin, pecan, or apple pie mixture.

Since pie plates may be either metal or glass, different methods of baking are required. If using a metal pie plate, bake the pie on a heavy duty cookie sheet which has been heated for about 5 minutes in the preheated oven for a evenly baked crust. If an ovenproof glass pie plate is used, cut the baking time listed by one-fourth or one-fifth.

With the 4th ball of dough rolled out, adjust it over the apple filling. Cut attractive slits in top to allow the steam to escape. Seal edges. Sprinkle the top crust lightly with sugar and cinnamon.

Do not handle dough more than necessary as dough will become tough.

Makes 2 single pie crusts and 1 double crust.

## Pumpkin pie

Pumpkins are the sign of fall and harvest season. Christmas and Thanksgiving are wonderful occasions to serve this special treat. The original pumpkin pie shell was its own exterior. The seeds were removed, then milk, sugar, eggs, and the spices were added before baking. Now we generally pour the mixture into a pie shell.

Put oven rack 4–5 inches from bottom of oven and preheat oven to 425°F.

2 eggs
1 15-ounce can of solid pack pumpkin *or* 2 cups cooked pumpkin
¾ cup granulated white sugar
       *or* sugar may be divided into
        ¼ cup brown sugar plus ½ cup granulated white sugar
½ teaspoon salt
1 teaspoon ground cinnamon
½ teaspoon ground ginger
¼ teaspoon ground allspice *or* nutmeg
¼ teaspoon ground cloves
1 12-ounce can of undiluted evaporated milk
1 9" pie shell

In a medium size bowl, slightly beat eggs. Add pumpkin, sugar, salt, spices, and milk to eggs. Pour mixture into unbaked pie shell made according to previous directions or a purchased pie shell. Bake at 425°F for 15 minutes using recommended procedures in pie crust directions. Reduce temperature to 350°F and bake for an additional 45 minutes. Insert knife into center of pie to check for doneness. When knife comes out clean, pie is done. Cool. Serve within 3 hours if pie is unrefrigerated. Do not leave pie out for extended periods. Always refrigerate uneaten portions.

May be served with sweetened whipped cream.

2 cups chilled whipping cream
¼ cup honey
½ teaspoon ginger

In a chilled bowl, beat chilled whipping cream with chilled beaters until stiff. Gradually add honey and ginger. Chill 1–2 hours before serving on top of pie. As an alternative, add 1 teaspoon vanilla and 2–6 tablespoons of powdered sugar instead of the honey and ginger.

Be ever watchful while whipping cream, as just a few seconds too long turns the mixture into butter. For best results, chill all metal equipment and cream.

Makes 6–8 servings.

## Raleigh pecan pie

Put oven rack 4–5 inches from bottom of oven and preheat oven to 450°F.

3 eggs (reserve 1 teaspoon of the egg white) slightly beaten
1 cup white corn syrup
1 cup dark brown sugar
2 tablespoons fine corn meal
2 tablespoons melted butter
1 teaspoon vanilla
¼ teaspoon salt
1½ cups pecan pieces
1 9" deep dish pie shell

Lightly beat the 1 teaspoon of egg white and brush the pie shell with it to keep the crust from getting soggy. Slightly beat the rest of the eggs in a medium-sized bowl, but not so much as to form a foam or the foam will obscure the nuts on top of the pie. Stir in the rest of the filling ingredients. Pour mixture into unbaked pie shell made according to previous directions or into a purchased pie shell.

Set the pie crust on a cookie sheet or pizza pan for safety in handling the pie when hot. Use recommended baking procedures in pie crust directions. To prevent over browning of the nuts, cover the pie with an inverted aluminum pie pan of the same size or make an aluminum foil rounded cap for the pie. Place covered pie in oven and bake at 450°F for 10 minutes. Reduce heat to 325°F. Bake an additional 15 minutes. Remove cover and continue baking another 25-35 minutes until filling puffs up all over and moves a little when shaken gently. Total baking time is about 50–60 minutes.

Cool pan on a cake rack or other device that allows air to circulate under the pan. Allow to cool until it is just slightly warm before cutting.

Makes 6–12 servings.

# Apple pie

Put oven rack 4–5 inches from bottom of oven and preheat oven to 350°F.

1 cup granulated white sugar
¼ teaspoon salt
1 tablespoon all-purpose flour
½ teaspoon cinnamon
½ teaspoon nutmeg
8 tart apples, approximately 2 pounds
1 teaspoon egg white
1 9" pie shell
2 tablespoons butter
1 upper pie crust
granulated white sugar and cinnamon (optional)

Combine sugar, salt, flour, cinnamon, and nutmeg in a large bowl. Peel, core, and thinly slice apples. Add sliced apples to sugar mixture. Stir gently until apples are well coated. Lightly beat 1 teaspoon of egg white and brush the mixture onto the 9" pie shell to prevent the crust from getting soggy. Place mixture in layers in the pie shell. Dot mixture with butter.

Roll out second crust to ⅛" thick. Adjust it over the filling to cover it adequately. Seal edges. Cut attractive slits in top to allow the steam to escape. Sprinkle the top crust lightly with sugar and cinnamon. Bake at 350°F for 50–60 minutes using recommended procedures in pie crust directions. Cool and, if desired, drizzle with the thin glaze used for *kransekake*. Serve with whipping cream or vanilla ice cream.

Makes 6–12 servings.

## More Norwegian recipes

For other traditional Norwegian recipes the following books have been published:

Brimi, Arne and Bengt Wilson. *A Taste of Norway: a cookbook based on nature's own ingredients.* Oslo, Norway: Norwegian University Press, 1987. 82-00-036065. Mr. Brimi's book has been translated from the Norwegian into English with American measurements.

Bø, Olav, Liv Gregersen Konsten, Oskar Steingrimsen. *Norsk mat med tradisjon.* Oslo, Norway: Forenede Margarinfabrikker A/S, 1980. This little book with only 39 pages has some beautiful pictures taken in traditional settings including a *stabbur.*

*Kitchen secrets of the Daughters of Norway.* Portland, OR: Grand Lodge Daughters of Norway, 1956.

*The Norwegian kitchen.* Editor, Kjell E. Innli; photographers, Per Eide and Bengt Wilson; recipes, the Association of Norwegian Chefs; translated by Melody Favish. Kristiansund: KOM, 1993.

Ojakangas, Beatrice. *The Great Scandinavian baking book.* Boston, MA: Little Brown and Company, 1988.

Scott, Astrid Karlsen. *Authentic Norwegian cooking.* Olympia, WA: Nordic Adventures, 1995.

Scott, Astrid Karlsen. *Ekte Norsk jul: traditional Christmas foods.* Crosby, ND: Journal Publishing Company, 1993.

*Takk for maten II.* Tacoma, WA: Embla Lodge No. 2, Daughters of Norway, 1994.

| Table grace | *Bordbønn* |
|---|---|
| Come, Lord Jesus, be our guest, | *I Jesu navn går vi til bords* |
| Let these gifts to us be blest, | *Å spise og drikke på ditt ord* |
| by His hand we all are fed, | *Deg Gud til ære, oss til gavn* |
| Give us, Lord, our daily bread. Amen. | *Så får vi mat I Jesu navn. Amen.* |

# Little Christmas Eve / *Lille julaften*

December 23, Little Christmas Eve or *lille julaften*, is the night *nissefar*, or the Father Christmas Elf, comes to decorate the tree and the house in Norway. This tradition of decorating the tree and house just a few days before Christmas is still followed by many people of Norwegian descent in the United States. Some may start decorating homes, yards, and trees during the Thanksgiving weekend to be taken down about a month later on New Year's Day. Others may put decorations up about the middle of December and take them down on Epiphany. Some may even leave their tree up as long as it looks good which can be as late as Valentine's Day when the hearts on the tree are just transferred to other areas of the home to celebrate the Day of Hearts.

# Christmas decorations / *Julepynter*

## Greens and flowers

A holiday tradition in the United States is to decorate our entry doors with local greens and pine cones attractively arranged in wreaths and swags. Other materials for making wreaths include dried grape vines, herbs and flowers. Generally, wreaths are not put on the doors of Norwegian homes except for funerals.

Decorating a fireplace mantle in garlands or greens, cards, and candles of many colors or just gleaming white candles make a home seem ready for Christmas. White candles are always my choice because I have found colored candles often leave the dye from the melted wax on wood and tablecloths. For those of us without a fireplace mantle, window sills, hutches, and buffets become the center of decorating.

During the holidays, flowers and greens used in Northwest and Norwegian homes include branches from the evergreen holly tree. Using holly during this time of year dates back at least to the Roman midwinter sowing and harvest celebration of *Saturnalia* held in December. The Roman naturalist of the first century, Pliny, wrote: *"A holly tree planted in a town house or a country house keeps off magic influences ... so powerful is the nature of the tree."* [1] In 1640, John Parkinson states that *"the branches with berries, are used at Christ tide to decke up our houses withall, but that they should defend the house from lightening, and keepe themselves from witchcraft, is a superstition of the Gentiles, learned from Pliny."* [2] The name holly comes from an old Norse word *hulfr*. Holly eventually came to represent the holy season for Christians, too. The white flower represented Christ's purity, the blood red berries were Christ's drops of blood, and the sharp-thorned leaves became identified with the crown of

---

[1] Pliny. *Natural history* with an English translation in ten volumes by W. H. S. Jones. Cambridge, MA: Harvard University Press, 1956. Vol. VII, page 85.

[2] Parkinson, John. *Theatrum Botanicum*. London: The Kings Majestyes especail priviledge, printed by Tho. Cotes, 1640. Page 1487.

thorns. Thus the Norwegian word for holly, *kristtorn,* means Christ's thorn. Be sure to wear gloves when handling this prickly plant.

Green trailing ivy, the brightly colored tall amaryllis, and a variety of Christmas cacti, blooming this time of year all, add an additional festive touch to holiday tables and corners of special rooms and kitchens. Using Christmas greens of berried juniper, pine, noble fir, silver fir, incense cedar, salal, and holly in decorating is limited only by your imagination.

Red tulips are a favorite flower in Norway during this special season. Called *tulipaner,* they are often combined with evergreens in a vase. Tulips are forced to bloom during the Christmas holidays by planting the bulbs many weeks ahead. Talk with your local florist about the process of forcing the blooms. These potted bulbs also make nice gifts to bring Christmas cheer to shut-ins and friends.

Another favorite colorful plant used during the Christmas season is the poinsettia. Originally from Mexico, it has been in the United States for over 150 years. During the holidays, it is probably the most common plant seen in our homes. Often the red leaves are called the flower, but the actual flower is the small yellow center of the plant. Mexican Native Americans considered it a " flower of purity. " During the sixteenth century, Christian missionaries to Mexico encouraged the native people's reverence for the red-leafed poinsettia. It was given a Christian meaning through a legend about a young girl from Cuernavaca, Mexico. An angel had appeared to the child, telling her to bring a weed to the chapel for the baby Jesus. When the green weed was placed on the altar on Christmas Eve, it became a flaming red star. Thus a common weed became one of Mexico's most prized flowers. The poinsettia comes in colors ranging from white to very deep reds. This plant is also popular in Norway where it is called *julestjernen,* or the Christmas Star. Interestingly enough, a Norwegian named Thormod Hegg was influential in developing the plant into something more compact and suitable for indoor use. In its natural state they can grow to be large ten-foot shrubs.

Mistletoe, known as *misteltein* in Norway, is often in the stores during the Christmas season, usually in small clear sacks. It can be found in Eastern and Southern states and also in Oregon growing on oak trees, sweet gum, and red maple, but it is also receives life from other types of trees. Mistletoe is a parasitic plant and has leather-like green leaves with yellowish flowers and waxy-looking white berries. The mistletoe traditions of bringing good luck and giving protection from evil spirits were passed down into both American and Norwegian cultures by the Celts. It is believed kissing under the mistletoe was brought to us by the Scandinavians through the Norse myth about Balder.

Balder, the son of Odin and Frigg, was considered the most noble and pious of the Norse gods. He was the beautiful summer sun god. Balder was haunted by terrible nightmares about the ending of his life. As his mother wanted to protect him from this unknown fate, she sent her maid servants to take oaths from all living creatures, plants, metals, and stones to not hurt Balder. All of these promised to spare Balder from any harm.

Meanwhile, the mistletoe clung to the oak for protection and was thought to be harmless, so no oath was taken. Loke, known as the evil one, found out that no pledge was received from the mistletoe. With the help of an elf skilled in making arrows, he fashioned a magic and deadly arrow from a mistletoe twig. Hodur, who was Balder's blind brother, was given the deadly arrow by Loke. Balder was at a contest where everyone was shooting arrows at him since he could not be injured by any living thing, metal, or stone. Hodur, as a participant, sent the magic arrow flying, thinking nothing would harm his beloved brother. When the mistletoe arrow pierced Balder, he fell dead immediately, causing great sorrow among the gods. The tears of Frigg became the white berries of the mistletoe. She blessed the plant even though it had caused her son's death through no fault of its own. Mistletoe then became a symbol of love. It was believed Frigg bestowed a kiss on anyone who passed under the mistletoe.

In days of old, meeting an enemy underneath a sprig of mistletoe meant weapons were laid down and the enemies were to embrace each other in friendship. Our custom of hanging the mistletoe in the doorway originally meant anyone entering had an invitation to seal his or her friendship with a kiss. Each young woman kissed under a berry-filled sprig would be given one of the elegant white berries as a token of good luck. When all the berries were gone, one no longer had the privilege of kissing under the mistletoe.

## Paper snowflakes and stars / *Papir snøfjoner og stjerner*

Paper snowflakes or stars cut to hang in windows, on the tree, or glued onto wrapping paper, represent the traditional weather and sparkling nights of the Northern Hemisphere during this time of year. Even if we don't have a white Christmas, we can always pretend we have snow by making snowflakes to fall around us. Snowflakes or stars are easy to make with:

Tissue paper, rice paper, construction paper or fadeless paper
Scissors
Newspapers
Paper toweling
Iron
Spray on adhesive
Concentrated water colors, food coloring, glitter, crayons, sequins
Thread or yarn
Needle

The paper you choose will depend on how much you want to spend and how fancy you want the snowflakes or stars to look. Determine the size of the snowflake or star by deciding where the snowflake or star will be placed. If it is used on a card or as a Christmas tree decoration, the paper size will be much smaller.

After choosing the paper and size of the flake or star, fold the paper in half. Then fold it again into quarters. If the paper is thin enough, fold it one more time. It can be folded more times, but it may be difficult to cut through it with scissors. The design cut in the paper may be simple or intricate. There is no set pattern for cutting, just experiment to see what type of cuts you like best. When folding and cutting paper, be careful to leave at least one small portion of each fold uncut so the flake or star stays in one piece.

Thin tissue paper or rice paper may be colored with vibrant colors from concentrated water colors in a bottle or with food coloring. After cutting the pattern desired, keep the paper folded and add the colors, one at a time. Work on a flat surface covered with newspaper. Some food coloring bottles come as a small squeeze bottle, or an eye dropper may be used. Be very careful with the color as you don't want to have it on everything in the house. It is best to start with the light shades and add the darkest colors last. Be sure the color penetrates all layers. Blot the folded star or flake between the paper toweling or newspaper to remove the excess moisture. Unfold. Place the star or flake between two dry papers. Press flat with an iron set to medium heat. Remove the top paper and set the colored star or flake aside to dry completely.

Snowflakes or stars made with heavier paper may be decorated by coloring with crayons, but be careful not to tear the delicate cuts. Of course, the paper may be colored with crayons before cutting if no particular pattern is desired. To decorate with glitter or sequins, place newspaper on a table or other flat surface, lay the flake or star on the newspaper, then spray on the adhesive on the top of the star or flake. Sprinkle colored glitter or sequins onto the adhesive. Let dry. Carefully remove the star or flake, gently shaking it and leaving extra sequins and glitter on the newspaper for easy cleanup.

If applying the star or flake to wrapping paper, spray the dry flake or star with a spray-on adhesive. Lay the pattern gently on the card or wrapping paper. Starting at the center, gently smooth the flake or star out. Press with fingers into place.

If hanging the stars or snowflakes, thread a needle with 7" of regular sewing thread or a 7" yarn strand, and poke the needle through the center fold's top edge, leaving 3½" of the thread or yarn strand on each side. Tie the two ends of the thread together to form a hanger for the snowflake or star.

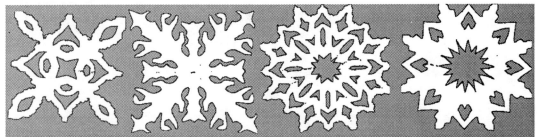

## Paper Santas and animals / *Papir julenisser og dyr*

*Julenisser*, cut in groups, holding hands and dancing are often used for decorating tables, mantles, and around the Christmas tree in Norway. In the United States small and large Santas and animals, especially reindeer, often decorate front doors, lawns, siding of homes, windows, and tables.

Tracing paper or cookie cutter
Pencil
Colored construction paper or similar paper
      heavy enough to stand on its own
      when cut in a grouping
Scissors

Select a pattern from those shown or a favorite cookie cutter. Fold paper into several layers no wider than the pattern and thick enough to make a chain, but not so thick the scissors won't cut the paper. If you have selected a pattern from below, trace around it using a pencil and tracing paper. Cut out the traced pattern with scissors. Place this pattern or the cookie cutter you have chosen on top of the folded paper. Trace around the outline of the pattern with a pencil. Cut around the pattern you have traced, being sure to leave the joined ends of the folds uncut so the chain will stay together. You may need to make several short chains if you want a long string of the same pattern, as construction paper does not come in long widths. Just tape, staple, or glue the ends together. Leave a small tab on the side of the first and last edge so the chains may be easily joined.

These chains may be left as is, or decorated as done for the snowflakes with colored pencils, crayons, or glitter.

## Incense of kings / *Kongerøkelse*

The smells of Christmas are with us whenever we think of Christmas. The pungent fragrance of cinnamon mixed with cloves and fresh greens take us back to a time and place we will never forget. To recreate some of the aromas of Christmas, mix a small potpourri of cloves, sticks of cinnamon, ginger, and fresh orange peel into a small saucepan filled with water. The pan can then be placed on the back burner of the stove. Let the contents simmer in the water and be careful to keep enough water in the pan so it doesn't burn. Little potpourri pots are now made especially for this. The water is heated with a small tea light candle. In Norway, this is known as *kongerøkelse* or incense of kings. It is kept burning during the holidays, filling homes with a spicy fragrance representing the gifts the Wise Men brought to Christ.

## Christmas straw and sheaves / *Julehalm og julenekker*

Straw and grains had many magical qualities in Norway. Much like reading tea leaves, it was believed the grains could predict the weather, love, marriage, and death. If the grains that fell on the floor were of good quality, it indicated a good harvest. If the grains were poor, a poor harvest was predicted. If barley grains were found, barley should be planted in the spring. If oat grains fell, the farmer should plant oats. Barley grains were thought to be a better omen than oat grains.

People would leave their regular beds during *jul* and sleep together on Christmas straw or hay called *julehalm* on the floor of the only room of the house or the main portion of the house. They believed this kept them safe from the wandering ghosts or *julereia* visiting during the holidays. The dreams you had while sleeping on the Christmas straw were said to come true. Unmarried people may even see their future spouse in dreams on these nights.

Ever mindful of the hospitality to be shown guests, the living left food and drink on the table for the *julereia* who came searching for food. They also found a place to rest in the beds abandoned by family members. The last grains were also left in the fields to feed the horses of these wandering spirits. In Christian times the invisible guests became the Holy Family searching for a place to stay. The straw then came to symbolize the bed of straw on which Mary gave birth to Jesus. It also represented the equality of men and women and the rich and poor during the Christmas season.

In those old days, on Christmas morning, breakfast was also served on the hay. It would be bad luck to drop something on the floor. If you found a grain under your place at the table you would probably die sometime during the next year—a frightful thought for anyone on Christmas morning.

A type of Christmas cake or *julekake* was made from the grain in the last straw gathered from the fields after the harvest. The cake was saved until the next spring when it was broken into pieces and, during the plowing, sown onto the fields for a good harvest.

The children bunched the last straw from the fields into what was called a *bruse*, which represented the hairy tuft on the forehead of a goat. Crosses were also made from the magical straw along with straw figures of men, women, and animals, perhaps in remembrance of the old fertility rites. Above the doors, straw crosses were fastened for protection to those within. These crosses and other straw figures are still seen today at many gift stores and Christmas bazaars.

Taking care of the birds and animals is as important today as it was hundreds of years ago. We often hang suet and provide seeds for the birds to eat during the winter season as snow covers the food supply of the birds.

A favorite symbol of Christmas in Norway is the *julenek*, a sheaf of grain hung out on a pole for the birds as a winter treat. In olden times this was done as an offering to the fertility gods. Perhaps with its magic, the birds would be prevented from damaging the next year's crop. It was also believed the sheaves would protect the house, cattle, and crops from witchcraft and other evils during the rest of the season.

The *julenek* came to the Ballard district in Seattle during the Christmas season several years ago, adding a festive touch to our business district. They decorated trees, light posts, and backyards of local residents. To make your own *julenek* all you need is a bundle of grain, such as wheat. A bundle would be about the size of what you can hold with two hands or about 5" in diameter. This is tied with a red ribbon, straw, or twine. The *julenek* may then be attached securely to a tree, roof, or other appropriate place so it doesn't blow away in a windstorm.

Birdfeeders of various types attract different birds. It is important to keep the feeders clean, dry, and filled with food to maintain a healthy bird population. Those filled with thistle seed are a favorite of pine siskins. Jays like peanuts, but so do the squirrels. Towhees, finches, chickadees, and Oregon juncos like millet and sunflower seeds. If you are lucky enough to live by a more forested area, quail are attracted to corn. Fill the bird bath with fresh water. If available, place a heater, made especially for keeping the water from freezing, into the bird bath.

The holly trees provide red berries much to the enjoyment of the birds who can strip a tree of the luscious berries after a snow storm. Other trees also provide nourishment and homes for the birds during the cold winter season.

A favorite bird in Norway during the winter season is the *dompap* or bullfinch with its red or rosy feathered breast. It was believed if the *dompap* was the first bird to eat from the sheaf of grain, it would be a good year. If the cheerful bird came out of the woods during the winter, the weather would be terrible with much cold and snow. Here in the Pacific Northwest, the chickadee with its black cap and friendly nature makes its home in the plentiful conifers during the winter season. Watching the chickadees eat from the feeders provides a relaxing pastime and pleasant break from the holiday rush.

In 1978 Paul Berg wrote about his Christmas experiences for his family. He served as president of Leif Erikson Lodge No. 1, Sons of Norway, in Seattle. In June of 1992, he passed away. His wife, Marian, kindly provided us with his story.

*In the autumn and winter of 1927 I was a 17-year-old youth, up in Guldalen, south of Trondheim, working in the woods. That was the first time I was away from my home farm in Rissa, west of Trondheim. That fall, we were in the forests cutting timbers and taking them by big carriers, using horses to bring them to the sawmills for cutting and distribution. Already I had thought about Christmas that year. The farmer and the business man for whom I worked, and where I was staying, were hoping to have me stay there for jul, but my mind was made up. There I sat in the middle of the woodpile, freezing and cold, and longing for my home and family. Early in the morning of julaften [Christmas Eve], I said goodbyes to the folks I had stayed with on the farm and took the train to Trondheim. I set out by train with 200 kroner. In Trondheim, I bought a small Christmas gift for my two brothers and a little something for all to enjoy for jul. I just couldn't go home in the cold winter in a threadbare wind jacket, so I spent a whole 40 kroner for a new vinterfrakk [winter overcoat]. The Kristiansund boat was anchored at a dock up in Nidelva in Trondheim, where I boarded, and the first stop was at Kvithild in Rissa. There my brother Oscar was on the dock to welcome me home. He had Blakke, our old black horse, and soon the two of us were aboard the sleigh with Blakke and on our homeward journey.*

*Mother had a bed in the living room and was almost completely bedridden for several years. She was a strong person in her younger years, but a stroke had befallen her and she was unable to do all of the things she had done before. This was Christmas time and we all pitched in to make it very pleasant for her.*

*The juletre was not put up in the house until Christmas Eve by tradition. First, we put up juleneket and fuglebordet [a gathering of wheat and oats arranged on a pole or on the big carriage house for the birds for Christmas.] Then the Christmas tree, which had been found two days earlier up in the hills, was brought in the house from the fjøset [cow barn] and placed in the stua [living room]. Also the Christmas trimmings which were kept in the storloft [big attic] upstairs were brought down and we three brothers decorated the tree. The candles were placed on the tree, but were not lit. After the tree was decorated, we went to the spisestua [dining room], and had our Christmas Eve dinner. We had roast pork and sviskegrøt [prune pudding]. After the meal, father read the entire Christmas story from the Bible. We then went back to the living room and lit the candles on the tree. This was when bestemor [grandmother] and bestefar [grandfather] came from their kammerset [living quarters] and took part in the singing of "Jeg er så glad hver julekveld." So that was a high time for all of us, Christmas Eve in Bergsaune. On Christmas Day we went to the church where I was baptized and confirmed two years earlier. That was the high time of all for me. Now I have celebrated jul in America, having left in March of 1928. In the last 41 years I have had my own family and have celebrated Christmas with the children and grandchildren in the traditional way it was done in my home in Norway. I hope that our children and grandchildren will have a traditional Christmas in the many years to come with a Christian home and julehygge [Christmas coziness]!*

# The Christmas tree / *Juletreet*

The tradition of our Christmas tree, similar to what we see today, came from Germany. According to legend, on a clear winter's night in the sixteenth century, Martin Luther walked home on Christmas Eve through the sparkling, white snow. That special evening, the stars were shining through the frost-covered branches of the evergreen forest. It was so beautiful he came home, cut a small fir tree, brought it into the house, put candles on it, and lit them one by one to bring the beauty of the night into his home. Decorated trees have been a part of holiday traditions since the 1700s in royal homes and for community trees. The idea of having a tree in private homes came to Norway in 1828. A German immigrant named August Imgart is credited with bringing the tree into our homes and the United States in 1847. The most common trees used for Christmas in the Northwest are fir and pine, but in Norway it is the spruce. These trees never fade in their evergreen color even in the darkest days of winter.

Whether cutting your own tree or buying one from a local lot, selecting the perfect tree may take some time. Christmas tree lots can be found on street corners to raise funds for groups or private enterprise. Some families still try to cut their own tree either in the forest or on a Christmas tree farm. Permits are needed for cutting trees in the national forests. Beginning on November 20, permits are sold at ranger stations or the national local office in your area. Call the Forest Service number listed under the United States Government in the blue pages of your phone book for costs and availability of permits. Trees from the forest are often a unique shape as they show signs of their struggle to survive in the wilds of the Northwest. Those on the U-cut tree farms have been cultivated and shaped to look their best. As it seems there are always at least two trees to consider, take along some bright or neon-colored ribbon, tape, or other material at least 1" wide and 6" long. This can be tied onto one of the branches of each tree being considered for your home. Then it is easy to make a selection from the marked trees of your most favorite at the tree farm.

One year my father, mother, and a family friend were cutting trees for themselves and me. The family friend and my father thought the perfect tree was the one with the double leader or two tops. It was a very different tree to decorate. Two stars topped my tree that year.

To keep your tree fresh, recut the trunk at least 1" above the original cut just before putting it in water and the Christmas tree stand. My dad now takes the piece of trunk leftover from the cut and makes a tree ornament to hang on the tree. Be sure the Christmas tree stand is clean. Rinse it with a solution of a capful of bleach mixed with water to reduce the number of organisms that may decrease the water uptake by the tree. If the tree isn't coming into the house for a few days, be sure to put it in a bucket of water outside immediately after cutting. Use lukewarm water as it is taken up by the tree more easily than cold water. Add fresh water daily.

Noel Wannebo Bruzzichesi of Seattle, was born in Minneapolis, Minnesota, in the late 1940s of Norwegian and Finnish heritage. Later, her family moved to New England where she spent her growing up years. She recalls her early Christmas memories and especially her Christmas trees fondly. Theodore Wannebo, Noel's father, is also part of the story and was present during the interview.

*We always had a tree that needed to be loved. We used to go out and get the tree up in the woods. We got a "Charlie Brown Christmas Tree," Dad always found the tree that needed to be cut. He used to say, "That one's too nice to cut," so he would never cut a good tree. The tree went into a huge stainless steel bucket filled with sand. That makes the best stand. In the sand it never tips over.*

*I was lucky because I had my grandparents, my mother's parents. They were Finnish. Christmas Eve was a family time centered around us kids. We either went to Grandma's and Grandpa's house or they came to ours. When my aunt, who was 14 years older than I, got married, her husband, Uncle Raymond, came with us. It was a nice Christmas exchange.*

*Gifts were always wrapped in white tissue paper with Christmas stickers on them. There are two Christmases I remember most. One, Dad painted my cradle gray and painted my cat's name on it. My cat's name was Heila. The other Christmas I remember is the year Dad gave Mom a garbage can for Christmas.*

*Theodore adds to the story, "We were just broke as heck. We always tried to get stuff for the kids. So I said [to Noel's mother], 'What do you want?' She said I gotta have a decent garbage pail. So I bought her a garbage pail. You know, one of those fancy ones you step on [to open the lid]. I wrapped it all up and she saw that big box and was imagining all sorts of things—fur coat, you know—she opens it up. I wish to this day I had a picture of her face! I've been paying for that garbage can ever since!"*

# Decorations for the tree / *Juletrepynter*

The traditional tree in Norway is decorated with vertical strands of small Norwegian flags, paper hearts called *julekurver* or *hjertekurver*, cone-shaped baskets known as *kremmerhus*, and white lights or candles. Straw goats and crosses, paper birds, and apples that are one of the few fresh fruits available in Norway during the winter also hang from the tree. The beautiful tree is topped with a radiant star, a symbol of the Star of Bethlehem.

Decorating a Christmas tree in the United States may follow a different, imaginative theme each year, or it may be decorated in a traditional way year after year. Perhaps you may want to try hanging your tree upside down from the ceiling. Strings of bright red cranberries and creamy white popcorn, paper chains, gingerbread cookies with ribbon, candy canes, and white or multicolored lights adorn the traditional tree in America. A glowing angel or twinkling star tops our favorite evergreen tree.

Rosemary Antel was born during World War II near Pittsburgh, Pennsylvania, of Norwegian heritage. With a Norwegian grandfather from her mother's side of the family, she recounts her Christmas history to Noel as a hybrid tradition.

*My grandfather insisted on celebrating Christmas Eve. My family would drive to his farm and my brothers and I would race to the kitchen door for the chance to be the one to ring the horse collar bells hung by the door for the season. Inside were wonderful smells of cookies, coffee, and a balsam fir tree. He always had popcorn balls and little baskets and paper cones filled with candy on his Christmas tree. Sometimes grandma made cookies to hang on the tree and there were always popcorn strings, cranberry strings, and paper chains. The grandkids were always put to work making these to keep them out of mischief. We'd go over to Grandpa's for Christmas Eve and then back home again, an hour trip each way, the kids sleeping on the way home. We did that as long as my grandmother and grandfather were strong enough to host Christmas Eve.*

*At that time, my mother's two younger sisters and younger brother lived with us as her mother had died and these aunts and uncle were still in high school and college. There was an abundance of adults in the family, and Mom's sisters and brother enjoyed taking care of us kids.*

*We would get back home about midnight and we would be sent upstairs to go to sleep. Then the crew of adults would go into action, putting up our tree, assembling toys, wrapping presents and filling stockings, starting with a huge orange in the toe. We would try real hard to go to sleep, but with all this scurrying and rustling downstairs, it was hard. Finally exhausted, we'd sleep but were up at daybreak attacking the stockings which we found hung on the foot of our bed. The rule was that we weren't to go downstairs to open presents until everyone else was up. Of course, we just couldn't wait and sneaked into the living room and found it transformed into a fairyland, a wonderland. We found a huge tree with an angel on top, floating on a cloud of angel hair with lights softly glowing through the cloud. There were greens and holly, mistletoe, candles in the windows, piles of colorful presents under the tree, and a manger scene under the tree, on a sheet that was sprinkled with glitter snow.*

One of the things I remember most was what my mother did for Christmas. She always did special things to take care of the birds at Christmas. If she could get my grandfather or one of my uncles to save a sheaf of oats for her from the summer harvest, she would tie it with a red ribbon and hang it in a tree. It was always the tree outside the kitchen window so she could watch the birds. She hung chunks of suet tied up in string bags in the tree. Sometimes she hung apples, ribbons saved from previous Christmases, and pine cones stuffed with suet and birdseed.

Then, of course, she'd bake for us. There were many things we just didn't get except at Christmas. She would make butter cookies or the fancy dark spicy cookies that had holes in them for ribbons and were decorated with icing and hung on the tree. She also made fruit filled cookies, at least a half dozen other special cookies and fruit cakes. Those were the things I thought of as being Christmas. We would have homemade cinnamon rolls and hot chocolate for Christmas breakfast and a big dinner.

My most memorable Christmas was the year I first tried to ski. My grandfather had made some homemade skis. Being a farmer, he could work with metal and work with wood. He had all those survival skills a good farmer had to have, being able to make whatever was needed on a moment's notice. He had made a very heavy pair of wooden skis with turned up toes, metal heel and toe pieces, and pieces of harness straps for bindings. I didn't ask anyone, but took a couple of old broom handles for poles and the skis, and carried them to the top of the hill in one of the pastures. I strapped the skis to my galoshes. Of course, nobody had told me how to do any of this, and I'm not even sure I had ever seen anyone ski, but I had this idea—you just put the skis on and went down the hill, like standing up sled riding. It was a steep hill, and before long I was going lickety-split. At the bottom of the hill was a barbed wire fence and I thought, "What do I do?" Panicked, I sat down. That was the end of my skiing! I didn't try skiing again until I moved to the state of Washington.

## Strings of cranberries, popcorn, cones, or cereal

Put on old clothes before starting this project so the cranberries do not stain anything special.

Fresh cranberries poured into a bowl
Freshly popped popcorn, unsalted and unbuttered (one large bowl makes a five foot chain)
Dried hemlock cones or other type of small cone
Dry cereal such as O's or round cereal
Sturdy white or red sewing thread or clear plastic fishing line
Long sharp needle
Scissors

Thread a long, sharp needle with a length of thread easily handled by you. Double the thread and fasten the end with a knot large enough to prevent the first cranberry from falling off the string. Do not exceed 6 feet as the thread will tangle. Take a cranberry and pierce the center of the cranberry with the needle and thread. Draw the needle and thread through until the cranberry reaches the knot. Tie another knot around the first cranberry to stop it from falling off the end. Continue adding cranberries, but without additional knots. Push each cranberry on tightly because the cranberries will eventually dry out, causing the thread to show. When as many cranberries as needed are on the thread, cut off the thread with the scissors and tie a knot large enough to prevent the last cranberry from pulling out of the string. Additional strings may be tied to the previous string to make handling easier, if longer strings are desired.

Popcorn, cone, and cereal strings are made in the same manner. You may want to combine several of these for a more colorful tree. The popcorn should be freshly popped because stale popcorn may shatter when threading.

## Christmas tree lights / *Juletrelyser*

There is something magical about this time of the year. The nights are long in the northern climates. We try to bring as much light into our world as possible, whether it is with the small white candles or strings of lights. Turn off all the lights, except those on the tree, and gaze at those hundreds of glowing lights. They seem to be the stars brought inside our homes. These lights bounce off the glass ornaments and the walls glow as they reflect the light so needed in these dark hours. Then the crystal birds are flying, the toy ornaments come alive, and Santa and *nisser* under the tree enjoy the festival of lights as much as we do.

## Christmas heart baskets / *Julekurver eller hjertekurver*

Several examples of heart baskets are shown here with different patterns and designs. Eventually try making your own designs to give to family and friends. Traditionally these hearts are filled with candy, nuts, small presents and surprises, and then hung on the Christmas tree. In some homes, a heart is put on the post of a bed or on a door handle in your bedroom on December. Then a small package or Christmas goody is put in it each day until Christmas Eve.

Colored construction paper, glossy wrapping paper, butcher paper or fadeless art paper
Glue or glue stick, tape, or staples and a stapler
Pencil
Scissors
Ruler
Glass, cup or other round object about 3½" in diameter

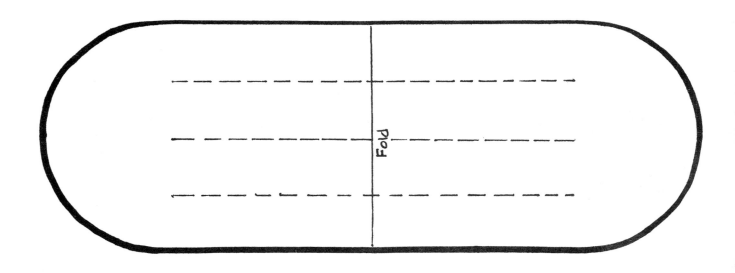

The basic heart pattern is the easiest example. Cut two pieces of paper the size of pattern. Traditionally, one piece of paper is red and the other piece is white. Fold the cut pieces of paper in half. Take one cut piece of folded paper (A) and place it still folded inside of piece two (B) to make a heart shape. Either tape, glue or staple the edges so a basket is formed.

Cut an additional strip of paper (C) about ½" wide and 7" long to form the handle. Fold this piece of paper in half. Either tape, glue or staple the handle in the middle of the heart where the V shape is formed.

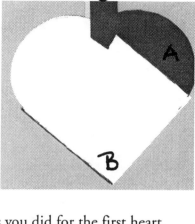

The woven heart is slightly more complicated. The first woven heart made is always the most challenging. As you gain experience, the ends weave into each other more easily and intricate patterns may be designed. Cut two pieces of paper, using the pattern in the first heart above. After you cut the two pieces of paper, fold each piece in half as you did for the first heart. This time cut three slits starting at the folded edge as shown in the example. Weave these two pieces together by beginning with the top strip 1. Push it, doubled, through the inside of strip 2. Open strip 1 and slip it over the top of the doubled strip 3. Next, weave the double strip 1 through the inside of opened strip 4. For the last one, open strip 1 and slip the loop over the top strip 5. Take alternate strips of colors opening the strip of one color and threading it through the other color. Now slide strip 1 down and weave strip 6 as you wove strip 1 the first time, except this time slip the loop over where you put strip 1 through the inside and slip it through where you put strip 1 over. This will create a beautiful woven basket that opens up to hold special items for Christmas. Add a handle as you did on the first basket above.

Many colors and types of paper may be used. For example, red and gold, red and green, silver and gold are common colors used for the baskets. Glossy wrapping paper is a favorite, but paper with prints on it, fabric, and fuzzy paper are options, too.

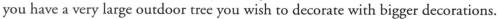

The size of the pattern may vary as well as the numbers and type of cuts made. Perhaps you have a very small tree for a special doll house you keep under the tree or you have a very large outdoor tree you wish to decorate with bigger decorations.

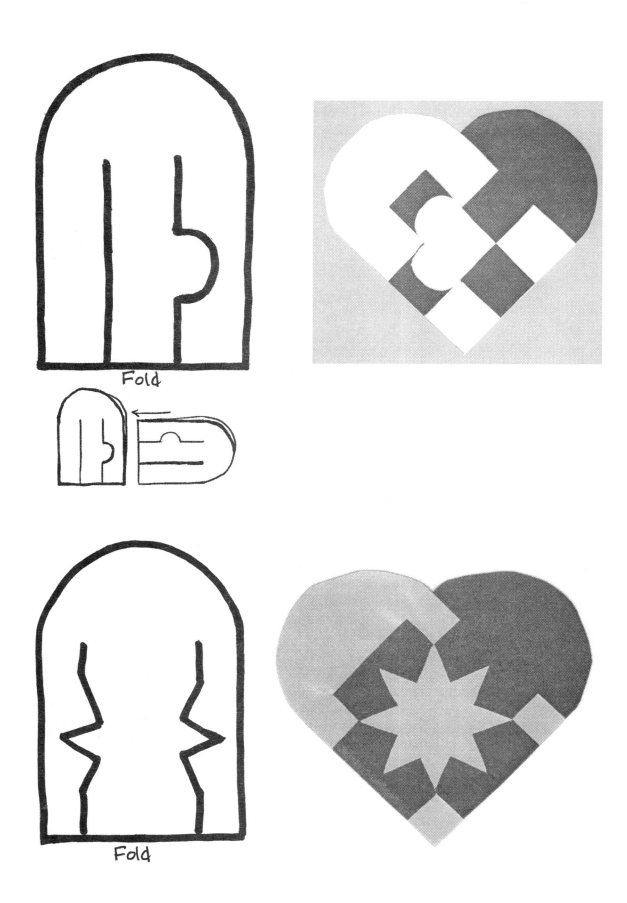

Fold

Fold

82

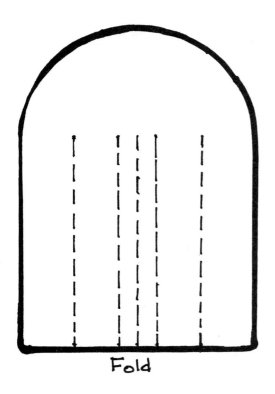

Fold

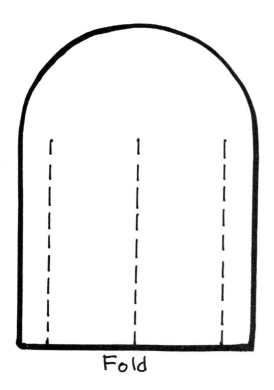

Fold

83

Another type of heart basket may be made with two circles. The circles are the same size. Draw two separate circles around the cup or glass on either the same color of paper or two different colors for contrast. Cut around the circles. Fold the circles in half. Place the ends of the folded circles inside each other. This forms a heart shape. Glue, staple or tape into place. Add a handle as you did on the first basket above.

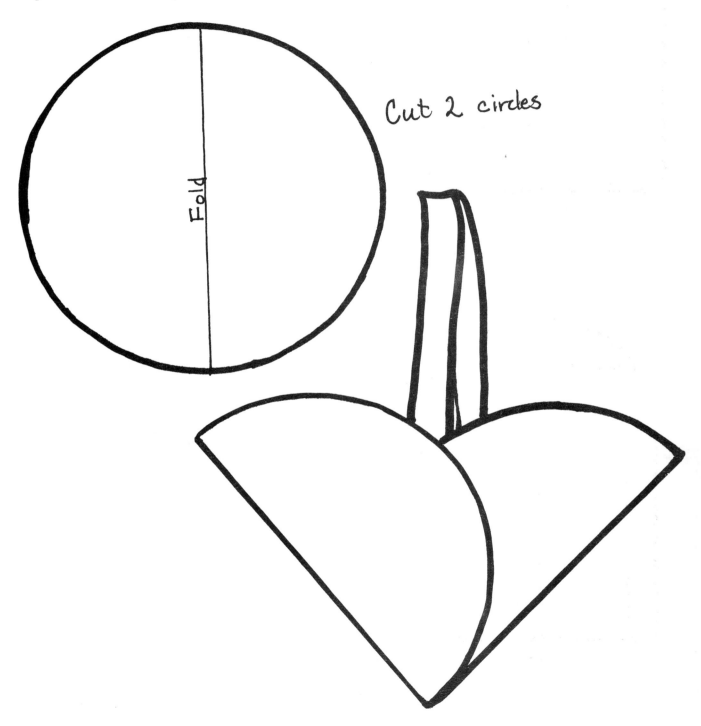

Fold

Cut 2 circles

## Cone shaped baskets / *Kremmerhus*

These cones are also traditionally filled with goodies just as the heart baskets. They make beautiful, simple gifts for special people in our lives.

Colored construction paper, glossy wrapping paper, butcher paper or fadeless art paper
Dinner plate or circular pan with a diameter of approximately 10"
Glue or glue stick, tape, or staples and stapler
Christmas stickers, hearts, stars, bells or pictures cut from old Christmas cards
Gold or silver glitter or use a glue with glitter in it called Glu Glitter™
Pencil
Scissors
Ruler
Yarn, ribbon, or a 7" by ½" strip of paper

With the pencil, draw a circle around the dinner plate. Cut around the circle. Fold the circle in half. Then fold it in half again so the size is now a quarter of the original size. Unfold the circle. Cut along the fold line into four equal parts. Cut off a small triangle piece at 1 and 2 from each corner as shown in example.\* Glue or staple side A behind side B. This makes a cone shape. Tie, glue, tape, or staple a handle made of yarn, ribbon or from the same paper as the basket. Add Christmas stickers or pictures cut from old Christmas cards to the outside of the basket.

\*As a variation, glitter may be added to the outside of the basket before it is formed into the cone shape. Cover the outside of the quarter of the circle with glue, then sprinkle the glue with the colored glitter. If using Glu Glitter™, it takes about ½ hour to dry. The nice thing about it is you can write with the tip of the bottle and it is not as messy as the two-step process. After this glue covered by glitter dries, glue or staple A and B together as described above.

Makes four baskets.

# Chains / *Lenker*

Colorful chains are a favorite of children in both Norway and the United States. We learned to make these simple decorations as very small children. The pieces are especially easy for young children to handle. Make the chains by interlocking the rings or links. Each ring symbolizes a circle of love. As the rings are linked together, the chain of love grows.

Colored construction paper, glossy wrapping paper, butcher paper or fadeless art paper heavy
   enough to hold the shape of a ring
Scissors
Glue or glue stick, tape or staples and stapler
Ruler
Pencil

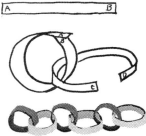

Measure paper into 5" by ½" lengths with pencil and ruler. Cut paper into strips. Join ends A and B of first strip into a circle with either glue stick, tape or staples. The next strip is put through the first circle, then the ends C and D of the second strip are joined together. As each strip is added, the chain becomes longer. Make the chain as long as necessary to decorate your tree, windows, and tables. The chains may hang straight from the top of the tree or encircle the tree in love by going around the tree.

## Santa's elves / *Julenisser*
## Gingerbread man and woman / *Pepperkakemann og pepperkakekone*

*Julenisser* or Santa's elves and *pepperkakemennesker* or gingerbread people are favorite decorations for Christmas both in Norway and the Puget Sound. There are several types to make for your tree, small gifts, or package decorations.

Red felt for *nisse* or brown felt for gingerbread figures
Flesh colored felt
Fabric pieces for the little packages for the *julenisser* to carry in their hands
Red or brown embroidery thread
Black embroidery thread
Yarn for hair
Pencil
Needle
Sewing thread

*Optional*
Glue
Fabric paint in various colors
Fine markers in various colors
Colored construction paper, butcher paper or fadeless art paper
Stars, hearts or other Christmas type stickers
Batting

Using the patterns provided, cut two *julenisser/pepperkakemenn* bodies out of the red or brown felt. Cut one *nisse* face out of the flesh-colored felt. Generally, the *pepperkaker* faces are done on the brown felt. Fasten the face to one of the bodies with either glue or small stitches. Embroider eyes, nose and a mouth for the face of the *julenisse/pepperkakemann*. These may also be drawn on with fabric paint or fine markers. Test the markers on the fabric to make sure the marker won't bleed. Just as each of own faces are unique, give each *julenisse/pepperkakekone* a different look. Attach small hands cut from the flesh- colored or red felt for the *julenisser*. The hands may also be embroidered on or marked with the fabric paint or markers. Use Christmas stickers or with the fabric pieces and construction paper make a star, a heart or a small package for the *julenisse* hands to hold. Stitch or glue the edges of the two body pieces together. Leave a small portion of one of the sides open to stuff a small amount of batting in the *julenisse/pepperkakekone* to give a little shape to the figure, if desired. Sew or glue the opening closed when finished stuffing. Add yarn hair made into braids, pig tails, curls or just a little hint of hair above the face. With different colored yarn, add a tassel onto the hat for the *julenisse*. Thread a needle with 7" of regular sewing thread or a 7" yarn strand. About a ¼" from the top of the hat, poke the needle through the layers of the *julenisse/pepperkakemann* body, leaving 3½" of the thread or yarn strand on each side of the head. Tie the two ends of the thread together to form a hanger for the *julenisse/pepperkakekone*.

## Paper angels / *Papirengler*

Make a choir of angels for the tree or use them for name cards on the table.

Heavy white paper, gold foil paper, silver foil paper, colored or glossy paper
Scissors
Colored pencils, crayons, felt pens, paints or Glu Glitter™
Pencil
7" heavy thread
Needle
Small bread and butter plate, saucer, or small cereal bowl

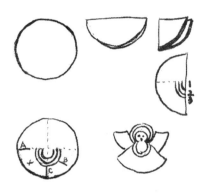

Draw a circle around a small bread and butter plate or small cereal bowl onto the paper. Cut out the circle. Fold it in half very lightly so as not to create a heavy crease. Fold it lightly in half again so it is now a quarter of its original size. Open it again so it is still folded in half. Now cut three half circles to the quarter fold mark. The first half circle (1) is a little bigger than the others as this will be the face of the angel. The other two cuts should be about ¼". The second cut (2) will form the arms and the last cut (3) will be the angel's halo. Unfold the circle. Make a short cut at A and one that is the same length at B. These will form the angel's wings. A last cut is made at C. After cutting A–C, slip opening A into opening B. Bring the long A wing around behind the halo. You may need to put a small dot of glue at X to get the wing to stay put. Fold the middle cut down to form the arms of the angel. If desired, draw faces and decorate the wings and dress of the angels with colored pencils, crayons, felt pens, paints, or Glu Glitter™. The angel is now ready for display. If hanging the angels, thread a needle with 7" of regular sewing thread or a 7" yarn strand. About a ¼" from the top and center of the head, poke the needle and thread through the paper leaving 3½" of the thread or yarn strand on each side. Tie the two ends of the thread together to form a hanger for the angel.

After making one angel, you may decide to decorate the angel before it is all assembled or decorate it after taking it apart so it lays flat, then reassemble it.

## Norwegian flags / *Norske flagg*

Traditionally the Norwegian flag's proportions are based on the size of one of the white bars in the flag. The blue cross is twice the width of a white bar. The two small red corners are six times the width of a white bar and the two large corners are twelve times the width of a white bar or twice the width of the small red corners. The flags on the Christmas tree are a reminder of the friendship among all peoples. Hang flags from other countries represented in your family for an international tree.

Felt or construction paper in red, white, and blue colors
Glue
Toothpicks or other small thin piece of wood
Gold (or some other color you like) cord, string or thread
Scissors
Ruler

The flags may be made of paper or felt. They may also be made in the shape of rectangles or, for more fancy flags, with a v-shape cut into the rectangle shape or v-shape. For a simple version based on the proportions for a Norwegian flag, cut a rectangle from the red felt 2" by 2¾". Cut 2 stripes from the blue felt, the first stripe is ¼" wide and 2" long and the second stripe is ¼" wide by 2¾" long. Cut 4 stripes from the white felt, the first two stripes are ⅛" wide and 2" long and the second two stripes are ⅛" wide by 2¾" long. Glue one of the long white stripes ¾" from the edge of the red felt. Then glue the long blue stripe next to the first white stripe. Take the second white long stripe and glue it next to the blue stripe. To make the cross, glue one of the short white stripes ¾" from the top edge, then glue the short blue stripe, and the last white stripe is glued next to the blue stripe. Let glue dry.

Glue a toothpick onto the back of the flag at the top, leaving a ¼" extension on each side of the flag. Let dry. Cut a 7" length of thread, then wrap and knot about 1¼" of each end of the thread around each end of the wood. Either cut off excess ends when finished tying or leave for a decoration.

## Ornaments from wood shavings

The patterns of these ornaments are only limited by your imagination and the material.

1" wide clear (without knots) white pine board, approximately 3 feet in length
Water
Container long enough to hold board (a bathtub is ideal)
Weight to hold down board
Craft glue
Wooden clothes pins or plastic paper clips (plastic clips will not leave a stain on the wet
      wood, but if you only have metal paper clips, use those)
String, thread, or cord
Vise
Smooth or jack plane
Rubber bands
Iron
Scissors

Place 1" x 3 foot board in a bathtub filled with enough water to cover the board. Soak the board by submerging it for 12–24 hours with a weight on top of it. When the wood is saturated with water, remove it from the tub. Place the board in a very sturdy vise with the 1" side up. Take the smooth or jack plane which has a sharp, cutting edge with a medium opening. Make some sample cuts by placing the plane at one end of the board and moving firmly forward with even pressure. If the opening is too large on the plane, the shavings will be too thick to curl easily. If the opening is too small, the shavings will be too thin and will break while forming the curls. Adjust the opening accordingly. Practice a few more times until long, smooth, uniform shavings can be achieved.

To make the shavings curl more, roll them tightly and secure with a rubber band until dry. If flat ornaments are desired, the curls can be dried and flattened with an iron on a medium setting. If using an iron, be sure to use an appropriate ironing surface, such as an ironing board.

Thin veneer strips may also be purchased at lumber yards. You will need to soak the strips before curling the strips as above.

Suggested patterns are shown. Glue areas of the curls which touch other curls. Hold together with paper clips until glue dries.

For the flat ornaments, take four flat 5" long strips of wood. Lay them across each other to form an eight-pointed star or cross. Try to keep the angles as even as possible. Hold the strips in place with small amounts of glue. Take some thread, leaving at least 2" at the end for hanging. Wrap the thread over one strip and then under the next strip several times. Turn the star over and repeat the same thing, but starting the "over" part on a strip where the thread is on the bottom instead of the top. The thread will then go over and under each strip on both sides so it looks like one continuous strip of thread. Tie the two ends together to form a loop to hang the ornament. Use scissors to cut the ends of the strips into various designs. Look at costumes from the Hardanger area of Norway for ideas on how to cut the ends.

Cut an 7" length of string, thread, or cord. Run string through an appropriate opening in the ornament. Tie a knot joining the two ends of the string so the ornament can be hung from the tree or window. These patterns are courtesy of Sons of Norway.

# Christmas caroling / *Julesanger*

Caroling and folkdancing at the Norse Home in Seattle have been a tradition in *Leikarringen* for many years. It is why this book was written. Typically, our visit to the Norse Home is our last performance of the year. Afterwards we meet at someone's home to eat holiday cookies and refreshments. It is a chance for us to enjoy each other's company before we take our Christmas break.

Another opportunity for caroling in Seattle is to visit the Hiram M. Chittenden Locks in Ballard or various parks along the waterfronts to sing with the people on the Christmas boats. Boats of all sizes and shapes are decorated with lights, trees, and other ornaments much to the delight of onlookers. During December the Christmas boats motor through the Locks. While they are there, carolers on board the boats lead the crowds in singing favorite Christmas songs. Later on, the boats cruise into Shilshole and Golden Gardens where the lights reflect off the water adding more stars to the night even if the sky is covered in clouds. Here more singers bundled in warm jackets, mittens, and hats eagerly await the arrival of the boats. Large bonfires are set to warm the hearts of everyone along with the singing. Hot cider and other refreshments are available for the participants. The boats eventually move down the shoreline to another group of carolers, but the glow of Christmas still remains in our hearts.

Perhaps your family or group would also like to start or revive the caroling tradition. Caroling at retirement homes, convalescent centers, and hospitals, or visiting people confined to their homes spreads Christmas joy for all participating, both carolers and listeners.

Confirm a date with family members or the organization you are in and with the place where you want to carol. If you will be outside for a time or if you would like to have a little practice before going out, plan a small meal with finger foods, some warm drinks, and easy cleanup about an hour before you venture out.

Plan what routes you will travel if you are visiting neighbors or shut-ins. This is especially important if you are in several groups who plan on meeting at different homes along the route. It helps to have a designated leader for singing. Keep in mind to sing softer or more quiet songs mixed with lively songs. Try to finish with an upbeat song such as *We Wish You a Merry Christmas* as you leave the house or building. Be sure to bring along this book to help you remember the tune and the words to those favorite carols. If members of your group play an instrument which cannot be damaged by cold or wet weather, encourage them to bring the instruments.

If you will be outside for any length of time, be sure to bring flashlights. To soften the light from the flashlights, wrap white or colored tissue paper around the lighted end. Fasten the paper with tape. This turns the flashlight into a small torch. Candles are an alternative for flashlights, but may not be as dependable for lighting stairs, etc. because the flame may go out with the smallest gust of wind. As it gets dark early in December, it is important to wear warm clothing with reflective tape or light in color so you can be seen by drivers as you walk and sing.

When you are finished caroling, join together again for a more substantial meal, hot drinks and dessert. Perhaps you will linger and sing a few more songs for your own enjoyment.

# Here we come a-wassailing / Wassail song

Tune: Yorkshire carol (17th century), harmonized by Sir John Stainer (1840-1901) (1871?)
English lyrics: Yorkshire carol (17th century)

*Lively / Livlig*

1 We Here we come a - was - sail - ing A - mong the leaves so green,____
2 We are not dai - ly beg - gars That beg from door to door, But
3 Good mas - ter and mis - tress As you sit by the fire, Pray
4 God bless the mas - ter of this house, Like - wise the mis - tress too; And

Here we come a - wan - d'ring, So fair____ to be seen.
we are neigh - bors' chil - dren, Whom you have seen be - fore.
think of us poor chil - dren, Who wan - der in the mire.
all the lit - tle chil - dren, That 'round the ta - ble go.

*Refrain / Refreng*

Love and joy come to you, And to you your was - sail too, And God bless you, and

send you a Hap - py New Year, And God send you a Hap - py New Year.

95

# Gloucestershire wassail / Wassail, wassail all over the town

Tune: Gloucestershire carol (18th century)
English lyrics: Gloucestershire folk (18th century)

Merrily / Muntert

1 Was - sail, was - sail, all o - ver the town,
2 Come, but - ler, fill us a bowl of the best,
3 Come here, sweet maid, in the frill - y white smock,

Was - sail, was - sail,

Our bread it is white and our ale it is brown;
Then we pray that your soul in heav - en may rest;
Come trip to the door and trip back the lock!

was - sail, was - sail,

Our bowl it is made of the good ma - ple tree,
But if you do bring us a bowl of the small,
Come trip to the door and pull back the pin,

was - sail, was - sail.

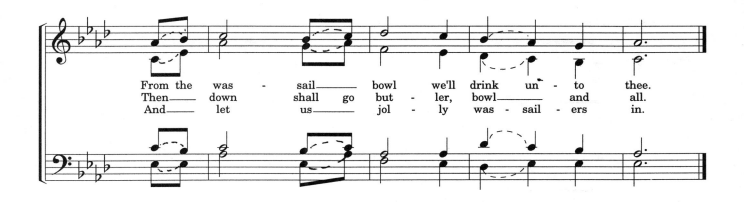

From the was - sail_____ bowl we'll drink un - to thee.
Then____ down shall go but - ler, bowl_____ and all.
And____ let us____ jol - ly was - sail - ers in.

# Christmas is here again / *Nå er det jul igjen*

Tune: Swedish carol (16th-18th century), harmonized by Darrel Eide (1997)
Norwegian lyrics: Norwegian folk based on Swedish text (16th-18th century)
English lyrics: Anonymous

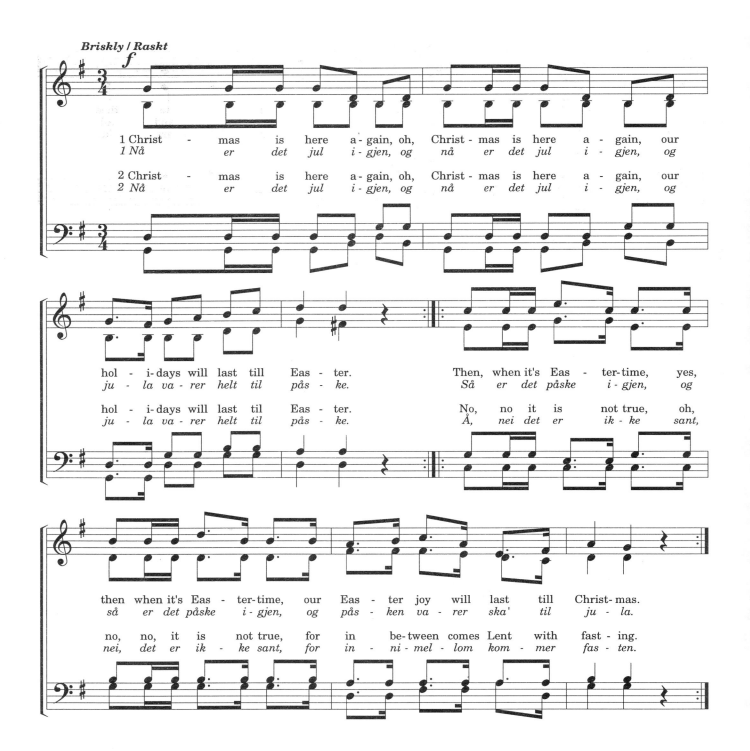

98

# A thousand Christmas lights are lit / *Nå tennes tusen julelys*

Tune: Emmy Köhler (Sweden) (1858-1925) (1898), harmonized by Paul Allen (1997)
Norwegian lyrics: Lars Søraas (1862-1925)
English lyrics: Liv Nordem Lyons (1984)

**Gently / Sakte**
*mp*

1 A thou-sand Christ-mas lights are lit. The earth is all a-blaze;
*1 Nå ten-nes tu-sen ju-le-lys. Det strå-ler rundt vår jord,*

The stars of heav-en greet man-kind in bless-ed Christ-mas days.
*og him-lens stjer-ner blin-ker ned til li-ten og til stor.*

2  Throughout the land, a message sweet
Lights hope and glad delight.
A child is born to save us all,
Our Lord has come tonight.

3  O, shining star of Bethlehem,
Send wishes from above,
For Christmas to forever mean
Eternal peace and love.

4  And kindle in our hearts a flame,
Of good will towards all men
To make the Earth a better place
Til Christmas comes again.

2  *Og over land og by i kveld
går julens glade bud
om han som fødtes i en stall,
vår Frelser og vår Gud.*

3  *Du stjerne over Betlehem,
send dine stråler ned,
og minn oss om at julens bud
er kjærlighet og fred.*

4  *Til hvert er fattig hjerte send
et lysstreif ifra sky.
Så finner det den rette vei,
og det blir jul på ny.*

# Deck the hall

Tune: Welsh carol (16th century)
English lyrics: Welsh folk (16th century)

**Gaily / Gladelig**
*mf*

1 Deck the hall with boughs of hol - ly, Fa la la la la, la la la la.
2 See the blaz - ing Yule be - fore us, Fa la la la la, la la la la.
3 Fast a - way the old year pass - es, Fa la la la la, la la la la.

'Tis the sea - son to be jol - ly, Fa la la la la, la la la la.
Strike the harp and join the cho - rus, Fa la la la la, la la la la.
Hail the new year lads and lass - es, Fa la la la la, la la la la.

Don we now our gay ap - par - rel, Fa la la la la, la la la la,
Fol - low me in mer - ry meas - ure, Fa la la la la, la la la la.
Sing we joy - ous all to - geth - er, Fa la la la la, la la la la.

Troll the an - cient Yule - tide car - ol, Fa la la la la, la la la la.
While I tell of Yule - tide treas - ure, Fa la la la la, la la la la.
Heed - less of the wind and weath - er, Fa la la la la, la la la la.

# O Christmas tree / O Tannenbaum

Tune: German carol (16th or 17th century)
German lyrics: German folk, verse 1; Ernest Gebhard Anschütz (1800-1861) (1824), verses 2 and 3
English lyrics: Anonymous

**Moderately / Moderat**
*mf*

1 O Christ-mas tree! O Christ-mas tree! Your leaves are so un-chang-ing!
2 O Christ-mas tree! O Christ-mas tree! Much plea-sure you can give me.
3 O. Christ-mas tree! O Christ-mas tree! Your can-dles shine so bright-ly!

Not on-ly green when sum-mer's here,
How of-ten has when the Christ-mas tree
From base to sum-mit, gay and bright,

but al-so when 'tis cold and drear. O O Christ-mas tree! O
af-ford-ed me the great-est glee! O O Christ-mas tree! O
there's on-ly splen-dor for the sight. O O Christ-mas tree! O

Christ-mas tree! Your leaves are so un-chang-ing!
Christ-mas tree! Much plea-sure you can give me.
Christ-mas tree! Your can-dles shine so bright-ly!

# Jingle bells / *Bjelleklang*

Tune: James S. Pierpont (1822-1893) (1857)
English lyrics: James S. Pierpont (1822-1893) (1857)
Norwegian lyrics: Juul Hansen (1913-1981) (c. 1960)
First secular American carol of international repute

Refrain / Refreng

Jin - gle bells! Jin - gle bells! Jin - gle all the way! Oh, what fun it is to ride In a
*Bjel - le - klang, bjel - le - klang, o - ver skog og hei! Hør på bjel - lens munt - re klang når —*

one-horse o - pen sleigh! Jin - gle bells! Jin - gle bells! Jin - gle all the way!
*Blak - ken drar i vei! Følg oss ut! Følg oss ut! O - ver mo og myr,*

Oh, what fun it is to ride In a one - horse o - pen sleigh!
*der hvor vei - en slyn - ger seg i — sko - gens e - ven - tyr!*

2   A day or two ago I thought I'd take a ride,
And soon Miss Fannie Bright was seated by my side;
The horse was lean and lank,
Misfortune seemed his lot,
He got into a drifted bank,
And we, we got upsot.
Jingle, bells! Jingle, bells! Jingle all the way!
Oh, what fun it is to ride in a one-horse open sleigh!
Jingle, bells! Jingle, bells! Jingle all the way!
Oh, what fun it is to ride in a one-horse open sleigh!

# The holly and the ivy

Tune: English carol (ca. 1700), harmonized by Sir John Stainer (1840-1901) (1871?)
English lyrics: English folk (ca. 1700)

1 The hol - ly and the i - vy, When they are both full grown, Of____ all the trees with - in the wood, The____ hol - ly bears the crown.

2 The hol - ly bears a blos - som, As white as lil - y flow'r, And____ Mar - y bore sweet____ Je - sus Christ, To____ be our sweet Sav - ior.

3 The hol - ly bears a ber - ry, As red as an - y blood, And____ Mar - y bore sweet____ Je - sus Christ, To____ do poor sin - ners good.

Refrain / Refreng

The ris-ing of the sun— And the run-ning of the deer, The play - ing of the mer - ry or - gan, Sweet— sing - ing in the choir.

# You, me, and the Chickadee / *Du og jeg og dompapen*

Tune: *Kväsarvalsen* by Arthur Högstedt (1877-1942) (1898) (Swedish), harmonized by Darrel Eide (1997)
Norwegian lyrics: Alf Prøysen (1914-1970) (1953)
English lyrics: Christine M. Anderson (1997)

2   Now Kari has cookies and milk on a tray
By the window there's hung some suet for a day.
But not a bird has been there to eat it yet
So now we must wait and not be upset.

And now we come you, me, and the chickadee,
Heisan and hopsan and fa-la-la
Yes, now we come you, me and the chickadee,
Heisan and hopsan and fa-la-la.

3   When Ola has set up a sheaf on a pole,
He'll gladly listen to a song of "mi fa so"
He likes to hear both peep-peep and fa-la-la
and now, yes, Ola can be very gla'.

For now we come you, me, and the chickadee,
Heisan and hopsan and fa-la-la
Yes, now we come you, me and the chickadee,
Heisan and hopsan and fa-la-la.

*2   Hu Kari har kaker og mjølk på et brett,
ved ruta der henger en strimmel med fett.
Men ingen har vært der og spist no' ennå,
så det må vi se å få retta på*

*Og nå kommer du og jeg og dompapen,
heisan og hopsan og trallalla.
Ja nå kommer du og jeg og dompapen,
heisan og hopsan og trallalla.*

*3   Han Ola har satt opp et nek på ei stang
og vil gjerne høre en lystelig sang,
han liker både kvittkvitt og trallalla,
og nå vil han Ola bil veldig gla.*

*For nå kommer du og jeg og dompapen,
heisan og hopsan og trallalla.
Ja, nå kommer du og jeg og dompapen,
heisan og hopsan og trallalla.*

# Let it snow! Let it snow! Let it snow!

Tune: Jule Styne (1905- 1994) (1945) (US)
English lyrics: Sammy Cahn (1913-1993) (1945) (US)

fi - nal-ly kiss good - night, How I'll hate go-ing out in the storm! But if

you real - ly hold me tight, All the way home I'll be warm. Oh, the

fire is slow - ly dy - ing, And, my dear, we're still good - bye-ing, But as

long as you love me so, Let it snow! Let it snow! Let it snow.

# The mouse's song / *Musevisa*

Tune: Norwegian folk melody, harmonized by Darrel Eide (1997)
Norwegian lyrics: Alf Prøysen (1914-1970) (1948)
English lyrics: Liv Nordem Lyons (1984)

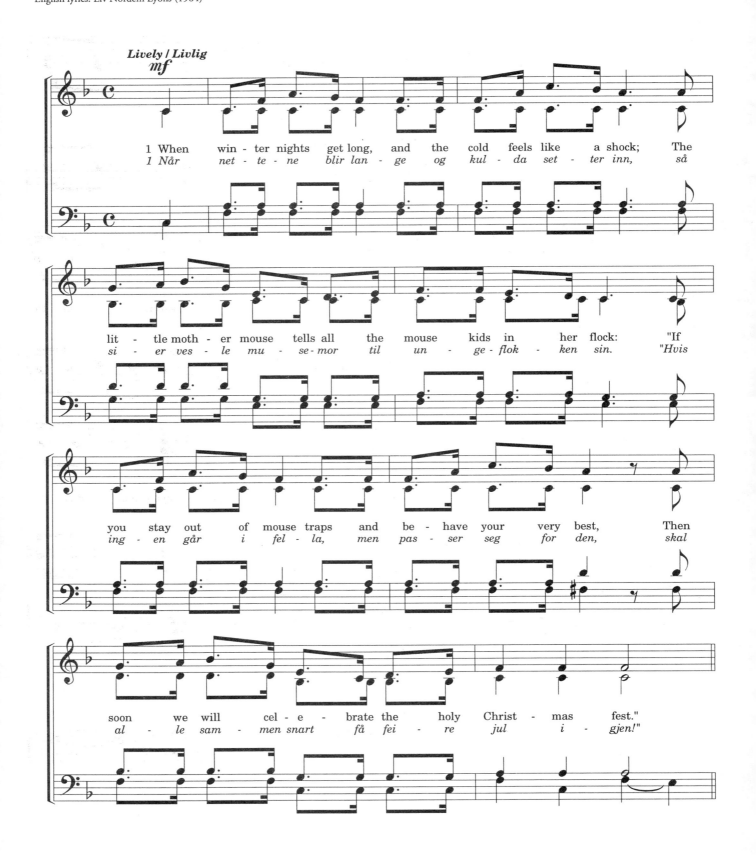

1 When win-ter nights get long, and the cold feels like a shock; The
*1 Når net-te-ne blir lan-ge og kul-da set-ter inn, så*

lit-tle moth-er mouse tells all the mouse kids in her flock: "If
*si-er ves-le mu-se-mor til un-ge-flok-ken sin. "Hvis*

you stay out of mouse traps and be-have your very best, Then
*ing-en går i fel-la, men pas-ser seg for den, skal*

soon we will cel-e-brate the holy Christ-mas fest."
*al-le sam-men snart få fei-re jul i-gjen!"*

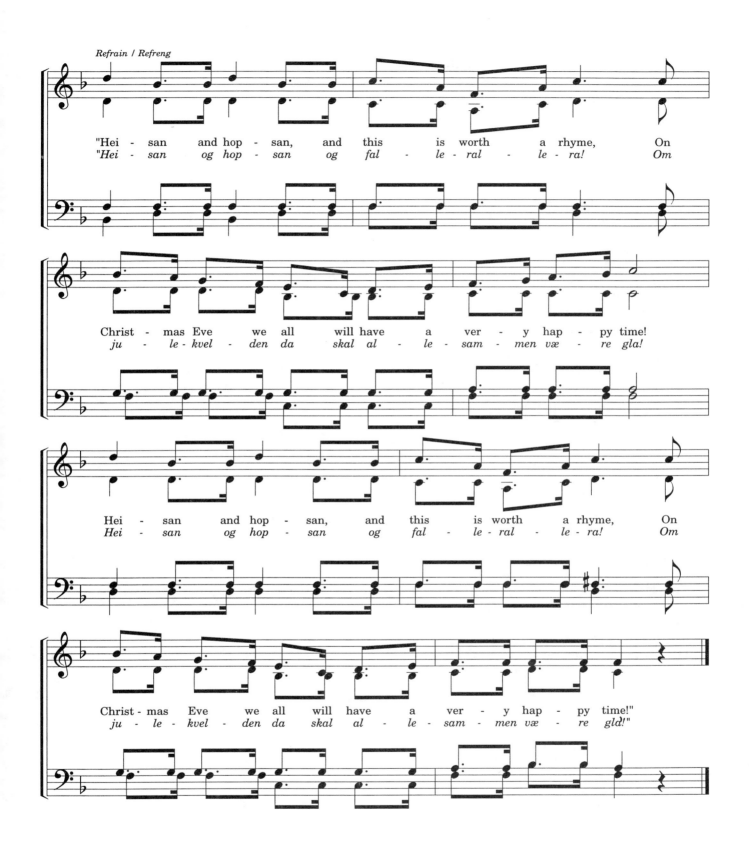

Refrain / Refreng

"Hei - san and hop - san, and this is worth a rhyme, On
"Hei - san og hop - san og fal - le - ral - le - ra! Om

Christ - mas Eve we all will have a ver - y hap - py time!
ju - le - kvel - den da skal al - le - sam - men væ - re gla!

Hei - san and hop - san, and this is worth a rhyme, On
Hei - san og hop - san og fal - le - ral - le - ra! Om

Christ - mas Eve we all will have a ver - y hap - py time!"
ju - le - kvel - den da skal al - le - sam - men væ - re gla!"

2   And mother mouse keeps busy, she takes a piece of coal
     And blackens walls and ceilings in her little mouse's hole.
     The kids, they clean the floor while dancing to a song,
     And even sweep the corners with their tails so long.
:/:  Heisan, hopsan, this is worth a rhyme,
     On Christmas Eve we all will have a very happy time. :/:

3   The evening then arrives they have all been waiting for
     Father mouse brings a worn out boot he places on the floor.
     They decorate the boot with spider webs and things,
     From the leather loop in back, there hangs a cork that swings.
:/:  Heisan, hopsan, this is worth a rhyme,
     On Christmas Eve we all will have a very happy time. :/:

4   And father mouse, he orders: "Come, form a circle now,
     The boot stays in the middle and we all will dance around.
     Go on and take each other's tails, yes, do just what I say,
     And one and two and three, and then we dance away."
:/:  Heisan, hopsan, this is worth a rhyme,
     On Christmas Eve we all will have a very happy time. :/:

5   Their Christmas dinner is some nuts brought out for all to eat,
     Some candy wrapping is dessert for those who go for sweets,
     And mother mouse, she watches a piece of bacon well,
     So no one eats it up, but sniffs the lovely smell.
:/:  Heisan, hopsan, this is worth a rhyme,
     On Christmas Eve we all will have a very happy time. :/:

6   The oldest in the family, grandmama mouse, is there,
     She's comfortably resting in her little rocking chair.
     The chair is not a real one, as everybody knows,
     She rocks on a potato till it makes her drowse.
:/:  Heisan, hopsan, this is worth a rhyme,
     On Christmas Eve we all will have a very happy time. :/:

7   They jump and hop and skip and sing with all of their might,
     Until their father says: "It's getting very late at night."
     The kids then go to bed, and father tucks them in,
     But even in their sleep they smile a happy grin.
:/:  Heisan, hopsan, this is worth a rhyme,
     On Christmas Eve we all will have a very happy time. :/:

8   And grandma mouse, she yawns and as she says to all:
     "Christmas Eve is fun for those who are big or very small.
     If we stay out of mouse traps and watch it where we go,
     we'll have another Christmas in a year or so."
:/:  Heisan, hopsan, this is worth a rhyme,
     On Christmas Eve we all will have a very happy time. :/:

2   Ja musemor er flittig, hun tar et stykke kull
     og sverter tak og vegger i sitt lille musehull,
     mens barna feier golvet og danser som en vind
     og soper borti krokene med halen sin.
:/:  Heisan og hopsan og fallerallera!
     Om julekvelden da skal allesammen være gla'! :/:

3   Omsider kommer kvelden som alle venter på
     og musefar han trekker fram en støvel uten tå,
     den pynter de med spindelvev og småspiker og sånn,
     og så putter de en flaskekork i hempa på'n.
:/:  Heisan og hopsan og fallerallera!
     Om julekvelden da skal allesammen være gla'! :/:

4   Og musefaren sier, nå skal vi danne ring,
     la støvlen stå i midten så går vi rundt omkring.
     Vi gir hverandre halen som vi kan leie i,
     og en og to og tre, og så begynner vi!
:/:  Heisan og hopsan og fallerallera!
     Om julekvelden da skal allesammen være gla'! :/:

5   Og julematen deres, det er ei lita nøtt,

     og så et stykke dropspapir for dem som liker søtt.
     Og musemor har stillet opp en fleskebit på skrå,
:/:  og den får allesammen lov å lukte på.
     Heisan og hopsan og fallerallera!
     Om julekvelden da skal allesammen være gla'! :/:

6   Ja musebestemora er også kommet inn,
     nå sitter hun og koser seg i gyngestolen sin.
     De æ'kke orntli gyngestol, d'er no' som alle vet,
     hun sitter der og gynger på en stor potet.
:/:  Heisan og hopsan og fallerallera!
     Om julekvelden da skal allesammen være gla'! :/:

7   Så hopper de, så danser de, så traller de en stund
     til musefaren sier: "Det er best vi tar en blund."
     Og ungene de legger seg, mens pappa holder vakt,
     men selv i søvne traller de i hopsatakt:
:/:  Heisan og hopsan og fallerallera!
     Om julekvelden da skal allesammen være gla'! :/:

8   Og bestemora gjesper, og sier slik som så:
     "D'er morosamt med jula for dessa som er små,
     (og) hvis ingen går i fella, men passer seg for den,
     skal alle om et år få feire jul igjen!"
:/:  Heisan og hopsan og fallerallera!
     Om julekvelden da skal allesammen være gla'! :/:

# We wish you a merry Christmas

Tune: English carol (16th century)
English lyrics: English folk (16th century)

*Brightly / Lystig*

1 We wish you a Mer - ry Christ - mas, We wish you a Mer - ry
2 Oh, bring us a fig - gy pud - ding, Oh, bring us a fig - gy
3 We won't go un - til we've got some, We won't go un - til we've
4 We wish you a Mer - ry Christ - mas, We wish you a Mer - ry

Christ - mas, We wish you a Mer - ry Christ - mas and a Hap - py New Year!
pud - ding, Oh, bring us a fig - gy pud - ding and a cup of good cheer.
got some, We won't go un - til we've got some, so— bring some out here.
Christ - mas, We wish you a Mer - ry Christ - mas and a Hap - py New Year!

*Refrain / Refreng*

Good tid - ings to you wher - ev - er you are;

Good tid - ings for Christ - mas and a Hap - py New Year.

# O come, O come, Emmanuel / *Å kom, å kom Immanuel* / Veni, Emanuel

Tune: French processional (15th century)
Original lyrics: Psalteriolum Cantionum Catholicarum, Köln (1710)
English lyrics: John Mason Neale (1818-1866) (1851)
Norwegian lyrics: Arve Brunvoll(1937- ) (1978)

1 O come, O come, Emmanuel, And ransom captive Israel, That mourns in lonely exile here Until the Son of God appears.

1 Å kom, å kom, Immanuel, og løys ditt bundne Israel, som sårt i utlægd ventar på den dag då dei Guds Son får sjå!

Refrain / Refreng

Re - joice! Re - joice! Em - man - u - el
Ver glad, ver glad! Im - ma - nu - el

Shall come to you, O Is - ra - el.
er født for deg, du Is - ra - el.

2   O, come, strong Branch of Jesse, free
     Your own from Satan's tyranny;
     From depths of hell your people save,
     And give them vict'ry o'er the grave.
     Rejoice! Rejoice! Emmanuel
     Shall come to you, O Israel.

3   O, come, blest Dayspring, come and cheer
     Our spirits by your advent here;
     Disperse the gloomy clouds of night,
     And death's dark shadows put to flight.
     Rejoice! Rejoice! Emmanuel
     Shall come to you, O Israel.

2   *Du Isais renning, kom, set fri*
     *ditt folk frå Satans tyranni,*
     *frå helheims djup og mørkers grav,*
     *gjev frelse med din kongestav!*
     *Ver glad, ver glad! Immanuel*
     *er født for deg, du Israel.*

3   *Du morgonrode, kom med ljos,*
     *å skin, du klare sol, for oss!*
     *Jag skoddeeim og tunge sky,*
     *så nattemørkret snart må fly!*
     *Ver glad, ver glad! Immanuel*
     *er født for deg, du Is-ra-el.*

# Joy to the world / *Gled deg, du jord*

Tune: George F. Handel (1685-1759), adapted 1742 by Lowell Mason(1792-1872) (1836) (US)
English lyrics: Isaac Watts (1674-1748) (1719)
Norwegian lyrics: Anonymous

2　Joy to the world! The Savior reigns!
　　Let all their songs employ,
　　While fields and floods,
　　rocks, hills and plains,
　　Repeat the sounding joy,
　　Repeat the sounding joy
　　Repeat, repeat the sounding joy.

3　He rules the world with truth and grace,
　　And makes the nations prove
　　The glories of
　　his righteousness
　　And wonders of his love,
　　And wonders of his love,
　　And wonders, wonders of his love.

2　*Gled deg, du jord, ditt lovsangskor*
　　*skal hylle kongen stor.*
　　*La mark og skog og berg og dal*
　　*og alt det skapte uten tal,*
　　*i stemme lovsangskor,*
　　*i stemme lovsangskor,*
　　*Istem, du jord, ditt lovsangskor!*

3　*Gled deg, du jord, han kommen er!*
　　*Lukk opp for ham din favn.*
　　*Gi rom i hvert et hjerte her,*
　　*forkynn hans ære fjernt og nær,*
　　*lovsyng hans store navn,*
　　*lovsyng hans store navn.*
　　*Lovsyng hans ære fjernt og nær.*

# What child is this?

Tune: English folk melody (16th century)
English lyrics: William Chatterton Dix (1837-1898) (ca. 1865)

# Little drummer boy

Tune: Katherine K. Davis (1892-1980), Henry V. Onorati (1912-1993), and Harry Simeone (1911- ) (1958)
English lyrics: Katherine K. Davis (1892-1980), Henry V. Onorati (1912-1993), and Harry Simeone(1911- ) (1958)

To lay be-fore the King, Pa - rum-pum-pum-pum, rum-pum-pum-pum,
That's fit to give our King. Pa - rum-pum-pum-pum, rum-pum-pum-pum,
·I played my best for Him. Pa - rum-pum-pum-pum, rum-pum-pum-pum,

H'rum - rum, h'rum - pum, h'rum - pum, h'rum - pum,

rum-pum-pum - pum - mm. So to hon - or Him, Pa -
rum-pum-pum - pum - mm. Shall I play for you, Pa -
rum-pum-pum - pum - mm. Then He smiled at me, Pa -

h'rum - pum, h'rum-pum. H'rum - pum, h'rum - pum,

rum-pum-pum - pum - mm. When we come._____
rum-pum-pum - pum - mm. On my drum?_____
rum-pum-pum - pum - mm. Me and my drum._____

h'rum - pum, h'rum-pum. H'rum - pum, h'rum - pum - pum-pum.

# O little town of Bethlehem / *Å Betlehem, du kongeby*

Tune: Lewis Henry Redner (1831-1908) (1868) (US)
English lyrics: Phillips Brooks (1835-1893) (1868) (US)
Norwegian lyrics: Trygve Bjerkrheim (1904- ) (1951)
Probably the best known American carol, first published in 1874

1 O lit-tle town of Beth-le-hem, How still we see thee lie!
*1 Å Bet-le-hem, du kon-ge-by, vi ser deg kvi-la der.*

A-bove thy deep and dream-less sleep The si-lent stars go by;
*Og o-ver deg så stil-le dreg dei stjer-ners sto-re her.*

Yet in thy dark streets shin-eth The ev-er-last-ing light.
*Men i dei mør-ke ga-ter eit æ-ve-lys skin-ned,*

The hopes and fears of all the years Are met in thee to-night.
*Til deg nå går dei tu-sen år sin leng-sel et-ter fred.*

2   For Christ is born of Mary,
    And, gathered all above,
    While mortals sleep, the angels keep
    Their watch of wond'ring love.
    O morning stars, together
    Proclaim the holy birth,
    And praises sing to God the king,
    And peace to all the earth!

3   How silently, how silently,
    The wondrous gift is giv'n!
    So God imparts to human hearts
    The blessings of his heav'n.
    No ear may hear his coming;
    But in this world of sin,
    Where meek souls will receive him still
    The dear Christ enters in.

4   O holy Child of Bethlehem,
    Descend to us, we pray;
    Cast out our sin, and enter in,
    Be born in us today.
    We hear the Christmas angels
    The great glad tidings tell;
    O come to us, abide with us,
    Our Lord Emmanuel!

2   *For denne natt ein frelsar stor*
    *Vart fødd, og englar kvad.*
    *Mens verda sov, dei song Guds lov,*
    *Og himmelen var glad.*
    *Å, morgonstjerner alle,*
    *Forkynn at han er fødd!*
    *Du stjerne-kor, pris kongen stor!*
    *Og fred på jorda mødd!*

3   *Kor stilt, kor stilt vår Herre gav*
    *Den julegåva god!*
    *Slik himmelen gjev jorda enn*
    *Si rike signingsflod.*
    *Vi merkar ei hans kome,*
    *Men til kvar open sjel*
    *Stig Jesus inn med nåden sin*
    *Og gjer ein syndar sæl.*

4   *Å, kongebarn frå Betlehem,*
    *Inn i vårt hjarta drag!*
    *Vi audmjukt bed: Stig til oss ned,*
    *Vert fødd i oss i dag!*
    *Vi høyrer englesongen*
    *Det glade bod fortel.*
    *Å kom til oss, å ver hos oss,*
    *Guds Son Immanuel!*

# Oh come, all ye faithful / *Å, kom nå med lovsang*
## Adeste Fideles

Tune: John Francis Wade(1711-1786), *Cantus diversi* (1751)
Original lyrics: John Francis Wade (1711-1786) (lyrics first published 1760)
English lyrics: Frederick Oakeley (1802-1880) (1852)
Norwegian lyrics:Per Lønning ((1928- )

2    The highest, most holy, Light of light eternal,
        Born of a virgin, a mortal he comes;
        Son of the Father now in flesh appearing!
        Oh, come, let us adore him,
        Oh, come, let us adore him,
        Oh, come, let us adore him, Christ the Lord!

3    Sing, choirs of angels, sing in exultation,
        Sing, all ye citizens of heaven above!
        Glory to God . . . . in . . . the . . highest:
        Oh, come, let us adore him
        Oh, come, let us adore him,
        Oh, come, let us adore him, Christ the Lord!

2    *Gud, evig Gud, og lys av lys det er han*
        *Til oss er han kommet som bror i dag.*
        *Sann Gud av opphav, født før alle tider.*
        *Kom, tilbe ham, Guds under!*
        *Kom, tilbe ham, Guds under!*
        *Kom, tilbe ham, Guds under: Vår Herre Krist!*

3    *Syng, englehærer, syng med salig jubel!*
        *Å syng, myriader, i himlens slott:*
        *Ære til Gud og fred blant oss på jorden!*
        *Kom, tilbe ham, Guds under!*
        *Kom, tilbe ham, Guds under!*
        *Kom, tilbe ham, Guds under: Vår Herre Krist!*

# Your little ones, dear Lord / *Her kommer dine arme små*

Tune: Johann Abraham Peter Schulz (1747-1800) (1786), harmonized by Fartein Valen (1858-1937)
Danish/Norwegian lyrics: Hans Adolf Brorson (1694-1764) (1732) (Danish)
English lyrics: Harriet Reynolds Krauth Spaeth (1845-1925) (1898)

1 Your little ones, dear Lord, are we, And come your lowly bed to see; Enlighten ev'ry soul and mind, That we the way to you may find.

1 *Her kommer dine arme små, o Jesus, i din stall å gå, opplys enhver i sjel og sinn å finne veien til deg inn!*

2 With songs we hasten you to greet,
And kiss the ground before your feet.
Oh, blessed hour, oh, sweetest night
That gave you birth, our soul's delight.

3 Oh, draw us wholly to you, Lord,
And to us all your grace accord;
True faith and love to us impart,
That we may hold you in our heart.

4 Until at last we too proclaim,
With all your saints, your glorious name;
In paradise our songs renew,
And praise you as the angels do.

2 *Vi løper deg med sang i mot,
og kysser støvet for din fot;
å salig stund, å søte natt,
da du ble født, vår sjeleskatt!*

3 *Velkommen fra din himmelsal,
til denne verdens tåredal;
hvor man deg intet annet bød,
enn stall og krybbe, kors og død!*

4 *Her står vi nå i flokk og rad
om deg, vårt skønne hjerteblad,
akk, hjelp, at vi og alle må
i himlen for din trone stå.*

# A child is born in Bethlehem / *Et barn er født i Betlehem*

Tune: Ludvig Mathias Lindeman (1812-1887)
Original lyrics from Latin carol *Puer Natus in Bethlehem*(14th century)
Text based on 15th century German translation
Danish/Norwegian lyrics: Nikolai Fredrik Severin Grundtvig (1783-1872) (1820) (Danish)
English lyrics: Liv Nordem Lyons (1984)

2   The child in a manger lay,
    a manger lay,
    While angels sang: Rejoice today!
    Hallelujah, hallelujah!

3   From Saba Wise Men traveled swift,
    they traveled swift.
    Gold, incense, myrrh, they brought as gifts.
    Hallelujah, hallelujah!

4   To heaven we our voices raise,
    our voices raise,
    The Holy Trinity we praise,
    Hallelujah, hallelujah!

2   *Hun la ham i et krybberom,*
    *et krybberom,*
    *Guds engler sang med fryd derom.*
    *Halleluja, halleluja!*

3   *Fra Saba kom de konger tre,*
    *de konger tre.*
    *Gull, røkels, myrra ofret de.*
    *Halleluja, halleluja!*

4   *Lov, takk og pris i evighet,*
    *i evighet,*
    *Den Hellige Treenighet!*
    *Halleluja, halleluja!*

# It came upon the midnight clear

Tune: Richard Storrs Willis (1819-1900) (1850) (US)
English lyrics: Edmund Hamilton Sears (1810-1876) (12/29/1849) (US)
First American carol of international repute

on   the   earth,   good   will   to   all,   From   heav-en's   all - gra - cious
bove   its   sad   and   low - ly   plains   They   bend   on   hov - ering
now,   for   glad   and   gold - en   hours   Come   swift - ly   on   the
peace   shall   o - ver   all   the   earth   Its   an - cient   splend - dors

king."____   The   world   in   sol - emn   still - ness   lay   To
wing,____   And   ev - er   o'er   its   ba - bel   sounds   The
wing;____   Oh,   rest   be - side   the   wea - ry   road   And
fling,____   And   all   the   world   give   back   the   song   Which

hear   the   an - gels   sing.____
bless - ed   an - gels   sing!____
hear   the   an - gels   sing.____
now   the   an - gels   sing.____

# Good Christian friends rejoice / *Jeg synger julekvad*
## In dulci jubilo

Tune: German carol (14th century)
Original lyrics: Latin carol(14th century)
English lyrics: John Mason Neale (1818-1866) (1853)
Norwegian lyrics: Magnus Bråstrup Landstand (1802-1880) (1856)

1 Good Chris-tian friends, re-joice,___ With heart and soul and voice,___
*1 Jeg syn-ger ju-le-kvad,___ jeg er så glad, så glad! Min*

Give ye heed to what we say:___ Je-sus Christ is born to-day!___
*hjer-tens Je-sus hvi-ler i stall og kryb-be trang,___ som*

Ox and ass be-fore him bow, And he is in the man-ger now.
*so-len kla-re smi-ler han på sin mo-ders fang.___*

Christ is born to - day!___ Christ is born to - day!
*Han er Frel - ser min!___ Han er frel - ser min!*

2  Good Christian friends, rejoice
   With heart and soul and voice;
   Now ye hear of endless bliss:
   Jesus Christ was born for this!
   He has opened heaven's door,
   And we are blest forevermore.
   Christ was born for this!
   Christ was born for this!

3  Good Christian friends, rejoice
   With heart and soul and voice;
   Now ye need not fear the grave;
   Jesus Christ was born to save!
   Calls you one and calls you all
   To gain his everlasting hall.
   Christ was born to save!
   Christ was born to save!

2  *Å Jesus, du barnlill,*
   *deg lenges jeg så til!*
   *Kom, trøst meg allesinne,*
   *tred inn om her er smått,*
   *la meg deg se og finne,*
   *å, da har jeg det godt!*
   *Drag meg etter deg!*
   *Drag meg etter deg!*

3  *Hvor er Gud Fader mild:*
   *Sin sønn had sende vil.*
   *Vi alle var fordervet*
   *i vår ulydighet,*
   *men han har oss ervervet*
   *all himlens fryd og fred.*
   *Eia, var vi der!*
   *Eia, var vi der!*

# The first Noël / *Bryt ut i sang!*
# The first Nowell

Tune: English carol (16th century), harmonized by Sir John Stainer (1840-1901) (1871)
English lyrics: English carol (16th century) (1833 first published)
Norwegian lyrics: Eyvind Skeie (1947-  ) (1979)

1 The first No - el the an - gel did say
*1Bryt ut i sang! Nå strå - ler frem*

Was to cer - tain poor shep - herds in fields as they lay;
*Guds nå - des lys i Bet - le - hem.*

In fields where they lay, keep - ing their sheep,
*Et barn er født, en frel - ser stor*

On a cold win - ter's night that was so deep.
*for al - le fol - ke - slag på jord.*

Refrain / Refreng

No - el, No - el, No - el, No - el,
La san - gen klin - ge, ren og ny:

Born is the King of Is - ra - el.
Kris - tus er født i Da - vids by!

2  They lookèd up and saw a star
   Shining in the east beyond them far;
   And to the earth it gave great light,
   And so it continued both day and night.
   Noel, Noel, Noel, Noel!
   Born is the King of Israel.

3  And by the light of that same star
   Three Wise Men came from country far;
   To seek for a king was their intent,
   And to follow the star wherever it went.
   Noel, Noel, Noel, Noel!
   Born is the King of Israel.

4  This star drew near to the northwest,
   O'er Bethlehem it took its rest;
   And there it did both stop and stay
   Right over the place where Jesus lay.
   Noel, Noel, Noel, Noel!
   Born is the King of Israel.

2  *En stjerne klar med nytent glans*
   *gir verden bud om æren hans.*
   *Nå stiger frelsens dag i øst*
   *og bringer alle håp og trøst.*
   *La sangen klinge, ren og ny:*
   *Kristus er født i Davids by!*

3  *Hør englesang! Se lysets prakt!*
   *Gå inn dit englene har sagt,*
   *og hils Guds egen kongesønn*
   *med jubelsang og takkebønn.*
   *La sangen klinge, ren og ny:*
   *Kristus er født i Davids by!*

4  *For dette barn skal vi engang*
   *få prise Gud med evig sang.*
   *Nå er det født en frelser stor,*
   *for oss og alle folk på jord!*
   *La sangen klinge, ren og ny:*
   *Kristus er født i Davids by!*

# I am so glad each Christmas Eve / *Jeg er så glad hver julekveld*

Tune: Peder Knudsen (1819-1863) (1859?)
Norwegian lyrics: Marie Wexelsen (1832-1911) (1860)
English lyrics: Peter Andrew Sveeggen (1881-1959)
Best known Norwegian carol

**Joyfully / *Muntert***

*mf*

1 I am so glad— each Christ-mas Eve, The night of Je - sus' birth!—
1 *Jeg er så glad— hver ju - le-kveld, for da ble Je - sus født.—*

Then like the sun— the star shone forth, And an - gels sang— on earth.—
*Da lys - te stjer - nen som en sol, og eng - ler sang— så søtt.—*

2  The little child in Bethlehem,
He was a king indeed!
For he came down from heav'n above
To help a world in need.

3  He dwells again in heaven's realm,
The Son of God today;
And still he loves his little ones
And hears them when they pray.

4  I am so glad each Christmas Eve!
His praises then I sing;
He opens now for ev'ry child
The palace of the king.

2  *Det lille barn i Betlehem,*
*han var en konge stor,*
*som kom fra himlens høye slott*
*ned til vår arme jord.*

3  *Nå bor han høyt i himmerik,*
*han er Guds egen sønn,*
*men husker alltid på de små*
*og hører deres bønn.*

4  *Jeg er så glad hver julekveld,*
*da synger vi hans pris.*
*Da åpner han for alle små*
*sitt søte paradis.*

# Savior of the nations, come / *Folkefrelsar til oss kom*
## Veni, Redemptor Gentium

Tune: Walther, *Geistliche Gesangbüchlein* (1524)
Original Latin lyrics: Attributed to St. Ambrose (340?-397)
German lyrics: Martin Luther(1483-1546) (1524)
English lyrics: William Morton Reynolds (1816-1876), verses 1-3a;
Martin L. Seltz (1909-1967), verses 3b
Norwegian lyrics: Bernt Støylen(1858-1937) (1905)

1 Savior of the nations, come; Show the glory of the Son!
1 Folkefrelsar, til oss kom, født av møy i armodsdom!

Ev'ry people, stand in awe; Praise the perfect Son of God.
Heile verdi undrast på kvi du soleis koma må.

2   Not of human seed or worth,
    But from God's own mystic breath,
    Fruit in Mary's womb begun
    When God breathed the Word, his Son.

3   God the Father is his source,
    Back to God he runs his course;
    Down to death and hell descends,
    God's high throne he reascends.

2   *Utan synd han boren er*
    *som all synd for verdi ber,*
    *Han er både Gud og mann,*
    *alle folk han frelsa kan.*

3   *Frå Gud Fader kom han her,*
    *heim til Gud hans vegar ber,*
    *ned han for til helheims land,*
    *uppfor til Guds høgre hand.*

# O welcome, glittering Christmas tree

## *Du grønne, glitrende tre / Sang til juletreet*

Tune: Christoph Ernst Friedrich Weyse (1774-1842) (Danish)
**Norwegian lyrics:** Johan Jacob Krohn (1841-1925) (1866?)
**English lyrics:** Liv Nordem Lyons (1984)

Lyrics (English):
1 O, welcome, glittering Christmas tree! A greeting meets you from near and far, Your Christmas lights and Norwegian flags, And on the very top the blinking star. The

Lyrics (Norwegian):
1 Du grønne, glitrende tre, goddag! Velkommen, du som vi ser så gjerne, med julelys og med norske flagg og høyt i toppen den blanke stjerne! Ja,

star is shin - ing And thus re - minds us, The star is shin - ing and
*den må skin - ne, for den skal min - ne, ja, den må skin - ne, for*

thus re - minds us a - bout our Lord,_____ a - bout our Lord._____
*den skal min - ne oss om vår Gud,_____ oss om vår Gud._____*

2     The first, joyful Christmas on earth
      Our Lord lit for us a guiding light
      To tell us all about Jesus' birth,
      God's Son, born on the darkest night.
      The star was blinking and angels singing
      The star was blinking and angels singing
      O'er Bethlehem, o'er Bethlehem.

2     *Den første jul i et fremmed land*
      *sin store stjerne vår Herre tente;*
      *den skulle vise vår jord at han*
      *den lille Jesus til verden sendte.*
      *I stjerneglansen gikk engledansen*
      *I stjerneglansen gikk engledansen*
      *om Betlehem, om Betlehem.*

3     The Christmas story again and again
      Was told us in our childhood home
      And when we follow His word,
      We then will live together in His love.
      The star is shining, the tree reminding,
      The star is shining, the tree reminding,
      Us of our Lord, us of our Lord.

3     *Om Jesusbarnet fortalte mor*
      *som mangen aften vi satt der hjemme;*
      *vi kan hans bud og hans milde ord,*
      *vi vet at aldri vi dem må glemme.*
      *Når stjernen skinner, om ham oss minner*
      *Når stjernen skinner, om ham oss minner*
      *vårt juletre, vårt juletre!*

# Winter wonderland

Tune: Felix Bernard (1897-1944) (1934) (US)
English lyrics: Richard B. Smith (1901-1935) (1934) (US)

Sleigh - bells ring, are you lis - t'nin'? In the lane snow is glis - t'nin', a
beau - ti - ful sight, we're hap - py to - night, ___ walk - in' in a win - ter won - der -
land! Gone a - way ___ is the blue - bird, here to stay is a new bird; He

sings a love song, as we go a-long, walk-in' in a win-ter won-der-land!

In the mea-dow we can build a snow-man,
In the mea-dow we can build a snow-man,

Then pre-tend that he is Par-son Brown;
And pre-tend that he's a cir-cus clown;

He'll say "Are you
We'll have lots of

mar-ried?" We'll say, "No, man! But you can do the job when you're in
fun with Mis-ter Snow-man, Un-til the oth-er kid - dies knock 'im

town!" La - ter on——— we'll con - spire——— as we dream——— by the
down! When it snows,——— ain't it thrill - in', Tho' your nose——— gets a

fire——— to face un - a - fraid, the plans that we've made,
chill - in'? We'll frol - ic and play the Es - ki - mo way,

1
walk - in in a win - ter won - der - land!

2
walk - in in a win - ter, won - der - land!

# Jolly old Saint Nicholas

Tune: Anonymous, United States (late 19th or early 20th century)
English lyrics: Anonymous, United States (late 19th or early 20th century)

# Lo, how a rose 'er blooming / *Det hev ei rose sprunge*
## Es ist ein Roess entsprungen

Tune: *Alte Catholische Geistliche Kirchengesäng*, Köln, Germany (1599), harmonized by Michael Prätorius (1571-1621) (1609)
Original lyrics: German (15th century)
English lyrics: Theodore Baker (1851-1934) (1894), verses 1 and 2; Harriet R. Krauth (1845-1925) (1875), verse 3
Norwegian lyrcis: Peter Hognestad (1866-1931) (1919,1921)

2 Isaiah 'twas foretold it,
  The rose I have in mind,
With Mary we behold it,
  The Virgin Mother kind.
To show God's love aright,
She bore to all a Savior,
When half spent was the night.

3 This flower, whose fragrance tender
  With sweetness fills the air,
Dispels with glorious splendor
  The darkness everywhere.
True Man, yet very God,
From sin and death he saves us
And lightens every load.

2 *Om denne rosa eine*
  *er sagt Jesajas ord.*
*Maria møy, den reine,*
  *bar rosa til vår jord.*
*Og Herrens miskunnsmakt*
*det store under gjorde*
*som var i spådom sagt.*

3 *Guds rose ljuvleg angar*
  *og skin i jordlivs natt.*
*Når hennar ljos oss fangar,*
  *ho vert vår beste skatt.*
*Me syng i englelag:*
*No er det født ein Frelsar,*
*og natti vart til dag.*

# Hark! The herald angels sing / *Høyr kor englar syng frå sky*

Tune: Felix Mendelssohn (1809-1847) (1840) (German)
English lyrics: Charles Wesley (1707-1788) (1739), alt. by George Whitfield (1714-1770) (1753) (English)
Norwegian lyrics: Kjetil Frøysa (1976)
Whole carol first published in 1856

**Moderately / Moderat**

1 Hark! The her - ald an - gels sing,—— "Glo - ry to the
*1 Høyr kor eng - lar syng frå sky:—— "Krist er fødd i*

new - born king; Peace on earth, and mer - cy mild,——
*Da - vids by." Kjem med frel - se til oss ned,——*

God and sin - ners rec - on - ciled." Joy - ful, all you
*gir oss med Gud Fa - der fred. Gla - de al - le*

na - tions, rise;—— Join the tri - umph of the skies;——
*folk stig fram—— for å hyl - le det Guds lam.——*

With an-gel-ic hosts pro-claim, "Christ is born in Beth-le-hem!"
*Vi tok del i det-te kor som nå brer seg o-ver jord.*

**Refrain / Refreng**

Hark! The her-ald an-gels sing, "Glo-ry to the new-born king."
*Syng med eng-le-ne i sky: "Krist er født i Da-vids by!"*

2 Christ, by the highest heav'n adored,
Christ, the everlasting Lord,
Late in time behold him come,
Offspring of a virgin's womb.
Veiled in flesh the Godhead see!
Hail, incarnate deity!
Pleased as man with us to dwell,
Jesus, our Emmanuel!
Hark! The herald angels sing,
"Glory to the newborn king!"

3 Hail the heav'n born Prince of Peace!
Hail the son of righteousness!
Light and life to all he brings,
Ris'n with healing in his wings.
Mild he lays his glory by,
Born that we no more may die,
Born to raise each child of earth,
Born to give us second birth.
Hark! The herald angels sing,
"Glory to the newborn king!"

2 *Krist av englar ære får.*
*Krist er evig Herren vår.*
*Han som har Gud sjølv til far*
*kom då tida mogen var.*
*Kledde seg i kjøt og blod;*
*nådig mellom oss han sto.*
*Han er frelsas trygge fjell,*
*Jesus, vår Immanuel.*
*Syng med englene i sky:*
*Krist er født i Davids by.*

3 *Syng ein song til Herrens pris!*
*Lovsyng han på englars vis.*
*Rettferds opphav, truas grunn*
*pris skal ha or kvart ein munn.*
*Født til frelse og til fred.*
*Døden har han kjempa ned.*
*Født til liv for syndig mann.*
*Vi skal oppstå liksom han.*
*Syng med englene i sky:*
*Krist er født i Davids by.*

# The bells of Christmas / *Det kimer nå til julefest*

Tune: Carl C. N. Balle (1806-1855) (1850) (Danish)
Norwegian/Danish lyrics: Nikolai Fredrik Severin Grundtvig (1783-1872) (1817) (Danish)
English lyrics: Charles Porterfield Krauth (1823-1883) (1867)
Best known Danish carol

1 The bells of Christmas chime once more; The heav'n-ly guest is at the door. He comes to earth-ly dwell-ings still With new year gifts of peace, good will.

1 *Det ki - mer nå til ju - le - fest, det ki - mer for den høy - e gjest som steg til la - ve hyt - ter ned med nytt - års - ga - ver, fryd og fred.*

2  O, come to David's city, all
   Where angels sing in praise to God
   O, come and listen to the word
   That shepherds in the fields once heard.

3  In Bethlehem our Christ was born
   Our Savior, now we death can scorn
   And praise with an eternal fest
   The coming of our heavenly guest.

4  Come, Jesus, glorious heav'nly guest,
   And keep your Christmas in our breast;
   Then David's harpstrings, hushed so long,
   Shall swell our jubilee of song.

2  *Å, kom bli med til Davids by*
   *hvor engler synger under sky!*
   *Å la oss gå på marken ut*
   *hvor hyrder hører nytt fra Gud!*

3  *I Betlehem er Kristus født*
   *som frelser oss fra synd og død.*
   *Nå kom den store løvsals-fest!*
   *Nå ble vår Herre hyttens gjest.*

4  *Kom Jesus! Vær vår hyttes gjest!*
   *Hold selv i oss din julefest!*
   *Da skal med Davidsharpens klang*
   *deg takke høyt vår nyttårs-sang.*

# Ring, O ye bells, O ring out / *Kimer, i klokker*

Tune: German hymn (1668), *Ernewerten Gesangbuch*, Stralsund, arranged by F. Melius Christiansen (1907)
Norwegian/Danish lyrics: Nikolai Fredrik Severin Grundtvig (1783-1872) (1856) (Danish)
English lyrics: Peter Andrew Sveeggen (1881-1959) (1919)

2  Christmas has come,
   with its sunlight our fears all dispelling,
   Come with the child of
   whom voices angelic are telling,
   Come from above,
   Bringing glad tidings of love;
   Glory to God in the highest!

3  Sing, oh ye children
   of earth to the uttermost nation;
   Mingle sweet music and
   sing in your rapt jubilation!
   Born is the child,
   pledge of God's Fatherhood mild;
   Glory to God in the highest!

2  *Julen er kommet*
   *med solverv for hjertene bange,*
   *jul med Gudsbarnet*
   *i svøp under englenes sange;*
   *kommer fra Gud,*
   *bringer oss glederikt bud,*
   *æren er Guds i det høye!*

3  *Synger og leker*
   *og klapper i eders små hender,*
   *menneskebarnene*
   *alle til jorderiks ender!*
   *Født er i dag*
   *barnet til Guds velbehag,*
   *æren er Guds i det høye!*

# Rudolph the red-nosed reindeer / *Rudolf er rød på nesen*

Tune: John D. Marks (1909-1985) (1949) (US), harmonized by Erik Leidzen and Stephen Bulla of The Salvation Army
English lyrics: John D. Marks (1909-1985) (1949) (US)
Norwegian lyrics: Arne Bendiksen (1926- ) (1959)

1 Ru-dolph, the red-nosed rein-deer had a ver-y shin-y nose,
1 *Ru-dolf er rød på ne-sen, og når det er vind og sno,*

and if you ev-er saw it, you would e-ven say it glows.
*blir han så kald på ne-sen så den ly-ser som en glo.*

All of the oth-er rein-deer, used to laugh and call him names,
*Reins-flok-ken er-tet Ru-dolf sa han var et sno-dig dyr,*

they nev-er let poor Ru-dolph join in an-y rein-deer games.
*"Hold deg på av-stand, Ru-dolf! Husk hvor lett det kan ta fyr!"*

**RUDOLPH THE RED-NOSED REINDEER**

Music and Lyrics by JOHNNY MARKS   Norwegian text by ARNE BENDIKSEN

149

# Santa Claus is comin' to town / *Julenissen kommer i kveld*

Tune: John Frederick Coots (1897-1985) (1934) (US), harmonized by Erik Leidzen and Stephen Bulla of The Salvation Army
English lyrics: Haven Gillespie (1888-1975) (1934) (US)
Norwegian lyrics:: Arne Bendiksen (1926- ) (1959)

**Brightly / Lystig**

1You bet-ter watch out, you bet-ter not cry, Bet-ter not pout, I'm— tell-ing you why: San-ta Claus is com-in' to town. He's mak-ing a list and check-ing it twice, Gon-na find out who's— naugh-ty and nice, San-ta Claus is com-in' to town. He sees you when you're

1Vær flit-tig og snill, og ik-ke vær slem, når det blir mørkt må du skyn-de deg hjem. Ju-le-nis-sen kom-mer i kveld. Da fin-ner han ut hvor hen han skal dra. Hven som skal få det de gjer-ne vil ha. Ju-le-nis-sen kom-mer i kveld. Han vet om al-le

sleep- in',   He   knows   when   you're   a - wake,   He   knows   if   you've   been
*sam - men*   *for*   *in - gen*   *lu - rer*   *han.*   *Han*   *vet*   *om*   *du*   *er*

bad   or   good,   So   be   good   for   good - ness   sake.   Oh!   You
*rik - tig*   *snill,*   *så*   *vær*   *snill*   *så*   *godt*   *du*   *kan.*   *Å!*   *Om*

bet - ter watch   out,   you   bet - ter   not   cry,   Bet - ter   not   pout,   I'm____
*al - le*   *kan*   *si*   *at*   *du*   *har*   *vært*   *grei,*   *tror*   *jeg*   *nok*   *sik - kert*   *han*

tell - ing   you   why:   San - ta   Claus   is   com - in'   to   town.
*kom - mer*   *til*   *deg.*   *Ju - le - nis - sen*   *kom - mer*   *i*   *kveld.*

151

# Up on the housetop

Tune: Benjamin Russell Hanby (1833-1867) (1850's or 1860's) (US)
English lyrics: Benjamin Russell Hanby (1833-1867) (1850's or 1860's) (US)

**Gaily / Gladelig**

1 Up on the house-top— rein - deer pause; Out jumps good old San - ta Claus,
2 First comes the stock-ing of lit - tle Nell; Oh, dear San - ta, fill it well;
3 Next comes the stock-ing of lit - tle Will; Oh, just see what glo - rious fill!

Down thro' the chim-ney with lots of toys, All for the lit - tle ones' Christmas joys.
Give her a dol - ly that laughs and cries, One that can o - pen and shut its eyes.
Here is a ham-mer and lots of tacks, Whis - tle and ball and a set of jacks.

*Refrain / Refreng*

Ho, ho, ho! Who would-n't go? Ho, ho, ho! Who would-n't go?

Up on the house-top, click, click, click, Down thro' the chim-ney with good Saint Nick.

152

# I saw three ships

Tune: English carol (15th century), harmonized by Sir John Stainer (1840-1901) (1878?)
English lyrics: English folk (15th century)

1 I saw three ships come sail - ing in, on
2 And what was in those ships all three, on
3 The Vir - gin Mary and Christ were there, on
4 Then let us all re - joice a - main, on

Christ - mas Day, on Christ - mas Day; I saw three ships come
Christ - mas Day, on Christ - mas Day; And what was in those
Christ - mas Day, on Christ - mas Day; The Vir - gin Mary and
Christ - mas Day, on Christ - mas Day; Then let us all re -

sail - ing in, on Christ - mas Day in the morn - ing.
ships all three, on Christ - mas Day in the morn - ing?
Christ were there, on Christ - mas Day in the morn - ing.
joice a - main, on Christ - mas Day in the morn - ing.

153

# In the barn there sits the elf / *På låven sitter nissen*

Tune: Norwegian folk melody, harmonized by Darrel Eide (1997)
Norwegian lyrics: Margrethe Munthe (1860-1931)
English lyrics: Michael Sevig (1977)

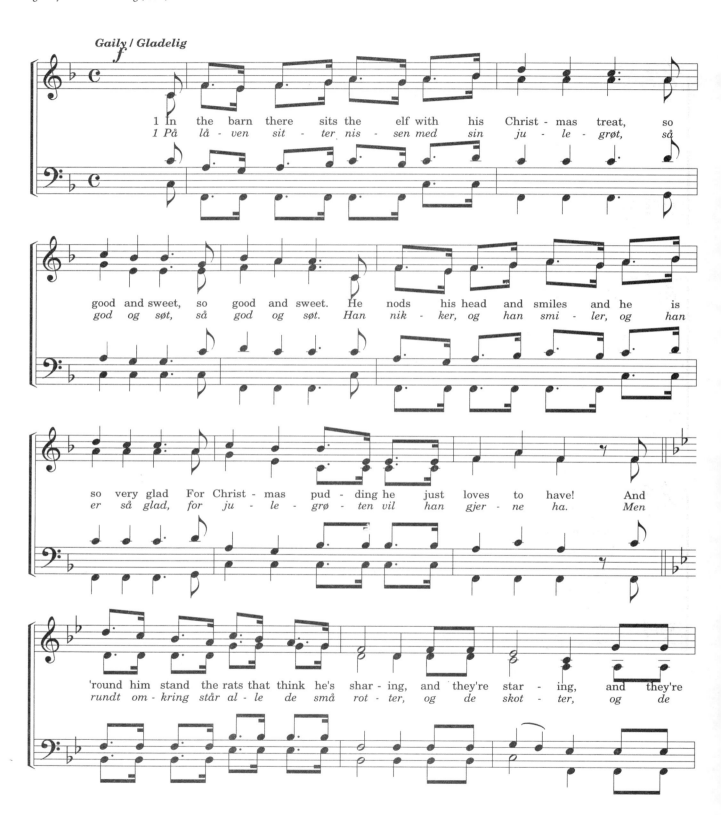

1 In the barn there sits the elf with his Christ-mas treat, so
*1 På lå-ven sit-ter nis-sen med sin ju-le-grøt, så*

good and sweet, so good and sweet. He nods his head and smiles and he is
*god og søt, så god og søt. Han nik-ker, og han smi-ler, og is han*

so very glad For Christ-mas pud-ding he just loves to have! And
*er så glad, for ju-le-grø-ten vil han gjer-ne ha. Men*

'round him stand the rats that think he's shar-ing, and they're star-ing, and they're
*rundt om-kring står al-le de små rot-ter, og de skot-ter, og de*

star - ing. They would al - so love to have some Christ - mas
skot - ter. De vil og - så gjer - ne ha litt ju - le -

pud - ding and they're dan - cing, dan - cing in a ring.
got - ter, og de dan - ser, dan - ser rundt i ring.

2  But the small elf starts to threaten with his
        big, big spoon,
   "You better watch out! You better leave soon!
   My Christmas pudding, that I want to eat myself,"
   And no one, no one's going to help himself!
   But the rats are now a-hopping and a-dancing,
   And they're swaying and they're prancing.
   They just want to have that pudding so they're dancing,
   And the elf is standing in the ring.

3  But the elf has a temper when things don't go well,
   So the elf jumps up and gives a yell,
   "If you don't quit right now, my friend, the cat, I'll tell.
   When he comes out, you'd better run or else!"
   Then the rats all run, they're scared and full of fright,
   Full of fright, full of fright,
   And they sway and prance to the left and to the right,
   And one, two, three, they're out of sight!

2  Men nissen, se han truer med sin
        store skje,
   "Nei, bare se og kom av sted,
   for julegrøten min den vil jeg ha i fred,
   og ingen, ingen vil jeg dele med!"
   Men rottene de hopper, og de danser,
   og de svinser, og de svanser,
   og de klorer etter grøten, og de stanser
   og de står om nissen tett i ring.

3  Men nissefar, han er en liten hissigpropp,
   og med sin kropp, han gjør et hopp.
   "Jeg henter katten hvis dere ikke holder opp!
   Når katten kommer, skal det nok bli stopp."
   Da løper alle rottene så bange,
   ja, så bange, ja, så bange,
   og de svinser og de svanser noen ganger,
   og en, to, tre så er de vekk!

# Away in a manger / *En krybbe var vuggen som ventet ham her*

Tune: James Ramsey Murray (1841-1905) (1887)
English lyrics: American (1885) (Anonymous, possibly German Lutheran community of Pennsylvania)
Norwegian lyrics: Agnes Landmark (1888-1959) verse 1; Eyvind Skeie (1947- ) (1979) verses 2-3

1 A - way in a man - ger, no crib for his
*1En kryb - be var vug - gen som ven - tet ham*

bed, The lit - tle Lord Je - sus laid down his sweet
*her, det lil - le barn Je - sus, vår Frel - ser, så*

head; The stars in the sky——— looked down where he
*kjær. Men stjer - ne - ne lys - te helt inn der han*

lay, The lit - tle Lord Je - sus a - sleep on the hay.
*lå, det lil - le barn Je - sus, på lei - et av strå.*

2  The cattle are lowing, the poor baby wakes,
But little Lord Jesus no crying he makes.
I love you Lord Jesus, look down from the sky
And stay by my cradle, till morning is nigh.

3  Be near me, Lord Jesus, I ask you to stay
Close by me forever and love me, I pray.
Bless all the dear children in your tender care
And take us to heaven to live with you there.

2  *Så enkelt og stille kom Gud til vår jord.*
*Så høyt er jeg elsket av Jesus, min bror.*
*Han kom fra Guds himmel, Gud selv var han lik,*
*men Jesus ble fattig, og jeg er blitt rik.*

3  *Fra krybben til korset gikk veien for deg,*
*slik åpnet du porten til himlen for meg.*
*Velsign oss, vær med oss, gi lys på vår vei,*
*så alle kan samles i himlen hos deg!*

# Christmas Eve song / *Julekveldsvise*

Tune: Arnljot Høyland (1924- ) (1952), harmonized by Darrel Eide (1997)
Norwegian lyrics: Alf Prøysen (1914-1970) (1952)
English lyrics: Liv Nordem Lyons (1984)

**Brightly / Lystig**

*mf*

1 Now we have washed the floors, and the fire-wood is in place, the
1 Nå har vi vas - ke gol - vet og vi har bø - ri ved, og

birds have got their sheaf of grain, our tree is trimmed so nice. Now
vi har sett opp fug - gel - band og vi har pyn - te tre. Nå

we'll sit down a little while, so we can catch our breath and
sett vi øss og hvi - le og pus - te på ei stund, i -

I will rock the crib so your broth - er gets some rest.
mens je rug - ge vog - ga, så bror din får en blund.

2   Come, sit down by the window and take a look with me,
    We'll try to find the Christmas star, wherever it might be.
    The brightest of them all, strong and clear, it comfort gives.
    You'll see it up above the house where midwife Matja lives.

3   The star is such a good one, it's blinking, do you see?
    And now I'll tell a story, so listen well to me.
    The first time it was shining, it made a golden bridge
    From heaven down to Earth and a stable and a crib.

4   A little boy was in the crib, a cuddly, healthy child.
    His mom was caring for him, his dad stood there and smiled,
    And shepherds in the neighborhood were also full of glee.
    They brought some newborn lambs for the little boy to see.

5   And even three wise men were riding on, day by day.
    Though none of them knew where, for they didn't know the
            way.
    The only one to lead them was the shining star above
    That twinkled on the firmament to show them where to go.

6   So this was the first time that the Christmas star was seen,
    And now all nations of the world know what its twinkling
            means.
    Whatever happens to us, it blinks and guidance gives,
    You'll see it up above the house where midwife Matja lives.

2   *Dra krakken bortått glaset, så sett vi øss og ser,*
    *og prøve finne leia der julestjerna er,*
    *den blankeste ta alle, hu er så klar og stor*
    *du ser a over taket der a Jordmor-Matja bor.*

3   *Hu er så snill den stjerna, hu blonke', kan du sjå?*
    *Og nå ska je fortælja og du ska høre på.*
    *Den fyste gong hu skinte så laga hu ei bru*
    *imilla seg og himmel'n og ei krubbe og ei ku.*

4   *I krubba låg en liten gutt så fresk og rein og go,*
    *og mor hass dreiv og stelte'n og far hass sto og lo,*
    *og gjetergutte deromkring dom kute tel og frå*
    *og bar med seg små lam-onger som guten skulle få.*

5   *Og tel og med tre vise menn, dom rei i flere da'r*
    *og ingen visste vegen og itte' hen det bar,*

    *men stjerna sto og blonke på himmelhveleven blå*
    *så ingen ta dom gikk bort seg og alle tre fekk sjå.*

6   *Ja, det var fyste gongen som julestjerna brann,*
    *men sea har a brønni i alle verdens land,*

    *og såmmå å som hende er stjerna like stor*
    *du ser a over taket der a Jordmor-Matja bor.*

# Go tell it on the mountain

Tune: African American spiritual (late 19th or early 20th century)
English lyrics: African American spiritual (late 19th or early 20th century)

**Joyfully / Muntert**

*Refrain / Refreng*

Go, tell it on the moun - tain,— O - ver the hills and ev - 'ry-where;—

Go, tell it on the moun - tain That Je - sus Christ— is born!—

1 While shep - herds kept their watch - ing O'er si - lent flocks by night, Be -
2 The shep - herds feared and trem - bled When, lo, a - bove the earth Rang
3 Down in a low - ly man - ger The hum - ble Christ was born; And

*Refrain / Refreng*

hold, through-out the heav - ens— There shone a ho - ly light.—
out the an - gel cho - rus— That hailed our Sav - ior's birth.—
God sent us sal - va - tion— That bless - ed Christ - mas morn.—

# O holy night / *O hellig natt*
## Cantique de Noël

Tune: Adolphe Charles Adam (1803-1856) (1847) (French)
Original French lyrics: Placide Cappeau (1808-1877) (1847)
English lyrics: John Sullivan Dwight (1818-1893) (ca. 1855)
Norwegian lyrics: Christine M. Anderson and Edward D. Egerdahl (1997)

thrill of hope, the wea - ry soul re - joic - es, For yon - der breaks a
*hå - pets strå - le går i - gjen - nom ver - den, og ly - set skim - rer*

new and glo-rious morn. Fall on your knees, Oh, hear the an - gel voic - es! O
*o - ver land og hav. Folk! Fall nå ned og hils gla - de - lig din fri - het. O*

night di - vine O night when Christ was
*hel - lig natt, du frel - ser til oss*

born! O night, O ho - ly night, O night di - vine!
gav. O hel - lig natt, du frel - ser til oss gav.

ho - ly night, O night di - vine!
natt du frel - ser til oss gav.

2  Truly He taught us to love one another;
   His law is love, and His Gospel is peace;
   Chains shall he break for the slave is our brother,
   And in His name all oppression shall cease.
   Sweet hymns of joy in the grateful chorus raise we,
   Let all within us praise His holy name;
   Christ is the Lord, Oh, praise His name forever!
   His pow'r and glory evermore proclaim!
   His pow'r and glory evermore proclaim!

2  *For frelser knuste våre tunge byrder,*
   *Vår jord er fri! Himlene åpnet nå er!*
   *Ute en slave, du ser en elskede bror,*
   *Og se din fiende skal bli deg så kjær.*
   *Fra himlene brakte Frelseren oss freden,*
   *For oss han steg ned i sin stille grav.*
   *Folk! Fall nå ned og hils gladelig din frihet.*
   *O hellig natt, du frelser til oss gav;*
   *O hellig natt, du frelser til oss gav.*

# Angels we have heard on high / *Engler kom fra høye himler*
## Les anges dans nos campagnes

Tune: French carol (18th century)
Original lyrics: French carol (18th century)
English lyrics: H. F. Hémy (1818-1888) after James Chadwick (1813-1882) (1860)
Norwegian/Danish lyrics: Helge Brønnum Jacobsen (Danish)

**Brightly / Lystig**
*mf*

1 An - gels we have heard on high, Sweet - ly sing - ing o'er the plains,
1 Eng - ler kom fra høye him - ler, kom med gle - des bud til jord

And the moun-tains in re - ply, Ech - o - ing their joy - ous strains.
ver - dens frel - ser født og båren opp - fylt - er guds eg et ord.

*Refrain / Refreng*

Glo - ri - a

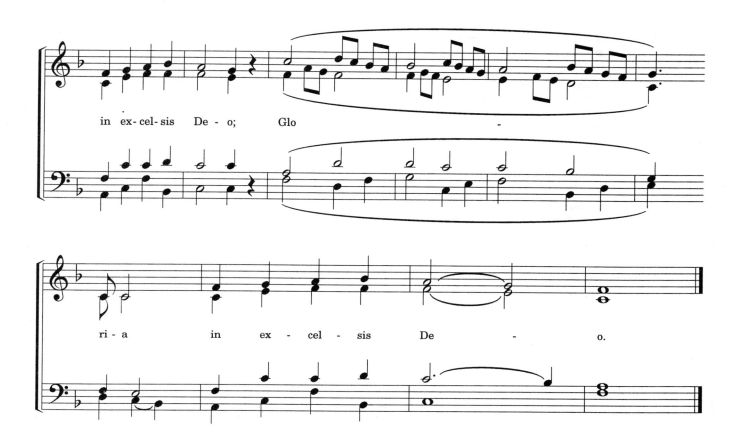

in ex-cel-sis De - o;    Glo - - - - ri - a    in ex - cel - sis    De - - o.

2  Shepherds, why this jubilee?
   Why your joyous strains prolong?
   What the gladsome tidings be
   Which inspire your heav'nly song?
   Gloria in excelsis Deo, Gloria in excelsis Deo.

3  Come to Bethlehem and see
   Him whose birth the angels sing;
   Come, adore on bended knee
   Christ the Lord, the newborn king.
   Gloria in excelsis Deo, Gloria in excelsis Deo.

2  *Hyrder på sin frelser ventet,*
   *voktet hjord i vinternatt.*
   *La dem så bli ditt eksempel,*
   *vent med dem på lysets skatt.*
   *Gloria in excelsis Deo, Gloria in excelsis Deo.*

3  *Se det barn som Gud har sendt oss,*
   *deg til glede, frelse, fred.*
   *Han på tronen, livets fyrste,*
   *vi for Han vil knele ned.*
   *Gloria in excelsis Deo, Gloria in excelsis Deo.*

# Child Jesus in a manger lay / *Barn Jesus i en krybbe lå*

Tune: Niels Wilhelm Gade (1817-1890) (1859) (Danish)
Danish/Norwegian lyrics: Hans Christian Andersen (1805-1875) (1849) (Danish)
English lyrics: Liv Nordem Lyons (1984)

**Moderately / Moderat**

*mp*

1 Child Je - sus in a man - ger lay, al -
*1 Barn Je - sus i en kryb - be lå, skjønt*

though he came from heav - en. His pil - low made of
*him - len var hans ei - e. Hans pu - te her var*

straw and hay and dark - ness all a - round him; but
*høy og strå, mørkt var det om hans lei - e. Men*

o'er the house a star was bright and ox - en kissed his feet that night.
*stjer - nen o - ver hu - set stod, og ok - sen kys - set bar - nets fot.*

Al - le - lu - ia, al - le - lu - ia, Child Je - sus.
Hal - le - lu - ja, hal - le - lu - ja, barn Je - sus.

2  My weary soul no more forlorn
   My pain now left behind.
   A child in David's city born
   Will comfort all mankind.
   With minds like children, faithful, mild,
   We all shall go to seek this child
   Halleluia, halleluia, Child Jesus.

2  *Hver sorgfull sjel blir frisk og glad*
   *og legger bort sin smerte;*
   *et barn er født i Davids stad*
   *til trøst for hvert et hjerte.*
   *Til dette barnet skal vi gå*
   *for barnesinn igjen å få.*
   *Halleluja, halleluja, barn Jesus!*

# I wonder as I wander

Tune: John Jacob Niles (1892-1980) (1934), based on an Appalachian folk melody
English lyrics: John Jacob Niles (1892-1980) (1934), based on an Appalachian carol

**Tenderly / Sakte**
*mp*

1 I wonder as I wander, out under the
2 When Mary birth-ed Je - sus, 'twas in a cow's
3 If Je - sus had want - ed for an - y small
4 I won - der as I wan - der, out un - der the

sky, how Je - sus the Sav - ior did come for to
stall, with wise men and farm - ers and shep - herds and
thing, a star in the sky or a bird on
sky, how Je - sus the Sav - ior did come for to

die for poor low - ly peo - ple like you and like
all, and high from the heav - ens, a star's light did
wing, or all of God's an - gels in heav'n for to
die for poor low - ly peo - ple like you and like

# The friendly beasts

Tune: French or possibly English carol (12th century), arranged by Leland B. Sateren(1954?)
English lyrics: Attributed to Robert Hobart Davis (US) (First known text 1934)

good. "I," said the don - key, shag - gy and brown, "I____ car - ried his
red. "I," said the sheep with the cur - ly horn, "I____ gave him my
high. Thus ev - 'ry beast by some____ good spell, In the sta - ble

moth - er____ up - hill and down; I____ car - ried his moth - er to
wool for his blan - ket warm, He____ wore____ my coat____ on
dark was____ glad____ to tell Of the gift____ he gave____ Em -

Beth - le - hem town."____ "I," said the don - key, shag - gy and brown.
Christ - mas morn."____ "I," said the sheep with the cur - ly horn.
man - u - el, The gift he____ gave Em - man - u - el.

# Silent night / *Glade jul*
## Stille nacht

Tune: Franz Xaver Gruber (1787-1863) (1818) (Austria)
Original lyrics: Joseph Mohr (1792-1849) (1818) (Austria)
English lyrics: John Freeman Young (1820-1885)
Norwegian lyrics: Bernhard Severin Ingemann(1789-1862) (1850)

1 Silent night, holy night! All is calm, all is bright. Round yon virgin, mother and child. Holy Infant, so tender and mild,

*1 Glade jul, hellige jul! Engler daler ned i skjul. Hit de flyver med paradis grønt, hvor de ser hva for Gud er skjønt,*

Sleep__ in heav-en-ly peace, Sleep__ in heav-en-ly peace.
*lønn-lig  i - blant oss de  går,  lønn-lig  i - blant oss de  går.*

2 Silent night, holy night!
  Shepherds quake at the sight.
  Glories stream from heaven afar,
  Heav'nly hosts sing, Alleluia!
  Christ, the Savior, is born!
  Christ, the Savior, is born!

3 Silent night, holy night!
  Son of God, love's pure light,
  Radiant beams from your holy face,
  With the dawn of redeeming grace,
  Jesus, Lord, at your birth,
  Jesus, Lord, at your birth.

2 *Julefryd, evige fryd,*
  *hellig sang med himmelsk lyd!*
  *Det er engler som hyrdene så*
  *dengang Herren i krybben lå,*
  *evig er englenes sang,*
  *evig er englenes sang.*

3 *Fred på jord, fryd på jord,*
  *Jesusbarnet blant oss bor!*
  *Engler synger om barnet så smukt,*
  *han har himmeriks dør opplukt.*
  *Salig er englenes sang,*
  *salig er englenes sang.*

# God rest you merry, gentlemen

Tune: English carol (16th century), harmonized by Sir John Stainer (1840-1901) (1867)
English lyrics: English carol (18th century)

1 God rest you merry, gentlemen, let nothing you dismay,
2 In Bethlehem, in Israel, this blessed babe was born,
3 From God our heav'nly Father, a blessed angel came;

Remember Christ our Savior was born on Christmas Day,
And laid within a manger, upon this blessed morn;
And unto certain shepherds, brought tidings of the same;

To save us all from Satan's pow'r, when we were gone astray;
The which his Mother Mary, did nothing take in scorn.
How that in Bethlehem was born the Son of God by name.

# Beautiful Savior / *Deilig er jorden* / Lovely is the earth
## Schönster Herr Jesu

Tune: Silesian folk melody (1842)
Original lyrics: *Gesangbuch*, Münster (1677))
English lyrics: Joseph Augustus Seiss (1823-1904)
Norwegian lyrics: Bernhard Severin Ingemann(1789-1862) (1850)

Calmly / Rolig
*mp*

1 Beau - ti - ful Sav - ior, King of cre - a - tion,
*1 Dei - lig er jor - den, prek - tig er Guds him - mel,*

Son of God and Son of Man!
*skjønn er sje - le - nes pil - grims - gang!*

Tru - ly I'd love thee, Tru - ly I'd serve thee,
*Gjen - nom de fag - re ri - ker på jor - den*

Light of my soul, my joy, my crown.
*går vi til pa - ra - dis med sang.*

2   Fair are the meadows, fair are the woodlands,
    Robed in flowers of blooming spring;
    Jesus is fairer, Jesus is purer,
    He makes our sorrowing spirit sing.

3   Fair is the sunshine, fair is the moonlight,
    Bright the sparkling stars on high;
    Jesus shines brighter, Jesus shines purer,
    Than all the angels in the sky.

2   *Tider skal komme, tider skal henrulle,*
    *slekt skal følge slekters gang.*
    *Aldri forstummer tonen fra himlen*
    *i sjelens glade pilgrimssang!*

3   *Englene sang den, først for markens hyrder;*
    *skjønt fra sjel til sjel det lød:*
    *Fred over jorden! Menneske fryd deg!*
    *Oss er en evig Frelser født!*

# The twelve days of Christmas / *Tolv juleting i Norge*

This is one of the most satarized pieces of Christmas music ever written. The total number of gifts the true love gave is 364, or one present for each day of the year except for the day just before Christmas. At one time this song was part of a game of forfeits. For each error in the song a price was paid. While the song now has a standard list of gifts, it is believed in its original form, at each new day in the song, a new singer had to add a new gift and recite the previous days without error. The song is believed to be full of symbolism, all but lost in today's world. The partridge represents fickleness, or in the church symbolizes abandonment of faith as the partridge abandons its young. At one time, if a young girl backed into a pear tree and then walked around it three times, she would see her true love. The hens are Breton hens and the four calling birds were once "collied" birds, meaning they were coal black. The five golden rings may refer to a ringed pheasant instead of the traditional rings we think of. As there were often penalties for not observing the rituals of the twelve days of Christmas, other parts of the song are believed to represent the payments for these failures.

# The twelve days of Christmas / *Tolv juleting i Norge*

Tune: English carol (17th or 18th century)
English lyrics: English folk (17th or 18th century ) (First published 1780)
Norwegian lyrics: Leikarringen of Leif Erikson Lodge No. 1 (1981)

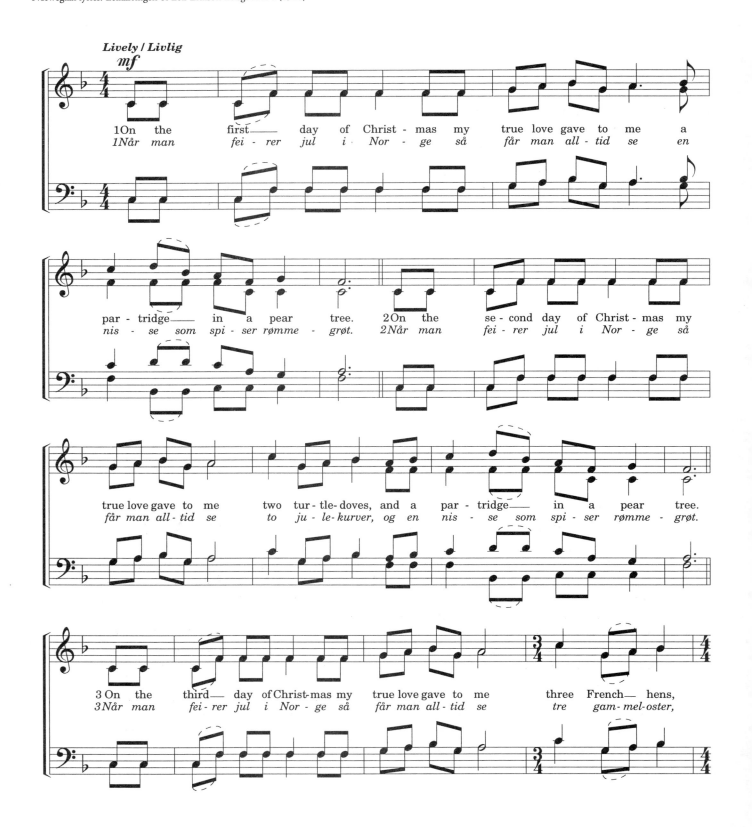

178

two tur - tle - doves, and a par - tridge____ in a pear tree.
*to ju - le - kurver, og en nis - se som spi - ser rømme - grøt.*

4 On the fourth____ day of Christ-mas my true love gave to me four call - ing birds,
*4 Når man fei - rer jul i Nor - ge så får man all - tid se fire pep - per - kaker,*

three French____ hens, two tur - tle - doves, and a par - tridge____ in a pear tree.
*tre gam - mel - oster, to ju - le - kurver, og en nis - se som spi - ser rømme - grøt.*

5 On the fifth____ day of Christ - mas my true love gave to me
*5 Når man fei - rer jul i Nor - ge så får man all - tid se*

five gold— rings, four call-ing birds, three French— hens,
*fem blanke— stjern, fire— pep-per-kaker, tre gam-mel-oster,*

two— tur-tle-doves, and a par-tridge— in a pear tree.
*to— ju-le-kurver, og en nis-se som spi-ser rømme-grøt.*

6 On the sixth— day of Christ-mas my true love gave to me
*6 Når man fei-rer jul i Nor-ge så får man all-tid se*

7 On the seventh day of Christ-mas my true love gave to me
8 On the eighth day of Christ-mas my true love gave to me
9 On the ninth day of Christ-mas my true love gave to me
10 On the tenth day of Christ-mas my true love gave to me
11 On the eleventh, day of Christ-mas my true love sent to me
12 On the twelfth day of Christ-mas my true love gave to me

*7 Når man fei-rer jul i Nor-ge så får man all-tid se*
*8 Når man fei-rer jul i Nor-ge så får man all-tid se*
*9 Når man fei-rer jul i Nor-ge så får man all-tid se*
*10 Når man fei-rer jul i Nor-ge så får man all-tid se*
*11 Når man fei-rer jul i Nor-ge så får man all-tid se*
*12 Når man fei-rer jul i Nor-ge så får man all-tid se*

# Good King Wenceslas

Tune: Latin Spring carol (13th century) (first published in the collection *Piae Cantiones* (1582))
English lyrics: John Mason Neale (1818-1866) (1853)

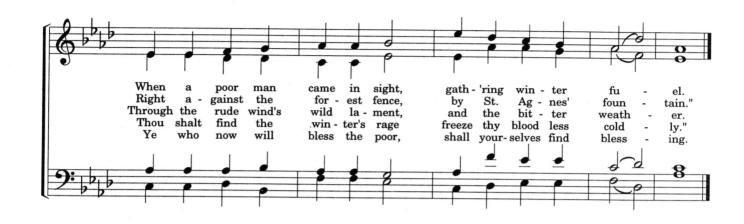

When a poor man came in sight, gath-'ring win - ter fu - el.
Right a - gainst the for - est fence, by St. Ag - nes' foun - tain."
Through the rude wind's wild la - ment, and the bit - ter weath - er.
Thou shalt find the win - ter's rage freeze thy blood less cold - ly."
Ye who now will bless the poor, shall your-selves find bless - ing.

# We three kings of Orient are

Tune: John Henry Hopkins(1820-1891) (1857) (US)
English lyrics: John Henry Hopkins (1820-1891) (1857) (US)

**Moderately / Moderat**
*mp*

Kings: We three kings of O - ri - ent are; Bear - ing
Melchoir: Born a king on Beth - le - hem's plain, Gold I
Casper: Frank - in - cense to of - fer have I; In - cense
Balthazar: Myrrh is mine; its bit - ter per - fume Breathes a
All: ·Glo - rious now be - hold him a - rise, King and

gifts we tra - verse a - far, Field and foun - tain,
bring to crown him a - gain; King for - ev - er,
owns a de - i - ty nigh; Prayer and prais - ing,
life of gath - er - ing gloom; Sor - rowing, sigh - ing,
God and Sac - ri - fice; Heav'n sings al - le -

moor and moun - tain, fol - low - ing yon - der star.
ceas - ing nev - er, o - ver us all to reign.
glad - ly rais - ing, wor - ship - ing, God Most High.
bleed - ing, dy - ing, sealed in the stone - cold tomb.
lu - ia: Al - le - lu - ia the earth re - plies.

*Refrain / Refreng*

Oh,_____ star of won - der, star of night,

star with roy - al beau - ty bright; west - ward

lead - ing, still pro - ceed - ing, guide us to your per - fect light!

# Bright and glorious is the sky / *Deilig er den himmel blå*

Tune: Jacob Gerhard Meidell (1778-1859) (c. 1840)
Norwegian/Danish lyrics: Nikolai Fredrik Severin Grundtvig (1783-1872) (1810) (Danish)
English lyrics: Service Book and Hymnal, 1958, alt.

1 Bright and glo - rious is the sky, Ra - diant are the
*1 Dei - lig er den him - mel blå,* *lyst det er å*

heav - ens high Where the gold - en stars are shin - ing.
*se der - på,* *hvor de gyl - ne stjer - ner blin - ker,*

All their rays to earth in - clin - ing Beck - on us to
*hvor de smi - ler,* *hvor de vin - ker* *oss fra jor - den*

heav'n a - bove, Beck - on us to heav'n a - bove.
*opp til seg,* *oss fra jor - den* *opp til seg.*

# Bright and glorious is the sky / *Deilig er den himmel blå*

Tune: Jacob Gerhard Meidell (1778-1859) (c. 1840)
Norwegian/Danish lyrics: Nikolai Fredrik Severin Grundtvig (1783-1872) (1810) (Danish)
English lyrics: Service Book and Hymnal, 1958, alt.

2    On that holy Christmas night
      Through the darkness beamed a light;
      All the stars above were paling,
      All their luster slowly failing
      As the Christmas star drew nigh,
      As the Christmas star drew nigh.

3    Sages from the East afar,
      When they saw this wondrous star,
      Went to find the king of nations
      And to offer their oblations
      Unto him as Lord and King,
      Unto him as Lord and King.

4    Him they found in Bethlehem,
      Yet he wore no diadem;
      They but saw a maiden lowly
      With an infant pure and holy
      Resting in her loving arms,
      Resting in her loving arms.

5    As a star, God's holy Word
      Leads us to our King and Lord;
      Brightly from its sacred pages
      Shall this light throughout the ages
      Shine upon our path of life,
      Shine upon our path of life.

2    *Der var midt i julenatt,*
      *hver en stjerne glimtet matt;*
      *men med ett der ble å skue*
      *én så klar på himlens bue*
      *som en liten stjernesol,*
      *som en liten stjernesol.*

3    *Han med sønn og stjernemann*
      *straks dro ut fra Østerland*
      *for den konge å opplete,*
      *for den konge å tilbede,*
      *som var født i samme stund,*
      *som var født i samme stund.*

4    *Glade uti sjel og sinn*
      *gikk de nu i hytten inn.*
      *Der var ingen kongetrone*
      *der satt kun en fattig kone,*
      *vugget barnet i sitt skjød,*
      *vugget barnet i sitt skjød.*

5    *Denne stjerne lys og mild,*
      *som kan aldri lede vill,*
      *er hans guddomsord det klare,*
      *som han lot oss åpenbare*
      *til å lyse for vår fot,*
      *til å lyse for vår fot.*

# The Christmas gift / *Julepresangen*

Tune: Norwegian folk melody, harmonized by Darrel Eide (1997)
Norwegian lyrics: Alf Prøysen (1914-1970) (1954)
English lyrics: Olive M. Sevig (1977)

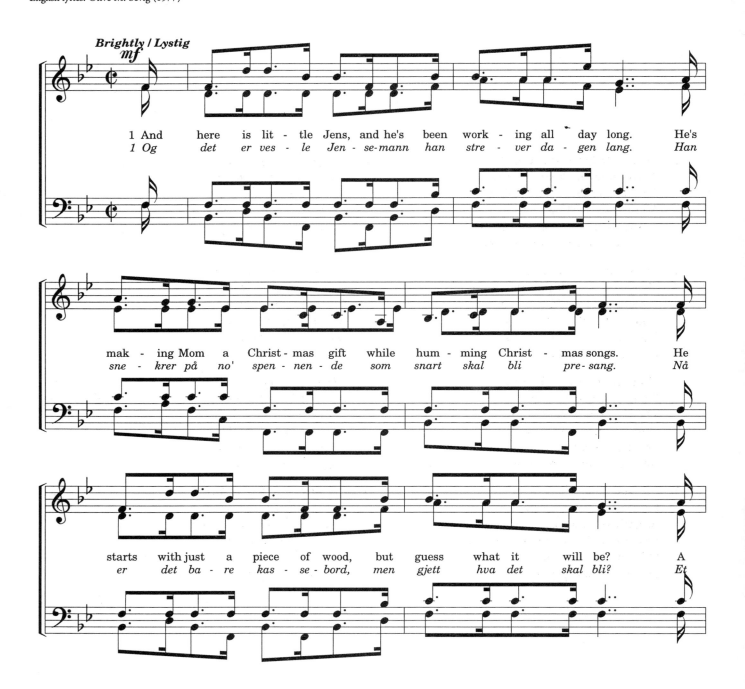

**Brightly / Lystig**
*mf*

1 And here is lit - tle Jens, and he's been work - ing all day long. He's
*1 Og det er ves - le Jen - se-mann han stre - ver da - gen lang. Han*

mak - ing Mom a Christ - mas gift while hum - ming Christ - mas songs. He
*sne - krer på no' spen - nen - de som snart skal bli pre - sang. Nå*

starts with just a piece of wood, but guess what it will be? A
*er det ba - re kas - se-bord, men gjett hva det skal bli? Et*

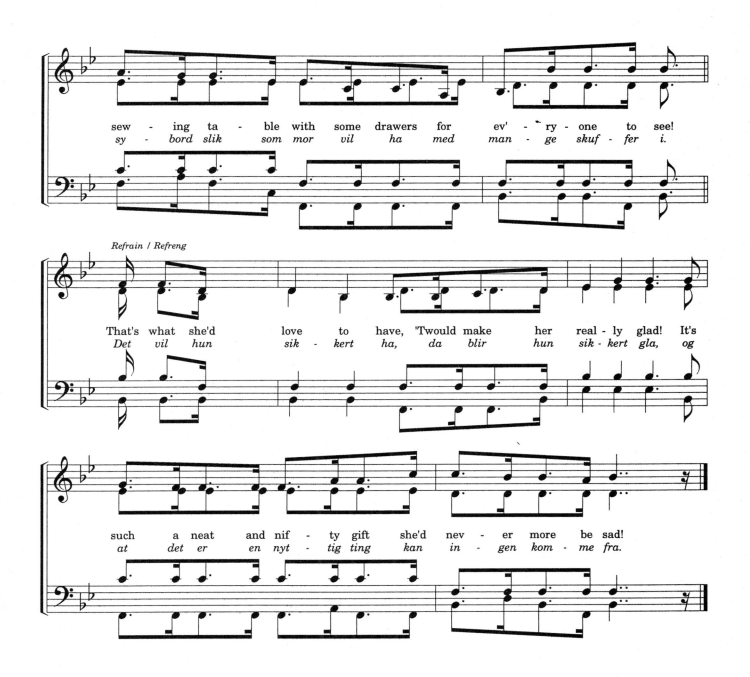

sew - ing ta - ble with some drawers for ev' - ry - one to see!
*sy - bord slik som mor vil ha med man - ge skuf - fer i.*

**Refrain / Refreng**

That's what she'd love to have, 'Twould make her real - ly glad! It's
*Det vil hun sik - kert ha, da blir hun sik - kert gla, og*

such a neat and nif - ty gift she'd nev - er more be sad!
*at det er en nyt - tig ting kan in - gen kom - me fra.*

2　When putting on the table legs there's something really wrong,
　　'Cause two of them are much too short, the other two too long.
　　He saws off one and then one more, I must say it's a sin.
　　It's now become a chest for Mom to put her knitting in.
　　That's what she'd love to have, 'twould make her really glad!
　　It's such a neat and nifty gift, she'd never more be sad!

3　A knitting chest is just as good a gift, in that he's right,
　　But Jens has trouble with the lid, it just will not fit tight.
　　He planes the lid and planes some more, just guess what it will be?
　　A basket for Mom's scissors and for her embroidery.
　　That's what she'd love to have, 'twould make her really glad!
　　It's such a neat and nifty gift, she'd never more be sad!

4　The basket is uneven so it must be evened off,
　　And Jens has endless energy, at that we cannot scoff.
　　He trims it here and trims it there, he never is dismayed.
　　It's now become a box where Mother's letters can be laid.
　　That's what she'd love to have, 'twould make her really glad!
　　It's such a neat and nifty gift, she'd never more be sad!

5　It seems the box is crooked so he planes a little here,
　　And then to make it even he just planes a little there.
　　This planing just goes on until poor Jens just knows he blew it.
　　It's now a board where Mom can give the birds oatmeal and suet.
　　That's what she'd love to have, 'twould make her really glad!
　　It's such a neat and nifty gift, she'd never more be sad!

6　And now the gift is ready, though his finger's black and blue,
　　But Jens is just delighted because with building he is through.
　　The gift is wrapped and ready. Can you guess? It's really cool!
　　A board on which his mom can make his sandwiches for school!
　　That's what she'd love to have, 'twould make her really glad!
　　It's such a neat and nifty gift, she'd never more be sad!

2　*Men bena er det verste, for når han får satt dem på,*
　　*så er de to for lange og de andre to for små.*
　　*Han sager av og sager av, til slutt så er det blitt*
　　*en kiste der hvor mor kan gjemme strikketøyet sitt.*
　　*Det vil hun sikkert ha, da blir hun sikkert gla,*
　　*og at det er en nyttig ting, kan ingen komme fra.*

3　*En kiste er jo vel så bra, bevare dere vel,*
　　*da er det bare lokket som han ikke kan få tel,*
　　*og etter som han høvler, ser han klart at det vil bli*
　　*et skrin der mor kan legge fra seg saks og broderi.*
　　*Det vil hun sikkert ha, da blir hun sikkert gla,*
　　*og at det er en nyttig ting, kan ingen komme fra.*

4　*Men så skal skrinet høvles fint og jevnes lite grann,*
　　*og den som jevner flittig, det er vesle Jensemann,*
　　*og etter som han jevner, er det opplagt at det blir*
　　*en eske der som mor kan gjemme brevark og papir.*
　　*Det vil hun sikkert ha, da blir hun sikkert gla,*
　　*og at det er en nyttig ting, kan ingen komme fra.*

5　*Nå skal han bare ta og høvle høyre siden her,*
　　*men etterpå så må han høvle venstre siden der,*
　　*og plutselig er esken blitt et lite fuglebrett*
　　*som mor kan ha ved vindu' sitt med havregryn og fett.*
　　*Det vil hun sikkert ha, da blir hun sikkert gla,*
　　*og at det er en nyttig ting, kan ingen komme fra.*

6　*Og så er gaven ferdig, selv om langemann er blå*
　　*og tommeltott har plasterlapp, så fryder han seg nå,*
　　*for gaven ligger pakket inn, og gjett hva mor skal få,*
　　*ei spekefjøl som mor kan smøre skolematen på.*
　　*Det vil hun sikkert ha, da blir hun sikkert gla,*
　　*og at det er en nyttig ting, kan ingen komme fra.*

# Christmas Eve / *Julekveld*

The high point of Christmas in Norway is Christmas Eve, December 24. By 5 P.M. the streets are hushed and still, and the bells of every church in the area ring out to announce the start of the festival. For once the churches are filled to capacity for the traditional Christmas service or *høgmesse*, also called high mass.

Later that evening, each home in Norway has many candles flickering brightly as the main Christmas meal is eaten. The Christmas story from the Bible is read, often followed by the singing of carols and presents being opened.

Candles have long been considered the symbol of spiritual light. We continue to light them during the holidays to bring us out of darkness. At one time the light was very protected, as starting the flame was not as easy as lighting a match today. In Norway, the Christmas candles needed to be large and tall enough to burn throughout the entire holiday season. If a family were careless and allowed the candles to burn out during Christmas Eve, some disaster, perhaps even death, might occur to loved ones before the next Christmas Eve. On Christmas morning the wax drippings were collected and mixed with crumbs from the feast on Christmas Eve. This potent mixture was then given to the animals. It was also believed candles radiated blessings to all they shined upon. Clothes or other personal belongs were often placed within reach of the light of the candle. At the end of the season, the ends of the candles were kept for consecrating the newborn calves throughout the next year to protect them in their new life.

The tradition of keeping candles in the window to provide a beacon for those coming home is alive today in both countries. On the East Coast of the United States, small glowing electric candles placed on the window sill are an inviting tradition, especially as part of Christmas at Colonial Williamsburg, Virginia. Gradually, this custom has moved west to the Puget Sound area for all of us to enjoy.

In Norway families will place candles and wreaths on the graves of relatives, creating a glow of light from the shielded candles in the cold, crisp snow. In a small way this is still keeping the old *jól* traditions of honoring the dead this time of year.

Alfred Blomlie came from a little town called Orkdal in Trøndelag. He arrived in America in 1925 when he was seventeen. He later settled in the Bremerton area of Washington State. During an interview with Noel, he recalled some Christmas traditions from when he was a young boy and from a trip he took to Norway in 1970 where he observed the candles in the snow.

*When I was a boy, we would go out into the woods around the farm and cut the Christmas tree and drag it through the snow. Sometimes the snow was up over our knees. That was on Christmas eve morning. Then we would put it up that evening. In those days we had candles instead of lights. We never touched anything before Christmas Eve.*

*Then at around six o'clock, the family had their dinner and also the church bells would start to ring at 6 o'clock, all over the country—in the cities and out in the farming areas. And that was beautiful.*

*When I was a boy, it wasn't as commercialized as it is today. For Christmas decorations we made those paper hearts, those ones with the lattice work and you also had candles instead of the lights [on the Christmas tree]. We never had a fire. You had to watch it close. That was Christmas Eve. It was also at that time, if there were any presents, we opened them. When I grew up, we didn't have very many presents.*

*Sometimes we walked around the tree and sang Christmas songs. We had different types of food. We had surkål, potatoes, but the national food for Christmas Eve is lutefisk and milk soup. But as I remember, back in those days, that's what we had out in the country, too, but now they have spareribs and sausage. We had lefse for one thing and julekake—lots of it—Christmas bread. Fattigmann on the holiday table—fattigmann, goro, and sandkaker—they had it on Christmas Eve, but that was more for dessert.*

*I've been in Norway once at Christmas after I came here and it was in 1970. They did the same thing then. My sister's husband, Johan, he was a locomotive engineer driving a train up through that valley and I rode with him. We came up there and we were looking for a place with Christmas trees. It was Christmas Eve. Johan stopped the train right there and he said, "There is a nice Christmas tree." We both got out of the locomotive—there was nobody else on the train. It was a good thing. I'll never forget that! "Are you going to leave it there now? Should we cut that tree?" "Ja," he said, "It'll be all right." There were 30 or 40 ore cars behind us. We got out and we cut that tree and went on up to the end of the line.*

*There's one thing I'd like to mention about Christmas time in Norway in 1970. When I came to Oslo, there was all this commercialized advertising. It's all over the world. I didn't remember that they had all that before Christmas.*

*There's another thing that impressed me. I took the train over the Dovre mountains. Every once in a while, you see a white church with floodlights in the woods. That really impressed me more than anything else. I guess it wasn't just for Christmas time, it's year round, but it was Christmas when I saw it for the first time and it was really impressive. Then, of course, the church bells Christmas Eve, they started to chime all over the country, not only in the cities but off in the countryside. There's another thing. People in Norway don't go to church much, but at Christmas time they all go. When the church bells start to ring, people who have somebody buried there at the church they come and put candles on the graves in the church graveyard. They started to do this about 20–25 years ago, after World War II. So that's another thing they started at Christmas time that must be very nice. Most of our relatives are buried at the big church in Orkdal. The family puts candles on these graves. We have a niece who was married to an English boy and I guess he started crying when he saw the lights on the graves—he had never seen anything so beautiful.*

## The Christmas Gospel / *Juleevangelium*

Christmas Eve in the United States is also filled with candlelight services. Starting at 5 P.M., churches have services for young families and continue with additional services, including carol and candlelight services starting at 11 P.M. and lasting until midnight. It is a time for reflection upon the season.

The most frequently told Christmas story from the Bible told this night is found in Luke 2: 1–20. Luke is believed to have been a Greek physician who probably wrote the story of the birth of Jesus sometime between AD 70 and 90. In our homes the story is symbolized in a Nativity scene or crèche with Mary, Joseph, and the baby Jesus lying in a manger protected by the walls of the stable. The setting is surrounded by shepherds, sheep, a donkey, and the Three Wise Men.

Luke 2: 1–20

*In those days a decree went out from Emperor Augustus that all the world should be registered. This was the first registration and was taken while Quirinius was governor of Syria. All went to their own towns to be registered. Joseph also went from the town of Nazareth in Galilee to Judea, to the city of David called Bethlehem, because he was descended from the house and family of David. He went to be registered with Mary, to whom he was engaged and who was expecting a child. While they were there, the time came for her to deliver her child. And she gave birth to her firstborn son and wrapped him in bands of cloth, and laid him in a manger, because there was no place for them in the inn.*

*In that region there were shepherds living in the fields, keeping watch over their flock by night. Then an angel of the Lord stood before them, and the glory of the Lord shone around them, and they were terrified. But the angel said to them, "Do not be afraid; for see—I am bringing you good news of great joy for all the people: to you is born this day in the city of David a Savior, who is the Messiah, the Lord. This will be a sign for you: you will find a child wrapped in bands of cloth and lying in a manger." And suddenly there was with the angel a multitude of the heavenly host praising God, and saying,*

*'Glory to God in the highest heaven,*
*and on earth peace among those whom he favors.'*

*When the angels had left them and gone into heaven, the shepherds said to one another, "Let us go now to Bethlehem and see this thing that has taken place, which the Lord has made known to us." So they went with haste and found Mary and Joseph, and the child lying in the manger. When they saw this, they made known what had been told them about this child; and all who heard it were amazed at what the shepherds told them. But Mary treasured all these words and pondered them in her heart. The shepherds returned, glorifying and praising God for all they had heard and seen, as it had been told them.*[1]

---

[1]Scripture quotation from the *New Revised Standard Version of the Bible*, copyright 1989 by the Division of Christian Education of the National Council of the Churches of Christ in the USA. Used by permission. All rights reserved. Page 58.

*Lukas 2, 1–20*

*I de dager gikk det ut bud fra keiser Augustus at all verden skulle innskrives i manntall. Dette var den første innskrivingen mens Kvirinius var landshøvding i Syria. Og alle dro av sted for å la seg skrive inn, hver til sin by. Også Josef dro fra byen Nasaret i Galilea til Davids by, som er Betlehem i Judea, fordi han var av Davids hus og ætt, og ville skrive seg inn sammen med sin trolovede, Maria, som ventet barn. Og mens de var der, kom tiden da hun skulle føde, og hun fødte sin sønn, den førstefødte, og svøpte ham og la ham i en krybbe. For det var ikke rom til dem i herberget.*

*Like i nærheten var det noen gjetere som lå ute og holdt vakt over dyrene sine om natten. Med ett sto det en Herrens engel foran dem, og Herrens herlighet lyste om dem. De ble redde og skalv; men engelen sa: "Vær ikke redde! Jeg kommer med bud til dere om en stor glede, som skal være for hele folket: I dag er det født dere en frelser i Davids by, han er Kristus, Herren. Og dette skal dere ha til tegn: Dere skal finne et lite barn som er svøpt og ligger i en krybbe." Og med ett var det hos engelen en himmelsk hærskare som priste Gud og sang:*

*'Ære være Gud i det høyeste,*
*og fred på jorden blant mennesker som har nåde hos Gud.'*

*Da englene var faret bort fra dem, opp til himmelen, sa gjeterne til hverandre: "La oss gå til Betlehem og se dette som har hendt, og som Herren har kunngjort for oss!" Så skyndte de seg dit, og fant Maria og Josef og det lille barnet som lå i krybben. Og da de hadde fått se det, fortalte de alt som var blitt sagt til dem om dette barnet. Alle som hørte det, undret seg over det de sa; men Maria gjemte alt dette i sitt hjerte og grunnet på det. Så dro gjeterne tilbake, med lov og takk til Gud for alt de hadde hørt og sett, slik som det var blitt sagt dem.*[1]

Legend tells us the animals talk at midnight on Christmas Eve, and the sweetest song is heard at that magic time by voices raised in harmony. During the late night services, hearing the clear voices singing Silent Night with the candles flickering and shining upon the expectant faces gives us a sense of peace.

---

[1]Scripture quotation from *Det Nye Testamente*. Oslo: Det Norske Bibelselskaps Forlag, 1967. Pages 132–133.

Elaine Marie Thoreson Anderson was born on January 1, New Year's Day, 1925, in Churchs Ferry, North Dakota. She and her family moved to Seattle in 1942. The Anderson family has traveled extensively throughout the United States and lived in the Pacific Northwest for the most part of their lives. Elaine now lives in Tacoma with her Danish-Swedish-American husband, Donald.

*My immigrant Norwegian grandparents kept their Christmas traditions as they brought them to Minnesota and North Dakota in the 1850s and 60s. Their first generation children, especially those who married Norwegians, kept many of the same traditions and shared them with their children, which is my generation. Now, however, with marriages into other ethnic groups and with families from different parts of the country, other traditions have crept into the Christmas season.*

*My three older brothers and I remember the Sunday School programs at the Lutheran Church on Christmas Eve with the big tree decorated with candles in holders on the branches. At the church we were always given little gift bags with fruits, candies, or nuts in them. At home maybe we would receive one or two little gifts and then something useful, like some clothing item as no one had much money. I do remember receiving my last doll with hair to comb and eyes that opened and closed when I was in the 4th grade. Since I was the only girl in my family, my mother loved sewing a special dress for every occasion, including Christmas, Valentine's Day, Easter, etc.*

*My grandmother baked, my mother baked, and I still bake the same cookies. There seems to be a compulsion that says we have to have rosettes, krumkaker, goro, fattigmann, and sandbakkelser or it isn't Christmas, and potato lefse is everyone's favorite. However, if I'm going to eat lutefisk, I have to eat it at Sons of Norway or some church dinner as my family has no interest in having it Christmas Eve.*

*One of my brothers and his wife have a family of nine children, and in the last 25 years we have spent most Christmas Eves with their extended family—maybe 40 or more of us. We have the meatballs, lefse, mashed potatoes, ham, gravlaks, pickled herring, Norwegian cookies, but we also have baklava (Greek), trifle (English), and American pies, cakes, salads, sweet potatoes, chips and dips, etc. The Christmas story from Luke is always read, Christmas songs are sung, and those children and grandchildren who play the violin and guitar accompany the singing or perform on their own. It's a wonderful family affair, families maintaining contact with each other. After this, each family goes to their own homes to their own Christmas celebrations or to their churches to attend Christmas Eve services.*

*Christmas Day is more for our family, but not very Norwegian. My younger brother's wife is from New Zealand, but even before she was in our family, we frequently had roast beef with Yorkshire pudding or the traditional American turkey with bread stuffing. Christmas Eve was always the time to open the Christmas presents for each other, and Christmas morning was the time to see what was in the stockings or the presents brought by Santa. Even though our children are mature adults, all of us still enjoy Christmas morning, sitting around enjoying each other's presents and each other's presence.*

## Christmas gifts / *Julegaver*

Among our families and friends, giving food such as homemade cookies, breads, jams, jellies, and other homemade gifts has long been a tradition. During the 1500s a Roman Catholic archbishop named Olaus Magnus was living in Norway in exile from Sweden. He wrote, *"There is a kind of bread which is round, thick and as long as a five-year-old child. During the days when the birth of Christ is celebrated, this kind of bread is given away everywhere, even to strangers, and with it is given other proofs of charity worthy of such a feast."* Perhaps this is the *julekake* many of us receive from friends or relatives who bake this wonderful bread made of spices and dried fruits.

Precious gifts of gold, frankincense, and myrrh were given to Jesus by the Wise Men. The golden treasure was for his kingship, frankincense was given for holiness, and myrrh to heal the suffering he must bear while here on earth. We often give family and loved ones more elaborate or meaningful gifts during the holidays as these represent the love we have for them. There are many Christmas stories telling of people who have sold their most precious possessions, such as their beautiful long hair, to purchase something for a dear one at Christmas.

Gifts were known to be given by the early Romans during their New Year celebrations. On through the centuries gift-giving has continued and changed, but still remains a part of the celebrations this time of year, whether given by the *julenisse*, Santa Claus, Saint Nicholas, or by family and friends. It is a way to share our love and talents with those whom we care about. Sometimes the gift may be a simple letter or card to a loved one across the miles. Since Christmas may be the only time we write and hear from some friends and relatives, it becomes a small gift of love and sharing of our lives.

The traditional gift of fruitcake is either loved or hated. Sometimes a brandy liquer may be poured over the fruitcake to add flavor. Those who don't like fruitcake have been known to pass along the gift of a fruitcake to an unsuspecting person who may also dislike this type of Christmas cake. Fruitcakes have been passed around for years this way. Commercial fruitcake usually comes in beautiful Christmas tins that can be used later for your favorite cookies.

Many people make jams or jellies from fruit picked during the year. Blackberries, raspberries, peaches, pears, and apples make attractive jellies or jams. Other ideas are to select interesting pastas and put them in beautiful jars which may have been a container for something else. Spiced tea is a very popular gift to make and receive. Home grown herbs can also be attractively packed into bottles or jars to give as gifts. Cheese balls and nuts are a favorite to make for friends or to bring to the numerous Christmas parties.

## Pomander balls

Pomander balls can be made by children as gifts for grandmothers, mothers, and aunts. The balls may be hung in a closet or throughout the house for a spicy fragrance during the Christmas season. The balls keep things sweet-smelling for over a year.

Start making the balls about six weeks before Christmas. This will allow them time to dry completely so mildew doesn't become a problem.

Medium-size oranges, lemons, apples, or pears
Whole cloves
Orris root, if available
Ground cinnamon
Knitting needle
Tissue paper
Pretty ribbon

With a knitting needle or similarly pointed object, pierce the orange, lemon, apple, or pear rind. If your fingers are sufficiently strong, the cloves can be stuck into the fruit without first piercing its skin. Cover the fruit completely. The cloves do not need to be in set rows or any particular pattern unless you choose to do so.

After covering the fruit with the cloves, mix an equal amount of orris root and ground cinnamon. If desired, just use ground cinnamon. Roll the clove-covered fruit in the powder until the ball is well covered with the powder. Place the covered fruit in tissue paper and wrap loosely. Place the wrapped fruit in a warm, but dry place. Check the pomander balls occasionally. If the balls dry too fast, they may shrivel into nothing. If they dry too slowly, they may mildew.

When the balls are dry, unwrap them and shake off the extra powder. Trim as you like with colored ribbons. Be sure to attach one ribbon about 7" long, folded in half, for a hanger.

## Santa / *Julenisser*

In the United States it is Santa, a bag of goodies, his sleigh and his reindeer. In Norway it is a *nisse* with his *grøt* or porridge and a big spoon, a *julenek* for the birds, and marzipan pigs.

Santa as we know him today, a jolly man with rosy-red cheeks, twinkling eyes, a long flowing white beard, long red coat, and a black leather belt was brought to life in pictures in 1931 by Artist Haddon Sundbolm, a Swedish-American as part of a Coca-Cola advertising campaign. Thus our legendary jolly-old elf grew to human size. Many of his characteristics may be found in the *nisse* of Norway and the *tomte* of Sweden with their bright red hats, white beards, and rosy cheeks.

In Norway the *nisse* is the ubiquitous symbol of Christmas—very similar in looks to our Santa Claus, but in miniature. He is small and elf-like, dressed in a sweater, traditional knickers with knitted stockings, and very sturdy shoes. His head is covered with a bright red stocking cap. A full-size *julenisse* can be seen visiting homes in Norway. He is laden with presents and asks everyone upon entry to the house, *"God dag, god dag, er det noen snille barn her?"* "Good day, good day, are there any good children here?"

On Christmas Eve, *julaften*, it is an old tradition to make a bowl of Christmas porridge called *julegrøt* for the *julenisse*. According to tradition, the *nisse* is the protector of the home and farm and expects special treatment on Christmas. He loves animals and is especially fond of horses. There are many stories of the *nisser* who weren't offered their holiday treat. They have been known to play tricks on the dairy maid, such as knocking over the pails of milk, blowing out lanterns, holding onto the hay as the dairy maid tried to move it, and then suddenly letting go so that the dairy maid falls over backwards. In fact, if the *nisse* were neglected, he was even known to tie animals' tails together. It was also wise to serve the *julegrøt* with an island of butter, called a *smørøye*, floating on the top.

## Sour cream porridge / *Rømmegrøt*

1 quart non-homogenized heavy whipping cream*
1 cup sour cream
1⅓ cups all-purpose flour (approximate)
2 tablespoons granulated white sugar
1½ teaspoons salt or salt to taste
1 pint whole milk
1½ cups of water (approximate)

*If only homogenized heavy whipping cream is available, the butter is more difficult to separate from the porridge. Additional melted butter may need to be added at serving time.

*The day before preparing:*

Pour cream and sour cream into a 3-quart non-reactive saucepan and stir until smooth. Let sit for 24 hours at room temperature until mixture turns sour.

*The next day:*

In the saucepan, simmer cream mixture slowly for about 15 minutes. Sift and blend flour into cream mixture stirring constantly. Lift saucepan off burner and dip off butter. It may take some time before the butter separates from the cream. Put butter into separate container to save for the *smørøye* when serving later. Combine milk and water in a separate small saucepan and warm slowly on low heat. Slowly add warm milk mixture to porridge while continuing to stir constantly until porridge is thick and smooth. Add sugar and salt. Remove from heat. Serve in bowls. With a spoon create a small indention in the porridge for the *smørøye*. Sprinkle sugar and cinnamon on top, if desired.

To prevent a layer of scum from forming on the top of the *rømmegrøt* when refrigerating, add melted butter to the top or lay a piece of plastic wrap over the top to seal out the air. It also freezes well. To thaw, warm porridge in oven at a low temperature.

Makes 6–8 servings.

Bergljot Ringset Roswick was born in 1919 in the small town of Liabygda in the county of Sunnmøre, Norway. She immigrated to the Seattle area in the late 1940s and now resides in Ballard. She was *Leikarringen's* dance director for many years. During her interview with Noel, she tells about her Christmases filled with old traditions.

*I grew up on a small farm on the west coast. It was like the old days, three generations lived there. Grandparents, parents, and kids. My grandmother believed in all the old tales and at Christmas time we followed them. It was all going on before Christmas, making all kinds of food and all these things so you will be very well prepared [for the holidays].*

*The food was pretty much the same everywhere. Everything was homemade as there was no place you could buy food in that little village where I came from. Two, three weeks before Christmas all the women were baking, baking and making all kinds of things. They always had a lot of lamb meat—lamb rolls and all those things. And, of course, cookies. All the old-fashioned cookies. And bread, there had to be at least four different types of bread. Dinner was pretty much the same. Of course, it was before the freezer, so often it was salted meat, meatballs, and then the lamb ribs and all those things. They didn't have those things during the rest of the year so it was great to get them.*

*And Christmas Eve you had to feed all the things. You had to put rømmegrøt up in the barn because if you didn't feed the fjøsnisse or the underground people that lived there, then they would cast a spell on the animals during the year so you had to feed them. I think I was 16 or 17 years old before I really understood that the cat and the mice had a field day because it was always gone Christmas morning. Grandmother used to tell us all kinds of stories about people that hadn't done this and how all their animals died, and it was because they were too stingy and they wouldn't give the food to the people there.*

*Grandmother never drank hard liquor or beer or anything. She was deadly against it, but she had a bottle of brandy for medical reasons. Christmas morning she used to go around and give everybody a drink because that meant you would have a good year. She had one of those plunk flasks that make a plunk, plunk, plunk sound when you pour it. But that was the only time you should taste it.*

*When I was 10 or 11 years old I guess, she told me and I tried this, but nothing came out of it. On Christmas Eve you put a bowl of milk, a bowl of water and a bowl of brandy in front of your bed and you had to stay awake until midnight and look down into them. If you saw a face in the water you would marry a poor guy, if you saw a face in the milk it would be middle class guy, but if it was in the brandy it would be rich guy. I probably went to sleep before I could try any of this because I can't remember if I ever saw anything. But I think I did it a couple of years. What my grandmother told me, I believed.*

*The church bell was ringing on Christmas Eve in between five and six. At six o'clock everything was supposed to be done in the barn, all the animals were fed. And then we sat down and had a big dinner, the whole family. Then, of course, we always walked around the Christmas* tree and sang the carols. This was every year, and then we got the presents. I guess it was the big thing. There wasn't much to the presents we got. That was before people got so elaborate on that.

Then on Christmas Day, we couldn't go any place. We could go to church, but that was across the fjord. We had to go across in a rowboat, so when the weather was nasty, nobody went. But you had to stay home the whole Christmas Day. We couldn't go to our neighbors or anything. I know my brother used to go out on the back porch and call, "What did you get for Christmas?" We had cousins up there, and it wasn't far and you could hear it. But that was the extent of it.

And then, of course, you couldn't wait until early the day after Christmas and then you ran around everywhere. That's when all the big parties started. There was nothing before Christmas. There were dinner parties in the middle of the day. For young people it was in the evening, but family parties were in the middle of the day. People you never had anything to do with all year, they invited you to Christmas parties so you went from one place to another all Christmas. All the way up to the 13th day of Christmas, the seventh of January. During that time you didn't do anything but party and take care of the farm, of course, you had to take care of the farm. When you went to someone's house they expected you to have a party back. That was the exchange.

I remember one time we went to a big farm in the area just outside Drammen and they had three big rooms, a living room and dining room, and another room, three big rooms with big doors in between. Everybody was dressed up. I don't think any one had costumes [ bunader ] on, but it was in those days when you had long gowns. We came in sleds. I think there must have been about sixty people. And when you came, you just lined up and then you had a polonaise. You danced this dance, and the people who had the party, they danced down the whole line and shook hands with everybody. I remember that. It made a great impression on me. But I imagine that's over with too now. I don't think they can keep those big houses now because they can't afford to have people working there now. I remember that.

There was some parties later on, too, and the Christmas tree stayed up until the second of February. It was called kyndelsmesse. [1] Then the Christmas went out. That was the way it was when I grew up.

As children in the Pacific Northwest, we always left some cookies and milk for Santa and a few carrots and perhaps a sugar cube for his reindeer by the fireplace on Christmas Eve. In the morning, we found a thank you note from Santa and the food was always gone, just as it was so long ago on the farm in Norway.

Agnes Marie Caroline Nelson Blomlie was born in 1917 in Bellingham, Washington, of Norwegian parents from Hasta in northern Norway. Here she tells a little bit about her holidays.

---

[1] *Kyndelsmesse* or Candlemas was a day commemorating the presentation of Christ in the temple and the purification of Mary. On this day a sacred cake, baked on Christmas Eve, was eaten.

*I always had fun when I baked. Boy, did I like that dough when you made those spritz and all the goodies. The dough was so good. We got to scrape the bowl.*

*We didn't have family [around us]. I never knew what it was to have a grandma and grandpa. I only had a cousin and one uncle in this country. It was all I had. I really was lonely. So I adopted my closest girlfriend who was from a Swedish family. I adopted her grandma and grandpa. That's where I picked up Swedish and sang Swedish songs. I had to because Grandma Asplind couldn't speak any English and I was always over there as a little girl, knocking on their doors, going there visiting. I felt very lonely. It was mostly the Asplinds that we were surrounded by. They were a big, big family and so I was always involved with them.*

*Even when we had our own family, I still felt lonely. Friends would have big families. We started going over to Puyallup and had many Christmases over there with my cousin and their kids, and we have many wonderful memories. I wanted to do the same thing, but on a bigger scale than my parents. I felt that way all my life. I never had a grandma to hug me.*

*Christmas Eve was always so much fun with our kids. We had a Santa Claus who came to our front door. He came to our side window, and he would knock on the window, and we would hurry up and have dinner. We would have a plate with all the Norwegian goodies for Santa Claus, and our little children were fighting about who was going to answer the door. Our oldest daughter, Sharon, she and her cousin who was 4 months older, they would argue about who was going to open the door for Santa Claus. Well, Santa Claus come tromping up the porch and knocked on the door. Both of the kids ran to their parents, ran to their mothers. My niece she had her head down, but she was peeking out. Someone else had to open the door for Santa Claus. Her first words were, shaking she said, "Santa Claus has shoes like my daddy." …. We laughed so hard.*

In 1822 *A Visit from St. Nicholas*, also known as *The Night Before Christmas*, was written by Dr. Clement C. Moore for his children. This famous poem has given many of us our picture of Santa Claus and Christmas in the United States.

'Twas the night before Christmas, when all through the house
    Not a creature was stirring, not even a mouse;
The stockings were hung by the chimney with care,
    In hopes that St. Nicholas soon would be there;
The children were nestled all snug in their beds,
    While visions of sugar-plums danced in their heads;
And Mamma in her 'kerchief, and I in my cap,
    Had just settled our brains for a long winter's nap;

When out on the lawn there arose such a clatter,
    I sprang from the bed to see what was the matter.
Away to the window I flew like a flash,
    Tore open the shutters and threw up the sash.
The moon on the breast of the new-fallen snow,
    Gave the lustre of mid-day to objects below,
When, what to my wondering eyes should appear,
    But a miniature sleigh, and eight tiny rein-deer,

With a little old driver, so lively and quick,
    I knew in a moment it must be St. Nick.
More rapid than eagles his coursers they came,
    And he whistled, and shouted, and called them by name;
"Now, Dasher! now, Dancer! now, Prancer and Vixen!
    On, Comet! on, Cupid! on, Donder and Blitzen!
To the top of the porch! to the top of the wall!
    Now, dash away! dash away! dash away all!"

As dry leaves that before the wild hurricane fly,
    When they meet with an obstacle, mount to the sky;
So up to the house-top the coursers they flew,
    With a sleigh full of Toys and St. Nicholas too.
And then in a twinkling, I heard on the roof,
    The prancing and pawing of each little hoof—
As I drew in my head, and was turning around,
    Down the chimney St. Nicholas came with a bound.

He was dressed all in fur, from his head to his foot,
    And his clothes were all tarnished with ashes and soot;
A bundle of Toys he had flung on his back,
    And he looked like a pedlar just opening his pack,
His eyes—how they twinkled! his dimples, how merry!
    His cheeks were like roses, his nose like a cherry!
His droll little mouth was drawn up like a bow,
    And the beard of his chin was as white as the snow;

The stump of a pipe he held tight in his teeth,
        And the smoke, it encircled his head like a wreath;
He had a broad face, and a little round belly,
        That shook when he laughed like a bowlfull of jelly.
He was chubby and plump, a right jolly old elf,
        And I laughed when I saw him, in spite of myself,
A wink of his eye, and a twist of his head,
        Soon gave me to know I had nothing to dread;

        He spoke not a word, but went straight to his work,
                And fill'd all the stockings; then turned with a jerk,
        And laying his finger aside of his nose,
                And giving a nod, up the chimney he rose;
        He sprang to his sleigh, to his team gave a whistle,
                And away they all flew, like the down off a thistle.
        But I heard him exclaim, ere he drove out of sight,
                "Happy Christmas to all and to all a good night!"[1]

## Letters to Santa / *Brev til Julenissen*

As we make our Christmas lists each year, many of us have fond memories of sending letters to Santa at the North Pole. Frequently the letters were filled with a list of all the toys we wanted. Sometimes we would ask about the reindeer, especially Rudolph,[2] or perhaps the elves. Santa, as busy as he was this time of year, often replied. How he got our letters with so little of an address, I don't know. When I was young, it was simply Santa Claus, the North Pole. The Post Office, despite all our complaints, does seem to get Santa's mail to him. Letters to Santa Claus may now be officially addressed:

        Santa Claus
        c/o Postmaster
        PO Box 9998
        North Pole AK 99705-9998

If you wish to contact *Julenissen*, he receives letters at:

        Julenissen
        PO Box 200
        1441 Drøbak
        NORWAY

Cyberspace also offers access to Santa and *Julenissen* via Internet and the World Wide Web. Since their addresses change from year to year, be sure to do a search on their names.

---

[1]From: Moore, Clement C. *A Visit from St. Nicholas*. New York: Spalding & Shepard, 1849.

[2]Rudolph's story was first published in 1947. He became familiar to us through an advertising campaign created by Robert L. May for Montgomery Ward stores in 1939.

On September 21, 1897, an editorial written by Francis Pharcellus Church appeared in *The New York Sun*. As a writer who specialized in theological and controversial subjects, he was assigned to respond to a letter from Virginia O'Hanlon. Almost a hundred years later, this letter still helps us reply, "*Yes, Virginia, there is a Santa Claus.*"

*Dear Editor:*

*I am 8 years old. Some of my little friends say there is no Santa Claus. Papa says, "If you see it in The Sun it's so." Please tell me the truth; is there a Santa Claus?*

*Virginia O'Hanlon*

*Virginia, your little friends are wrong. They have been affected by the skepticism of a skeptical age. They do not believe except they see. They think that nothing can be which is not comprehensible by their little minds. All minds, Virginia, whether they be men's or children's, are little. In this great universe of ours man is a mere insect, an ant, in his intellect, as compared with the boundless world about him, as measured by the intelligence capable of grasping the whole of truth and knowledge.*

*Yes, Virginia, there is a Santa Claus. He exists as certainly as love and generosity and devotion exist, and you know that they abound and give to your life its highest beauty and joy. Alas! how dreary would be the world if there were no Santa Claus! It would be as dreary as if there were no Virginias. There would be no childlike faith then, no poetry, no romance to make tolerable this existence. We should have no enjoyment, except in sense and sight. The eternal light with which childhood fills the world would be extinguished.*

*Not believe in Santa Claus! You might as well not believe in fairies! You might get your papa to hire men to watch in all the chimneys on Christmas Eve to catch Santa Claus, but even if they did not see Santa Claus coming down, what would that prove? Nobody sees Santa Claus, but that is no sign that there is no Santa Claus. The most real things in the world are those that neither children nor men can see.*

*No Santa Claus! Thank God, he lives, and he lives forever. A thousand years from now, Virginia, nay ten times ten thousand years from now, he will continue to make glad the heart of childhood.*

*Francis Pharcellus Church*

# The mound dweller / *Haugebonden*

*Haugebonden* is the name of a traditional ballad from the Telemark region of Norway, although it is sung along the coast up to Trondenes and in Agder. It has more than a hundred verses. As part of a living tradition, different areas of Norway sing slightly different variations. While it is not necessarily sung at Christmas time, a translation of the song will give you an idea of what a powerful time of year Christmas or *jól* time is. Invisible guests and the dead wandering the land where they had lived is a strong belief in Norse culture and in Europe.

In the story there is a boat. In Viking times, boats and the sea were very much a part of people's lives even in death. A boat carried the dead into the afterlife either at sea or on land. Sometimes the graves were under stones in the shape of a ship. Inland the boats were buried, anchored and covered to form burial mounds or barrows. A large wooden chamber would even be built on or under a boat for the burial place of the wealthy. These burial mounds have been found all over Norway and often have trees growing on them. In fact, the Gokstad ship was found in a barrow known in the local area for centuries as *Kongshaugen*. As the tradition of burying people in mounds with their possessions was stopped sometime after AD 1000 with the arrival of Christianity in Norway, the farm in this story must be very old. It is not known how old the song is other than it may be from the Middle Ages.

*Haugebonden*, translated as the dead farmer who lives in the mound, is thought to be the first owner of a farm, long since departed from the living world, but still keeping a watchful eye on "his" farm. Sometimes this person is called *haugkallen* or the old man of the mound. Often he makes his presence known on Christmas Eve. The farmer now living on the farm is careful not to change too many things as this might disturb *Haugebonden* and make him angry. In this particular song, the farmer's sons have changed too much. *Haugebonden* is quite angry, but realizes the farmer has been good to him for many years. To honor *Haugebonden*, each Christmas Eve beer is poured over the roots of the tree growing on the mound.

In 1984, this song was translated by Harald Knutsen for *Norsk Folkedans Stemne* held at the Sons of Norway Trollhaugen Lodge at Stampede Pass in Washington State. It is adapted here for a more readable Christmas story.

*It was Holy Christmas Eve. The farmer went out to get branches to make brooms. When the farmer came to a grove, he heard Haugebonden sing, "How nice of you! The good farmer has come to listen to Haugebonden dance and sing."*
*"Do you hear, good farmer? Why aren't you disciplining your sons? Even though it is a Holy Christmas Eve, they are dancing on the head of my grave."*
*Haugebonden was very angry and made his displeasure known by asking again, "Do you hear, good farmer? Why aren't you disciplining your sons? Even though it is a Holy Christmas Eve, they are playing on my slopes."*
*"Even though it is a Holy Christmas Eve, they are throwing drinks on me. If it weren't for you, good farmer, they would have lost their hearing and their voices."*

*"They hit me so badly with a big beer stein. If it weren't for you, good farmer, they would have to flee your house. They gave me such a bad wound with the sharp spear. If it weren't for you, good farmer, I would have to torment them until they left. Oh, they gave me such a bad cut with their silver knife. If it weren't for you, good farmer, they would have lost their lives."*

*The good farmer finally gets a chance to speak: "Oh, you have been out in my boat [barrow or mound]. For eight years I have received no rent although the boat still passes time in the ground. Oh, you have been out in my boat, and for nine years I have received no rent. Still the years go on by."*

*Haugebonden decides the good farmer is not so bad after all. "Now I have been on your land all these years. No rent have you asked for and none have you received."*

*"Now go to the stern, there you will find some good tidbits. There you will find my gold chest. The key sticks out from the lock."*

*"I should give you a silver bowl, standing on four gold legs. Fifteen men can get a good drunk from it and you can float in it. Out there stands a little gold goblet. Nine times it has been used as a payment for murder."* [Murder in those days could be paid for by offering blood money compensation to the family of a murdered victim.]

*"I should give you a shirt sewn out of white silk. My daughter Dónsi made it when she stayed home as a young girl. And out there lays the blue muffler I had sewn out of white silver. This my daughter Ingjeri sewed when she stayed home as a young girl. Out there lays a silken sock which was knit with lilies and with wreaths. It never went on Malfri's foot except on Christmas day when she danced. And out there lays a silken cloth which is woven with red-gold thread and it never went on Haugebonden's table except at Christmas when he dances and sings."*

*"I should give you a little miller's pond where fifteen mills work with vanes made of white whalebone and beams of strongest iron."*

*Haugebonden at last tells a little about his farm and family when he was alive, "Lunden is the name of my farm. Under this grassy hillside I lie. Myself, I am called good Gullstein and my wife is called Malfri."*

*Once again the visit of the farmer is acknowledged, "How nice of you! The good farmer has come to listen to Haugebonden dance and sing."*

The story continues, but it gives us the idea of how rich the burial mounds were and how important it was to keep the spirits happy. Maybe such good fortune will be found by you, but only if you are nice to the spirit of the old farm.

## Other favorite Christmas stories and events

Now is a great time for families to be together reading favorite Christmas stories or attending special holiday events in the city or nearby neighborhoods. Local newspapers usually have a special section during Thanksgiving filled with more events than anyone can attend. From old-fashioned hay rides, farm implement parades, tree lightings, visiting Vikings, and Santa with his reindeer, the season provides opportunities to experience Christmas many ways.

The annual Yulefest celebration is held at the Nordic Heritage Museum located at 3014 NW 67th, Seattle WA 98117. It is usually the weekend before Thanksgiving. The event includes folkdancing from the Nordic countries, food, crafts, and entertainers. The Christmas season for *Leikarringen* begins here. For more information call the Museum at 206-789-5707.

Holiday bazaars are found at almost every church, nursing home, Sons of Norway hall, and Daughters of Norway meeting place. They are a great way to raise funds for the organization and allow us to gradually prepare for the holiday season by purchasing baked goods and small homemade items.

Businesses have staff parties to celebrate both the holiday and the end of the year. If businesses have done well, there may even be a bonus handed to employees just before or during the party. There is much to eat and to drink with a taxi cab ride home provided by employers so workers may travel safely through the holiday evening.

The day after Thanksgiving is considered the busiest shopping day of the year. Businesses do all they can to encourage people to visit their local shopping districts and to make a special trip downtown. Seattle features The Bon Marché Holiday Parade with Santa through the downtown area. The southeast side of The Bon Marché building is the place to be at dusk for the traditional holiday lighting of the Christmas star. Almost as tall as the building itself, the radiant star is an impressive sight to behold. The Westlake area across the street from The Bon features many activities all day for shoppers and sightseers alike.

Bergen Place is a small park and gathering place in the heart of Ballard, the Nordic community of Seattle. It is the scene of lively entertainment, usually starting the first weekend after Thanksgiving. *Julenissen* even makes a stop!

Participating in a sing-along Messiah or just listening to the presentation is a favorite event, too. First United Methodist Church, 811 5th Avenue, in downtown Seattle, has an annual sing-along for all types of singers. The church, filled with a thousand voices, brings new meaning and power to the songs and words in the Messiah. It is usually held the first Friday in December. For more information call 206-622-7278.

Visiting Santa at Frederick & Nelson was always a favorite occasion for those growing up in the Seattle area. But times change and stores don't survive. Now Santa comes to Nordstrom and The Bon Marché. Breakfast with Santa may also be something your child and you would enjoy. The Olympic Four Seasons Hotel in downtown Seattle is the location for a breakfast benefitting The Children's Hospital. The Bon Marché also features a brunch benefitting the Make-A-Wish Foundation® of Washington.

Handcrafted items from Northwest artists, food, Frosty the Snowman, and entertainment by musicians, singers, dancers and magicians are featured at The Winter Festival and Crafts Fair held at the Phinney Neighborhood Center, 6532 Phinney Avenue North in Seattle. It is held the first Saturday in December and information is available by calling 206-783-2244.

*The Nutcracker Suite,* written by Tchaikovsky and performed by the Pacific Northwest Ballet through the month of December, is a favorite of both children and adults. It features a growing Christmas tree and set by Maurice Sendak.

For those more inclined to run, not walk, there is the Jingle Bell Run. It is a 5K run starting at Westlake Center in downtown Seattle. It is held the first Sunday of December.

The belief of spirits walking the earth this time of year is reinforced in Charles Dickens' famous story called *A Christmas Carol* written in 1843. It has been produced in many ways for people to enjoy the warmth and spirit of Christmas. You may prefer to curl up with the book by the fireplace on a snowy winter evening. There are also many plays, movies, or public storytellings available to learn of Scrooge, the Ghost of Christmas Past, the Ghost of Christmas Present, the Ghost of Christmas Yet to Come, and Tiny Tim.

Special Christmas stories include *The Gift of the Magi* written by O. Henry in 1906 about the love between Della and Jim who gave each other their greatest possessions. Our pioneer Christmas past is celebrated in "Mr. Edwards Meets Santa Claus" by Laura Ingalls Wilder from the book *Little House on the Prairie.*

Skiing is popular in Norway and the Pacific Northwest, especially during the holidays and throughout the winter into Easter vacation. Norwegians are said to be born with skis on their feet and Norwegian-Americans have carried on this tradition. The snow in Norway may be just outside the door, but here one needs to travel an hour or two to be in the mountains covered with snow. For over 4000 years Norwegians have been skiing. The love of this sport has been passed down through the centuries and across the ocean to those of Norwegian descent in the Pacific Northwest. Skis were known in the Midwest as early as 1840. John Tostensen of Telemark, Norway, came to the United States in 1837 when he was ten years old. Later he was called Snowshoe Thompson because during the 1850s–1860s, he used homemade skis to carry mail across the Sierra Nevada mountains between Nevada and California. He was considered to be the first skier in the West even though his nickname was Snowshoe. Competitive downhill skiing took place in California in the 1860s. The first ski club in the United States was named Nansen Ski Club and was organized in 1872 in Berlin, New Hampshire.

Leavenworth, a popular area for cross country skiing, also hosts its annual Christmas lighting ceremonies on the first and second Saturdays of December. Festivities start around 11 A.M. and include performances by school bands, choirs, and Bavarian bands in the bandstand at the centrally located town square. Santa and his reindeer visit in the afternoon. Later, as darkness begins to settle in over the Cascades, thousands of lights illuminate the trees, garlands, and store fronts of this small mountain village. Call the Leavenworth Chamber of Commerce at 509-548-5807 for more information.

The Zoo in Point Defiance Park in Tacoma celebrates the holidays with Zoolights from 5 P.M.–9 P.M. A half-a-million colorful lights in animal shapes, nursery rhymes, and local landmarks decorate the grounds and buildings. It is a fun, brisk nighttime walk or drive through the park. For more information call the Point Defiance Zoo and Aquarium at 253-591-5337.

Poulsbo warms the heart with its lighting of the yulelog and torchlight parade at dusk along the waterfront the first Saturday in December. Father Christmas, Lucia and her Viking escort arrive by boat during this annual event. Information is available by calling 360-779-4848.

Woodland Park Zoo in Seattle features Holiday Zoobilee every weekend in December. It includes a visit with Santa, storytelling, puppet shows and live entertainment. Call 206-684-4800 for more information.

Football Bowl games for those less adventurous couch potatoes may be seen during the Christmas season as college Bowl games culminate on New Year's Day.

Christmas movies, such as *It's a Wonderful Life* and *Miracle on 34th Street,* may be seen many times on television or your VCR. For some, it has become such a tradition that movie watching marathons have started. At one time you could watch one of these films each day on different channels.

Sledding takes on many forms from inner tubes, plastic disks, to wooden flyers for those young at heart who like to fly out of control down a steep snow- covered hill or closed street. Ski facilities also have special sledding and snowboarding areas to cater to those family members who don't ski.

Ice skating and speed skating are both popular in Norway and in the United States. In the Pacific Northwest, it rarely gets cold enough for the lakes to freeze so indoor skating is the only way to enjoy this sport. If one has been fortunate enough to live in the Midwestern or the Northeastern United States, there is the fun of having a backyard skating rink or visiting the lake filled with other skaters trying new turns or just enjoying the fun of skating.

Driving or taking a brisk walk through local neighborhoods, such as Olympic Manor and Candy Cane Lane in Seattle, to see a variety of decorated homes with thousands of lights in all colors is spectacular. Many neighborhoods take it upon themselves to create a theme for their outdoor decorations. The impact created makes it a must-see area. One neighbor in Ballard has decided to cover his entire roof and much of the exterior of the house and yard with brightly colored flashing and chasing lights. The effect is overwhelming. One always wonders how long it took to put up, how long it takes to take down, and what must their electric bill be in January? Hopefully they will continue their effort as the lights seem to make us happy.

The Norwegian Ladies Chorus of Seattle gives a concert of favorite Christmas songs in Norwegian and English on the first Sunday of December. Traditional cookies, coffee, and additional entertainment round out the program.

In Seattle *Voices of Christmas* is a multicultural celebration of the many ways the winter holidays are commemorated throughout the world. Performances by the Seattle Group Theatre are held through December.

Many *juletrefester* are held for the children of Norwegian-Americans in the Pacific Northwest in churches, lodges, and private homes. The Christmas songs sung in Norway so long ago are remembered, along with favorite American songs.

School pageants are now winter festivals or singalongs with many of the favorite secular songs of the season. Check with your local school on the dates. Church Sunday School programs are prevalent, too. The Christmas story is told as only children can tell it. Mary and Joseph, Jesus, the Wise Men, angels and even the sheep and donkeys somehow take on a new life of their own. One just never knows what will happen!

The Scandinavian Hour on KBLE Radio 1050 AM is hosted, as of this writing, by Ron Olsen and Doug Warne. Some Saturdays and Sundays before Christmas and on Christmas day, Scandinavian Christmas music is played. Check with the radio station for times and dates of these special programs.

## Walking around the Christmas tree / *Går rundt juletreet*

A long lasting tradition in Norway is the ritual of walking around the tree at Christmas time. On Christmas Eve, families and friends can be found holding hands and walking around the tree singing carols. If the tree is large or there are few family members, teddy bears, dolls and other stuffed toys with arms may be added to fill out the circle to reach around the tree. While the origin of this tradition is unknown, some believe it originated with the Swedish practice of dancing around trees or Maypoles.

Traditionally, the first circle goes to the right, the second circle goes to the left, the third circle goes to the right and so on. At the end of each verse or song, the circles change direction. This activity is done not only on Christmas Eve, but throughout the holiday season especially at *juletrefester*, known as Christmas tree parties, held before Christmas in the Pacific Northwest and after Christmas in both Norway and this area.

Sigfrid Ohrt left Norway at the age of ten in 1901 and settled in the Pacific Northwest in 1919. Here she tells about her Christmas celebration in Eidsness, a rural community near Bergen, Norway.

*Our mother seldom left her home; she was so busy there. But she did go to the Christmas program at the schoolhouse with us. We danced around the Christmas tree and sang Christmas carols. They had one ring of adults. And the next [ring] would be coming the opposite direction with teenage children and at the outside were the little ones. We'd go in different directions. That was the highlight of our celebration. It was a free and easy evening. That was where I drank my first cup of cocoa; we really thought that was something special.* [1]

[1]Used by permission from: Rasmussen, Janet E. *New land, new lives : Scandinavian immigrants to the Pacific Northwest.* Seattle, WA: Norwegian-American Historical Association and University of Washington Press, 1993. Pages 44–45.

# Young one, young one / *Jomfru, jomfru*

Tune: Norwegian folk melody from Østby
Norwegian lyrics: Norwegian folk from Østby
English lyrics: Christine M. Anderson and Theresa Appelö Bakken (1997)

**Briskly / Raskt**

*mp*

Young one, young one, young one, you are so dear. Here is the car-ou-sel
*Jom - fru, jom - fru, jom - fru, jom - fru kjæ - re. Her er ka - ru - sel - len*

that runs in the eve - nin', ten for the grown ones and five for the small, hur - ry
*som skal gå til kvel - den, ti for de sto - re og fem for de små, skyn - da*

so, hur - ry so, now the car - ou - sel can go.
*på, skyn - da på nå skal ka - ru - sel - len gå.*

Ha, ha, ha, yes it goes so well for An - der - sen and Pet - ter - sen and Lund- strøm, oh, swell!
*Ha, ha, ha, det går jo så bra for An - der - sen og Pet - ter - sen og Lund- strøm å ja!*

Join hands and form a circle around the Christmas tree. Starting with the left foot, take 16 walking steps to the left. On the last steps, when singing *skynda på, skynda på nå skal karusellen gå*, increase the tempo of the singing and dancing through the rest of the dance. At *ha, ha, ha* face into the circle and take 8 side steps starting with the left foot while continuing to move to the left. Repeat the refrain starting at *ha, ha, ha*, but this time the circle moves to the right using 8 side steps. Be careful to keep the handhold so everyone stays in the circle and no one falls down.

# I traveled over sea and land / *Jeg gikk meg over sjø og land*

Tune: Norwegian folk melody, harmonized by Rosemary Antel (1997)
Norwegian lyrics: Norwegian folk
English lyrics: Christine M. Anderson (1997)

2    I traveled over sea and land
And then I met an old, old man.
He asked of me, he said to me,
"Where, O where can your home be?"
Oh, I have a home in Pointing Land,
In Pointing Land, in Pointing Land,
And all of you who point, point can,
You all have a home in Pointing Land.

3    I traveled over sea and land
And then I met an old, old man.
He asked of me, he said to me,
"Where, O where can your home be?"
I have a home in Limping Land,
In Limping Land, in Limping Land,
And all of you who limp, limp can,
You all have a home in Limping Land.

4    I traveled over sea and land
And then I met an old, old man.
He asked of me, he said to me,
"Where, O where can your home be?"
I have a home in Hopping Land,
In Hopping Land, in Hopping Land,
And all of you who hop, hop can,
You all have a home in Hopping Land.

5    I traveled over sea and land
And then I met an old, old man.
He asked of me, he said to me,
"Where, O where can your home be?"
I have a home in Clapping Land,
in Clapping Land, in Clapping Land,
And all of you who clap, clap can,
You all have a home in Clapping Land.

*2    Jeg gikk meg over sjø og land,
Da møtte jeg en gammel mann.
Han spurte så, han sagde så:
"Hvor hører du vel hjemme?"
Jeg hører hjemme i pekeland,
I pekeland, i pekeland,
Og alle de som peke kan,
De hører hjemme i pekeland.*

*3    Jeg gikk meg over sjø og land,
Da møtte jeg en gammel mann.
Han spurte så, han sagde så:
"Hvor hører du vel hjemme?"
Jeg hører hjemme i hinkeland,
I hinkeland, i hinkeland,
Og alle de som hinke kan,
De hører hjemme i hinkeland,*

*4    Jeg gikk meg over sjø og land,
Da møtte jeg en gammel mann.
Han spurte så, han sagde så:
"Hvor hører du vel hjemme?"
Jeg hører hjemme i hoppeland,
I hoppeland, i hoppeland,
Og alle de som hoppe kan,
De hører hjemme i hoppeland.*

*5    Jeg gikk meg over sjø og land,
Da møtte jeg en gammel mann.
Han spurte så, han sagde så:
"Hvor hører du vel hjemme?"
Jeg hører hjemme i klappeland,
I klappeland, i klappeland,
Og alle de som klappe kan,
De hører hjemme i klappeland.*

Join hands and form a circle around the Christmas tree. Starting with the left foot, take 16 walking steps to the left. On the last step, take a ½ turn to the right on your right foot. Now the circle will move to the right or counterclockwise direction, but instead of walking you will perform each different action sung in the verse. In the first verse, everyone will stamp as they are in Stamping Land when moving to the right.

In the last part of the second verse, everyone will point in Pointing Land.
In the last part of the third verse, everyone will limp in Limping Land.
In the last part of the fourth verse, everyone will hop in Hopping Land.
In the last part of the last verse, everyone will clap in Clapping Land.

Additional verses may be added if you wish to make up some.

# Here we go around the mulberry bush

## Så gå vi rundt om en enebærbusk / Vaskekjerringen

Tune: Norwegian(?) folk melody, harmonized by Darrel Eide (1997)
English lyrics: English based on Original Mother Goose rhyme (18th century)
Norwegian text: based on Original Mother Goose rhyme (18th century)

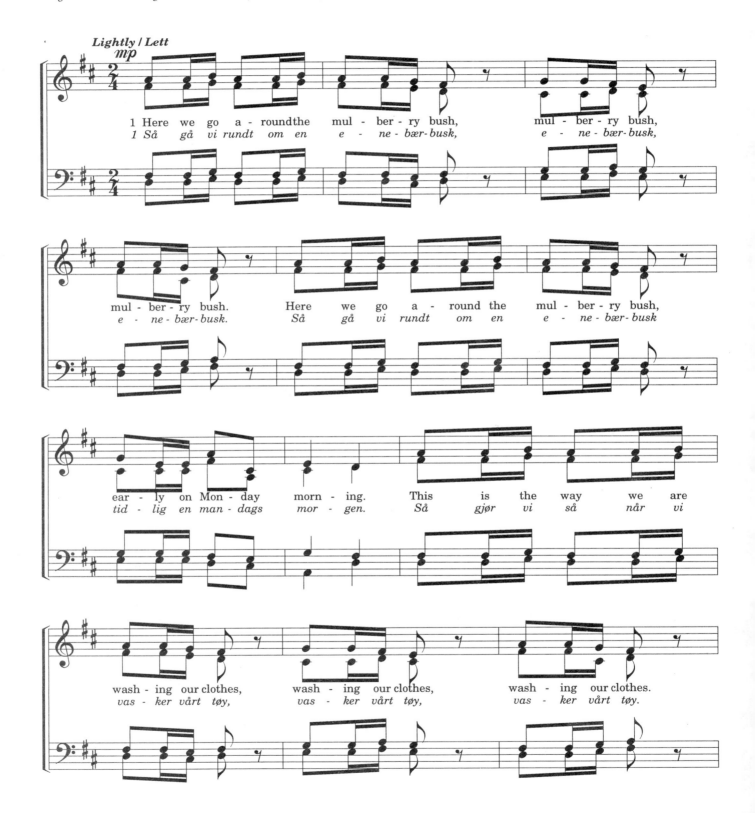

This is the way we are wash-ing our clothes ear-ly on Mon-day morn-ing.
*Så gjør vi så når vi vas-ker vårt tøy, tid-lig en man-dags mor-gen.*

2 Here we go around the mulberry bush,
mulberry bush, mulberry bush.
Here we go around the mulberry bush
early on Tuesday morning.
This is the way we are rinsing our clothes,
rinsing our clothes, rinsing our clothes.
This is the way we are rinsing our clothes
early on Tuesday morning.

3 Here we go around the mulberry bush,
mulberry bush, mulberry bush.
Here we go around the mulberry bush
early on Wednesday morning.
This is the way that we hang up our clothes,
hang up our clothes, hang up our clothes.
This is the way that we hang up our clothes
early on Wednesday morning.

4 Here we go around the mulberry bush,
mulberry bush, mulberry bush.
Here we go around the mulberry bush
early on Thursday morning.
This is the way that we roll up our clothes,
roll up our clothes, roll up our clothes.
This is the way that we roll up our clothes
early on Thursday morning.

2 *Så går vi rundt om en enebærbusk,*
*enebærbusk, enebærbusk.*
*Så går vi rundt om en enebærbusk*
*tidlig en tirsdags morgen.*
*Så gjør vi så når vi skyller vårt tøy,*
*skyller vårt tøy, skyller vårt tøy,*
*Så gjør vi så når vi skyller vårt tøy*
*tidlig en tirsdags morgen*

3 *Så går vi rundt om en enebærbusk,*
*enebærbusk, enebærbusk.*
*Så går vi rundt om en enebærbusk*
*tidlig en onsdags morgen.*
*Så gjør vi så når vi henger opp tøy,*
*henger opp tøy, henger opp tøy.*
*Så gjør vi så når vi henger opp tøy*
*tidlig en onsdags morgen.*

4 *Så går vi rundt om en enebærbusk,*
*enebærbusk, enebærbusk.*
*Så går vi rundt om en enebærbusk*
*tidlig en torsdags morgen.*
*Så gjør vi så når vi ruller vårt tøy,*
*ruller vårt tøy, ruller vårt tøy.*
*Så gjør vi så når vi ruller vårt tøy*
*tidlig en torsdags morgen.*

5 Here we go around the mulberry bush,
mulberry bush, mulberry bush.
Here we go around the mulberry bush
early on Friday morning.
This is the way we are ironing our clothes,
ironing our clothes, ironing our clothes.
This is the way we our ironing our clothes
early on Friday morning.

6 Here we go around the mulberry bush,
mulberry bush, mulberry bush.
Here we go around the mulberry bush
early on Saturday morning.
This is the way we are washing our floors,
washing our floors, washing our floors.
This is the way we are washing our floors
early on Saturday morning.

7 Here we go around the mulberry bush,
mulberry bush, mulberry bush.
Here we go around the mulberry bush
early on Sunday morning.
This is the way we are walking to church,
walking to church, walking to church.
This is the way we are walking to church
early on Sunday morning.

8 This is the way we are walking back home,
walking back home, walking back home.
This is the way we are walking back home
early on Sunday afternoon.

5 *Så går vi rundt om en enebærbusk,*
*enebærbusk, enebærbusk.*
*Så går vi rundt om en enebærbusk*
*tidlig en fredags morgen.*
*Så gjør vi så når vi stryker vårt tøy,*
*stryker vårt tøy, stryker vårt tøy.*
*Så gjør vi så når vi stryker vårt tøy*
*tidlig en fredags morgen.*

6 *Så går vi rundt om en enebærbusk,*
*enebærbusk, enebærbusk.*
*Så går vi rundt om en enebærbusk,*
*tidlig en lørdags morgen.*
*Så gjør vi så når vi vasker vårt gulv,*
*vasker vårt gulv, vasker vårt gulv.*
*Så gjør vi så når vi vasker vårt gulv*
*tidlig en lørdags morgen.*

7 *Så går vi rundt om en enebærbusk,*
*enebærbusk, enebærbusk.*
*Så går vi rundt om en enebærbusk*
*tidlig en søndags morgen.*
*Så gjør vi så når til kirke vi går,*
*kirke vi gå, kirke vi går.*
*Så gjør vi så når til kirke vi går*
*tidlig* **en** *søndags morgen.*

8 *Så gjør vi så når vi hjematt går,*
*hjematt går, hjematt går.*
*Så gjør vi så når vi hjematt går*
*tidlig en søndags middag.*

This song is a Mother Goose rhyme. It is an action song about the many household duties needing to be done during the week. It is a fun way to learn the days of the week in Norwegian.

Join hands and form a circle around the Christmas tree. Starting on the left foot, take 16 walking steps to the left. When the refrain starts describing the action of the day at *Så gjør vi så når vi vasker vårt tøy...,* drop hands with each other. Using your own two hands, pretend you are using a washboard by holding your fists so it looks as if you are scrubbing your clothes up and down on an old-fashioned washboard.

For each day, repeat the first part of the dance, taking 16 steps in the opposite direction as the previous verse. This next verse would start on the left foot, but move to the right or counterclockwise direction.

In the second verse, the clothes are being rinsed. With both hands, pretend you are rinsing the clothes by moving your hands in a circular motion at about thigh level. This verse will start on the left foot and move to the right.

In the third verse, the clothes are being hung to dry. Using both your hands, take your pretend clothes and hang them up on the clothesline. So the movement goes up and down, with the up being well above your head.

In the fourth verse, the clothes are rolled and dampened to prepare them for ironing. This time with both hands, pretend you are taking the clothes and wringing them into a tight roll.

In the fifth verse, the clothes are ironed. With your right hand make small back and forth actions pretending you are ironing on an ironing board. Your left hand is held at about waist height pretending to hold down the clothes you are ironing.

In the sixth verse, it is time to wash the floor. Standing on your feet, bend over. With your two hands, pretend you are washing the floor by making small circular motions with both hands just above the floor.

In the seventh verse, it is time to take a partner to church. So drop hands with one of the people you are walking with, link elbows with your partner and walk the entire dance to the left as couples.

In the last verse, drop linked arms, turn and walk in the opposite direction with your partner. Link the elbows that were not linked before and return home on Sunday afternoon.

# O Christmas with joy / *Å jul med din glede*

Tune: Norwegian folk melody (18th or 19th century)
Norwegian lyrics: Gustava Blom Kielland (1800-1889)(late 19th century)
English lyrics: Liv Nordem Lyons (1984)

glad are we. We swing 'round in a cir - cle and curt - sey and bow.
*glad er vi. Vi svin - ger oss i kret - sen og nei - er og buk - ker.*

2   You wise men from the East,
    Who followed a star,
    We know of the child you are seeking,
    We pray we may join you in your holy quest,
    And follow the star brightly beaming.
    We are clapping our hands,
    We're singing and we laugh,
    So glad are we, so glad are we,
    We swing 'round in a circle
    and curtsey and bow.

3   I reach out my hand
    In a gesture of joy.
    Now hurry, and give me your other.
    Then we will create an unbreakable bond
    And promise to care for each other.
    We are clapping our hands,
    We're singing and we laugh,
    So glad are we, so glad are we,
    We swing 'round in a circle
    and curtsey and bow.

2   *I Østerlands vise,*
    *I tre stjernemenn,*
    *Vi vet jo hvorhen I skal drage,*
    *For vi ville også så gjerne derhen,*
    *Og eder på reisen ledsage.*
    *Vi klapper i hendene,*
    *Vi synger og vi ler,*
    *Så glad er vi, så glad er vi,*
    *Vi svinger oss i kretsen*
    *og neier og bukker.*

3   *Så rekker jeg deg*
    *Nå med glede min hånd,*
    *Kom, skynd deg og gi meg den andre.*
    *Så knytter vi kjærlighets hellige bånd,*
    *Og lover å elske hverandre.*
    *Vi klapper i hendene,*
    *Vi synger og vi ler,*
    *Så glad er vi, så glad er vi,*
    *Vi svinger oss i kretsen*
    *og neier og bukker.*

Join hands and form a circle around the Christmas tree. Starting on the left foot, take 8 walking steps to the left. On the last step, take a ½ turn to the right on your right foot. Starting with your left foot, go in the opposite direction, now to the right or counterclockwise direction. When the refrain of *Vi klapper i hendene* starts, all face toward the Christmas tree. Drop hands in the circle and clap your own hands 16 times with each beat of music. At *Vi svinger oss i krestsen og*, turn in place on your right foot to the right or clockwise direction using 4 steps. At *neier og*, everyone places their right foot behind their left foot and does a small curtsey, using 4 counts, then everyone will fold their arms across their chest and take a bow, using 4 counts at *bukker*. As a variation, only the girls will curtsey at *neier* and only the boys will bow at *bukker*.

Repeat movements in each verse until the last verse. At the beginning of the last verse, move toward the tree a little bit. A friendship chain is made by crossing your arms. Usually your right arm goes over your left arm. Give your right hand to the person on your left. They will give you their left hand. Give your left hand to the person on your right. They will give you their right hand. Stand in place. Move arms back and forth in time to the music in a somewhat sawing motion. Repeat the last half of the dance as usual.

# The thief, the thief / *Tyven, tyven*

Tune: Norwegian folk melody
Norwegian lyrics: Norwegian folk
English lyrics: Christine M. Anderson (1997)

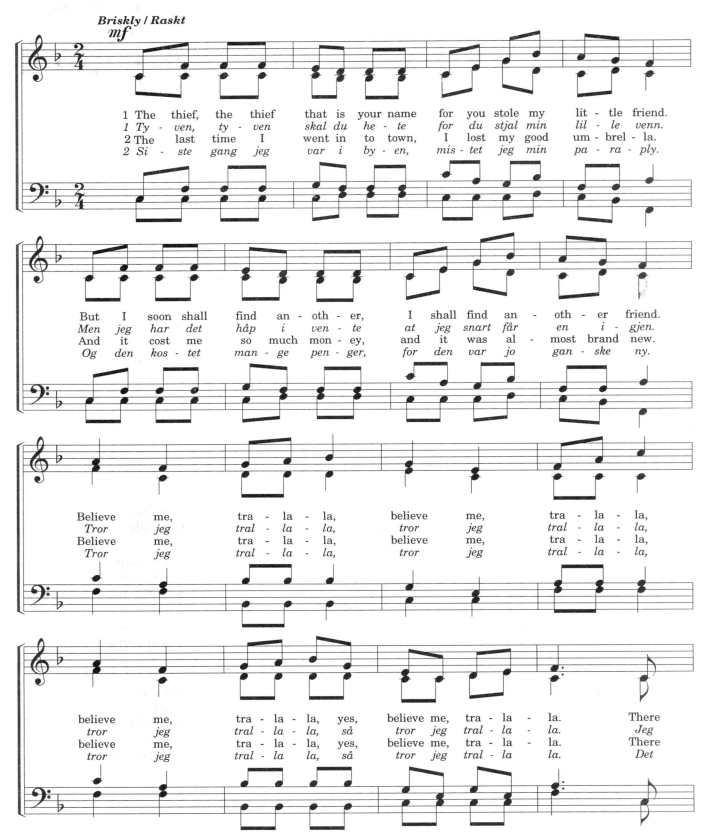

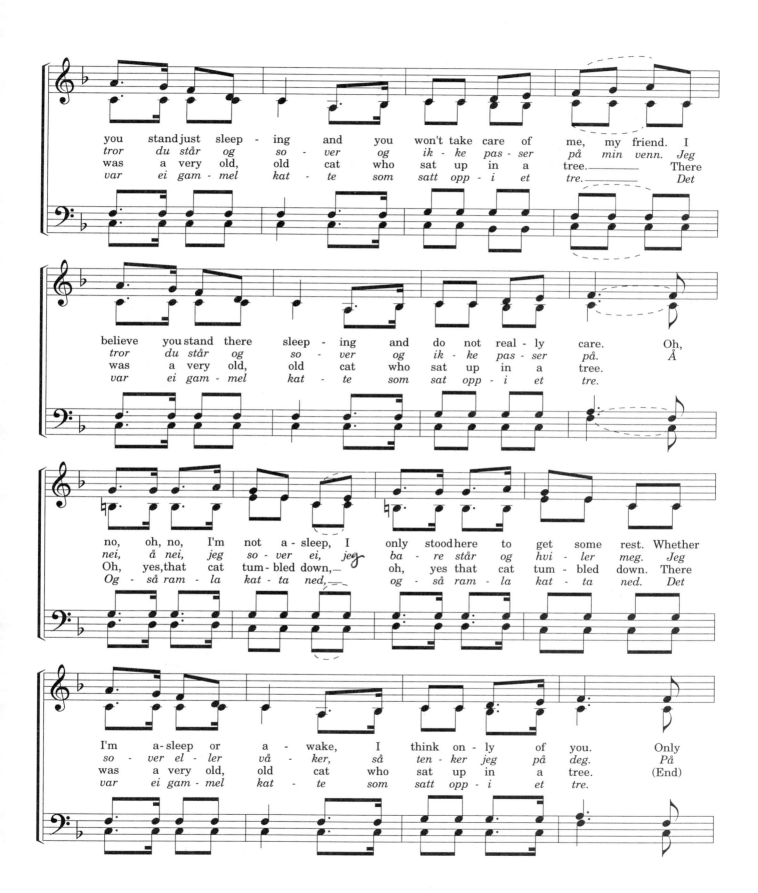

you, only you, my lit - tle friend, only you, only you, my lit - tle friend. Whether
deg, på deg, min lil - le venn, på deg, på deg, min lil - le venn. Jeg

I'm a - sleep or a - wake, I think on - ly of you.
so - ver el - ler vå - ker, så ten - ker jeg på deg.

This song is often sung at Christmas around the tree, but the dance may also be done away from the tree.

Form a circle of couples facing into the circle with the girl on the boy's right side. Girl places left hand on boy's right shoulder. Boy places his right arm around girl's waist. One or more people are in the center of the circle playing the thief.

The thief takes some skipping steps alone for a little bit in the center of the circle, or outside the circle if dancing around the tree. Then the thief lightly taps a person of the same sex in the circle and takes this person as a partner. The new couple skips together once around the circle then goes back to the place they left.

The person who just lost his or her partner is now the new thief. The new thief takes another partner the same way as the first thief did by skipping around the circle until s/he finds a new partner. It is best if the thief finds a new partner quickly. Continue to do this through all the verses.

# Christmas Day / *Juledag*

In Norway, on December 25 everyone was to remain at home to enjoy each other's company and some quiet time. According to oral tradition, if the day was clear it would be a good year. There was to be no compulsory work until the new year. The symbol on the calendar stick is a baby in a manger.

In the Pacific Northwest, Christmas Day may be just as event filled as Christmas Eve in Norway. Bright and early in the morning, children run to the Christmas tree to see what Santa has left them. For some, church services follow at 10 A.M. and then a brunch. Others may have a restful time with family and a warm fire burning in the fireplace, followed by a dinner with more family and friends. Jigsaw puzzles, walks, special television programs, movies on video, visiting, and quiet reflection fill the day.

Theodore Wannebo was born in Biwabik, Minnesota, on March 26, 1927. He now lives in Bremerton where he is active in Oslo Lodge No. 35, Sons of Norway. His daughter, Noel, interviewed him about the Christmas traditions he celebrated. Ted's grandparents came from Namsos, Norway.

*We lived in town down by the depot because Pa was a railroader. Then Pa bought some land from his father about six miles out of town. There was a nine-room house with two porches on a farm on the Iron Ore Range. Our winters were pretty rough up there, a lot of snow. There were about 18 people in the house in the 1930s, all family. When I was very young, we would have the big holiday dinner on Christmas Day. There was always plenty of food.*

*In the range area, it was common to have homemade wines and beer, which I remember helping my dad make. My mother would cook at least for a week before Christmas, going through 100-pound bags of flour and sugar in preparation for the holidays.*

*I can remember they kept a tree and everything. Christmas was fun and exciting for us kids. We used to have midnight mass on Christmas Eve and come home to a big turkey dinner at 1 A.M. or so. The Christmas tree was decorated after that by the grownups who partied a little and decorated it. The kids wouldn't see the tree until Christmas morning. The tree decorations were candles clipped on and carefully lit for a short time, glass balls, mostly strung cranberries and popcorn and popcorn balls which all of us then got to eat later.*

*We kids never saw a gift until then either. The one or two gifts we each got was special and not obscured with a lot of paper wrapping. As we kids got older we would stay up and open the gifts at night on Christmas Eve. It was all a mystery to the little ones until we figured Santa out.*

*In 1937, we moved to Two Harbors, which is strongly Scandinavian. Then we celebrated our Christmas Eve with dinner and presents and could sleep in the next morning. The tree stayed up from Christmas until New Year's. Christmas Eve was for family. After Christmas, came the visiting with friends with a lot of fancy cooking prepared in advance. New Year's was the party time for the grownups.*

*During World War II, Christmas was celebrated with family even though some of the family was away. Sugar and meat were harder to get, but the traditions were kept for the most part. Pork pies were a family tradition reserved for Christmas and my mother would make a large number and put them in the icebox with a lock so they would still be around at holiday time.*

Born in the early 1950s in Corvallis, Oregon, Christine Anderson grew up in a number of towns in western Washington with a Norwegian-American mother and a Swedish-Danish-American father. Her Norwegian roots are in the southeastern portions of Norway. Christmas time is shared with a large extended family.

*When I was growing up in Tacoma everyone gathered at my aunt's and my mother's brother's house for Christmas Eve. We have done this for the last 30 years or so. My grandparents, other uncles and their families would get together and there would be up to 40 people for Christmas Eve. Everything would be set out picnic style on tables in the living room with an adults' table and a kids' table. The packages would be mounded around the Christmas tree. You can imagine packages for 40 people. Those packages went out to the middle of the room.*

*I always made a kransekake, my dad made the krumkaker and goro with my mother and they brought that with my mother's extremely popular gravlaks, and other people brought things, too. We had turkey and ham, mashed potatoes and gravy and whatever kind of cooking my uncle happened to be into that year. One year it was Cajun and that was a little hot for me.*

*My aunt read the Christmas story. When I was little, all the cousins would get up and give a musical or dramatic show for the grownups, and now that the cousins have children, the tradition continues. Then everyone opened the presents. Everyone received a little something. It might be homemade jelly or a small Christmas ornament. My cousins drew names so their gifts were a little more substantial.*

*After all the singing, visiting, and eating, my family attended Christmas Eve services at Emmanuel Lutheran. Everyone used to be given candles when they arrived at church. Near the end of the service, the lights would be turned off. We would start singing Silent Night. As we started the quiet, but moving melody, the young people in the church would form a cross down the center aisle; the pastor would light his candle from the altar candle. His was the first candle at the head of the cross. He would turn and pass the flame onto the candle of the person in front of him. The church would get brighter and brighter as the light was passed down the cross. Then the young adults forming the cross would light the candles of the closest people in the pews next to them. Each person would light the candle of the person next to them. It was so beautiful! Everyone's faces were glowing from the small flame of the candles. After doing this for years, the fire department or the insurance company said we could not do it anymore. Too much of a fire hazard, they said. Now there is just a cross down the center aisle with the young adults holding the flickering candles. It is still beautiful, but I miss the warm glow of hundreds of candles.*

*We always had Sunday School Christmas programs when I was small. I remember practicing for one program. Our leader had us sing "Glory in 'Eggshells' Deo" instead of Excelsis because that was the best way to sing the word. I thought it was pretty funny. I still sing it that way, though!*

*When my family moved to Indiana in 1962, things were quite different. It was just our little family of five. We went to church and had a tree, did all the baking, of course, and kept our traditions. I liked Christmas and winter time in Indiana because there was so much snow. We three kids could ice skate in the back yard and build tunnels and igloos in the high drifts.*

*It has been a long time since I was very young, but Santa still comes to our house Christmas Eve to leave my family small packages. There are no young children at home, but the surprises of Santa still arrive. Santa now has many helpers bearing gifts. Our Santa may not even know what he is bringing, but in the morning he is as surprised as everyone else.*

*Even though we kids are all grown, I faithfully put out my stocking. We always have an orange, tangerine, or Mandarin orange in our stocking to eat while we open our presents. Along with this, usually comes our new toothbrush and perhaps a small tube of toothpaste. In the past, after we learned to drive, our stockings were filled with window and lock defroster. Eventually Santa had given us so much defroster our shelves were full. Finally Santa got the message we couldn't use all the defroster during our mild winters, so for several years we haven't received any. I often wonder, "What is the shelf life of defroster?"*

*Christmas Day morning is spent quietly at home with my immediate family. Later on in the day my aunts, uncles and cousins come over and we open even more presents from them if they haven't been with us the night before. Sometimes friends drop by, too, for a casual Christmas buffet with a standing rib roast, an assortment of vegetables, potatoes, an abundant supply of potato lefse, and leftovers from the night before with new additions, including more holiday cookies and such. Perhaps a little bit of the koldtbord has come down though the generations.*

*The fabulous popcorn balls my dad's mother made were memorable, and nowadays we put the popcorn balls in the microwave to make them soft and gooey in grandma's style and we eat those throughout the day. My mom and dad work together before Christmas to make potato lefse and holiday cookies. They don't make sandbakkelser, rosettes and fattigmann so much anymore. So we only have those on Christmas Day if someone else makes them.*

*I have collected ornaments for my tree from friends and family, and I love to have lots of lights on the tree. I also have a Scandinavian scene with a tomte and other Swedish and Norwegian figures. Some of my friends believe I collect horned animals, especially different types of reindeer and sheep, so they are all out at Christmas. My aunt from North Dakota worked in a florist shop, and she always sent us ornaments at Christmas, like bells one year and a group of angels which I still have to this day. Lately I've been collecting angels, made out of porcelain shells, and crystal ornaments. My brother gave me a tiny little Santa which I always put near the top of the tree. I am very fond of hearts also. I usually have a friend over to help decorate the tree and have a little dinner and a glass of wine. It is so much fun every year to open the Christmas ornament boxes. I think about and remember the friends or family associated with each ornament.*

*The Christmas that stands out most in my mind was when I was in the fourth grade and found out about Santa Claus. That year my mother had given me a doll she had when she was the same age. It is a really large doll, about three feet high. Mom had it refurbished as it was made of some type of clay. It needed a new leg and it also needed new hair. She made two new dresses for it. She even gave me some of the clothes her mother had made for the doll.*

*Another vivid Christmas memory I have from that same year was I loved to play the game SORRY, but my grades weren't very good in math. My grandfather said for every game of SORRY we played, I needed to recite my multiplication tables. The sevens, eights and nines were always the worst for me so we practiced them the most. By the end of that Christmas I knew my tables! My grandfather never grew tired of playing SORRY with me, but he always made sure I did my tables for another game. In my mind, I can still see us playing in the corner of the living room by the window in the house on Winnifred Street.*

*I like Christmas because I get to visit with relatives I don't see except at these family holiday gatherings. I associate Christmas with lots of family and lots of fun. It's really important to me that the family stays connected through these holiday gatherings, and I hope the next generation will continue the traditions.*

# The day after Christmas / *Annen juledag*

On December 26 our family is around the dinner table visiting with friends. The excitement of Christmas Eve and Christmas Day has passed and we relax. Employees of the largest company in the Northwest, Boeing, are on vacation from December 24 through January 1. Other adults take time off to share it with their families and friends at home. Children are on school vacation. Colleges and universities are closed, and students travel to a home they haven't seen in months.

There is a belief in Norway everyone who visits during these holidays must have some food to eat. Otherwise, the Christmas spirit leaves the house. If guests refuse to eat or do not take some food with them, the spell of Christmas will be broken and the Christmas spirit will be carried away with the guest who refuses.

In Norway the day after Christmas was known as *Staffansdagen,* or Saint Stephen's Day in memory of the martyr, Stephen. As a young boy, Saint Stephen worked as a stable boy and was considered the protector of horses. But the horse was also sacred to the god Frey. People raced their horses from farm to farm and also around their own houses. It was believed water held special powers on *Staffansdagen* so horses were raced to wells, springs with running water in the middle of winter, brooks, or rivers. The first horse to drink the water would be the strongest in the next year. The races were called *Stefanskeid* or *Staffankut* and dates back to the thirteenth century. It was a day to taste the Christmas brew at each farm visited, too. For a special treat and when romance is in the air, mountain resorts in the Cascade mountains offer sleigh rides with horses so some of the Saint Stephen tradition lives in the Northwest.

The joyous celebrations of *juletrefester* usually follow Christmas Day in Norway and in the Pacific Northwest. People continue celebrating the holidays with more food, singing, walking around the Christmas tree singing songs, and playing singing games around the tree.

Bergljot DeRosa, known as Bella, settled in Tacoma in 1922 at the age of 20. Here she describes what Christmas was like in Trondheim, Norway, where she was born.

*Christmas Eve, we had just for ourself. We had spareribs. In different parts of the country, they used different kind of food. In cities, seems like it was altogether different than out in the country. When you live in town, you have to buy it in the stores.*

*My mother had the most children, and my father's relatives always chose to come to us for Christmas Day. How they took interest in us children! We got handmade gifts, little fur collars and little mittens, and stuff like that. And we sang around the Christmas tree, and they all took part in it. That's when we had our big dinner. We had reindeer roast. Mother ran strips of pork, they call it spekk, into the meat, because there's no fat in there, see. There they don't roast meat in the oven, because it shrinks too much, and they don't fry meat. They roast it in a big pot. You brown it and then you cook it in milk or cream; and that gravy was, I believe, the best thing. Then we had tyttebær [ lingonberries ] and multekrem [ cloudberry cream ].*

*Then, of course, there was Christmas parties afterwards. I counted ten we went to one year. I remember I went to Glassmaker Petersen where they had a ballroom and we even had [dance] cards that we carried. At Christmas, we got to put fine little patent leather shoes on, and we felt like we didn't touch the ground. We felt so light, because we always had to have heavy shoes on. Oh, it was so good to dress up for Christmas!*[1]

Illustration by B. Bergstrøm, 1869.

[1]Used by permission from: Rasmussen, Janet E.. *New land, new lives : Scandinavian immigrants to the Pacific Northwest*. Seattle, WA: Norwegian-American Historical Association and University of Washington Press, 1993. Pages 63–64.

# The Christmas goat and the days after Christmas
## *Julebukken og romjulen*

When young people in Norway say they are going on a *julebukk*, Norwegians know *romjulen*, or the days of December 27–31, have arrived. Perhaps the word *rom jul* comes from the ancient Roman celebrations and feasts during the winter solstice, which these days slightly resemble. The Roman festival *Saturnalia* lasted seven days and was known for its freedom from all restraints, and for parties, riots, and other debauchery. During these holidays all public business was suspended so courts and schools were closed just as they usually are today.

It was believed a spirit in the form of a goat haunted the fields in Norway during summer. During the winter the goat disappeared into the cold mountains. As the *jul* season approached, he would reappear as someone clothed in a goat's skin and carrying a goat's skull or mask, looking like a goat. The goat was joined by other participants dressed in masks resembling horses, bears, or even people. Disguises were made of wood, fur, leather, or cloth. While visiting the farms, they would be allowed to sample the food and beer of the season. If the goat was not allowed to partake of the holiday fare, undesirable things might happen. Others think the goat represents the devil or even the goats who drew the chariot of the Norse god of Thunder called Thor, son of Odin and Jord.

The goat's procession from the mountains to the farm now has become a part of the Christmas fun of *romjulen* in farming communities and city neighborhoods. The mischief caused by *julereia* is now caused by the *julebukker*. These days children are dressed in costumes similar to American Halloween type costumes or old clothes. Usually, one person in the group continues to dress like a goat or *julebukk*. Sometimes a musician playing an accordion or harmonica may accompany the group. Participants sing, dance, and tell jokes while traveling from house to house asking for goodies or small gifts. A loud racket and banging tools let the hosts know guests have arrived. It is still considered bad luck to send the visitors away empty-handed, for then they are " carrying Christmas out with them. " Adults often join in·this ancient holiday tradition as they continue visiting and sharing the joy and light of the season by getting together with friends, family, and especially Grandmother during the long nights.

In the United States *romjul* is preserved mainly in the farming communities of Minnesota, Wisconsin, the Dakotas, and Iowa. Now called *julebukking* or some say *julebugging,* the participants leave etiquette behind. They alter voices, limp, stamp, and dress in costumes. Heads, hands, and bodies are covered, being sure to wear someone else's shoes and coats to prevent recognition. As in Norway, the *julebukker* come to share in the Christmas goodies. The participants move from one house to the next with the hosts of the previous house joining in the fun of pounding on windows, stomping through the house with snow-covered shoes, and enjoying a warm visit with friends as the *old goats* underneath the disguises are slowly identified.

# After Christmas dream / *Romjulsdrøm*

Tune: Thoralf Borg (1895-1969)(1964), harmonized by Darrel Eide (1997)
Norwegian lyrics: Alf Prøysen (1914-1970)(1964)
English lyrics: Christine M. Anderson and Jan Alfred Andersson (1997)

**Brightly / *Lystig***
*mf*

1 It would be best to be four dur-ing rom-jul'n, and
*1 En skul-le vø-ri fi-re år i rom-jul'n og*

know a young girl who is near-ly five. So both could dress up with very beau-ti-
*kjint ei jin-te som var nes-ten fem. Og beg-ge skul-le kledd seg ut med*

ful masks,——— and go for jul-bukk to their grand-ma's home. And
*mas-ker,——— og køm-mi jul-bokk tel et bæss-mor-hem. Og*

the clocks would all be set to a-round noon, and all the roads would be so easy to
*klok-ka skul-le va-ra midt på da-gen, og væ-gen skul-le va-ra lett å*

234

walk. And all of the big dogs would be kept in - side and all of
*gå. Og æil - le bik - kjer skul - le va - ra in - ne, og æil - le*

the cars would be stand - ing still.
*bi - ler skul - le bæ - re stå.*

2    And if we should meet other children on the way,
who laugh and say they want to go with us,
then we should have a brother in the fifth grade
who clears the way so we can walk in peace.
And our grandma's house should also be sleeping
Behind the curtains she should not see us
before we can tip-tip-toe in through the door
and put on party masks before we knock.

3    So we can tramp, tramp in with very heavy heels
and speak in such high voices: Good evenin'
and deep from the chair will our grandma answer:
"Now comes julbukk once more to old, old me!"
It would be best to be four during romjul'n
when the Christmas lights would burn all day long
And our world was just a warm home with four walls
and heaven was our own grandmother's lap.

2    *Og hvis en møtte onger etter væga
som lo og sa dom ville vara med,
da sku en hatt en bror i femte klassen
som rødde væg så folk fekk gå i fred.
Og bæssmorhuset skulle mæssom såvå,
og bak gardina skulle ingen sjå,
før dom fekk stiltre seg på tå i gangen
og feste maske før dom knakke på.*

3    *Så sku dom klampe inn på tunge hæler
og kvinke julbokkmål"Godkvell, godkvell."
Og djupt i stolen sku a bæssmor svara:
"Så kom det julbokk åt en stakkar lell!"
En skulle vøri fire år i romjul'n
da julelysa brente dagen lang,
og væla var et hus med fire vegger,
og saligheta var et bæssmorfang.*

# New Year's Eve / *Nyttårsaften*

The intoxicating last night of the year on December 31 is for fireworks, merrymaking, music, champagne cork popping, and singing *Auld Lang Syne* into the new year morning and beyond, while dancing to rock and roll, George Gershwin, a graceful European waltz, or sensual tango. Children try to stay awake to bring in the new year with their parents, but the Sandman calls the children's name too soon and they are asleep before the ratchety sounding noise makers are shaken. Others choose a quiet evening at home playing cards or games with close friends, watching old movies on the VCR, and making a light meal and drinking a glass of champagne or sparkling cider at midnight to toast in the new year.

One celebration in Seattle is at the Seattle Center where there is a gala for those who want to dress in their best clothes, and other parties for those who don't mind celebrating outside, dressed in warm clothes. The Space Needle elevator takes the last few moments of the year to travel to the top of the Needle to set off the flashing lights of the new year's date at the magic stroke of twelve midnight. Then the fireworks begin their blazing glory. Not as elaborate as Fourth of July, it is still an impressive sight to see at the start of the new year. In New York City it's the Ball dropping in Times Square. Happy New Year!!

Today the celebrations are much the same in Norway as they are here. Making as much noise as possible, perhaps to frighten all those evil spirits away is a tradition over many centuries. In some homes the custom continues of making predictions for the new year from molten lead or the wax of the Christmas candles poured onto a flat surface and hardened into magical shapes. *Godt nyttår*!!

# New Year's Day / *Nyttårsdag*

January 1 is the beginning of a new year and hopefully a prosperous one. New Year's resolutions are spoken or written and sometimes broken not long after. The symbol on the calendar stick is an hour glass. According to the oral tradition associated with this day in Norway, clear weather meant a good year. Red clouds would mean war. Snow or frost on the trees would mean a good crop of grain. In the western part of Norway, onshore winds meant a good year for fishing. Mild weather during the month of January meant the corn would freeze and the hay would be rotten. For Christians, it is the celebration of the circumcision of Jesus and his naming day.

In the Pacific Northwest, the day is filled with watching parades and football games on the television. The Rose Bowl, Orange Bowl, Citrus Bowl, Cotton Bowl, and the Sugar Bowl provide the football junky with games from morning until late in the night.

The Rose Bowl is considered the queen of the Bowl games, but it originally started in 1890 as a community parade and picnic. Prizes were given for the most beautifully decorated buggies and tally-hos. Today floats, bands, and equestrians are part of the Pasadena Tournament of Roses Parade. All floats are completely covered with natural materials with the best use of roses weighing the most heavily in the judging of the entries. The first football game was played in 1902, but was replaced by a polo match the next year. Other athletic events followed through the years until 1916 when football became a permanent part of the Tournament of Roses.

Being staunch University of Washington Husky fans, the Rose Bowl represents the Pacific-10 teams and is rarely missed on New Year's Day, my mother's birthday. Family and friends watch the game together, joining in a birthday dinner of duck cooked southern style with all the trimmings, which is delayed only if the Huskies are playing.

# Epiphany / *Helligtrekongersdag*

 The Epiphany celebration on January 6 commemorates the coming of the Magi to Christ. The Magi are often referred to as the three wise men from the East called Casper, Melchior, and Balthazar. It is celebrated as the first appearance of Christ to people who were not Jewish. The calendar stick symbol represents these three wise men. According to folk belief, whatever the weather was like on this day, for the next three weeks it would remain the same. In Norway it is also called *trettendedagen* or the thirteenth day of Christmas while it is considered the twelfth day of Christmas in the United States and England.

The story of the Magi was written by Matthew, who according to tradition, was a tax collector before following Christ. It is generally believed to be written between the years of AD 70 and 90.

Matthew 2: 1–12

> *In the time of King Herod, after Jesus was born in Bethlehem of Judea, wise men from the East came to Jerusalem, asking, "Where is the child who has been born king of the Jews? For we observed his star at its rising, and have come to pay him homage." When King Herod heard this, he was frightened, and all Jerusalem with him; and calling together all the chief priests and scribes of the people, he inquired of them where the Messiah was to be born. They told him, "In Bethlehem of Judea; for so it has been written by the prophet:*
> > *'And you, Bethlehem, in the land of Judah,*
> > *are by no means least among the rulers of Judah;*
> > *for from you shall come a ruler,*
> > *who is to shepherd my people Israel.'"*
>
> *Then Herod secretly called for the wise men and learned from them the exact time when the star had appeared. Then he sent them to Bethlehem, saying, "Go and search diligently for the child; and when you have found him, bring me word so that I may also go and pay him homage." When they had heard the king, they set out; and there, ahead of them, went the star that they had seen at its rising, until it stopped over the place where the child was. When they saw that the star had stopped, they were overwhelmed with joy. On entering the house, they saw the child with Mary his mother; and they knelt down and paid him homage. Then, opening their treasure chests; they offered him gifts of gold, frankincense, and myrrh. And having been warned in a dream not to return to Herod, they left for their own country by another road.*[1]

*Matteus 2, 1–12*

> *Da Jesus var født i Betlehem i Judea på kong Herodes' tid, kom det noen vismenn fra Østerland til Jerusalem og spurte: "Hvor er jødenes konge som nå er født? Vi har sett hans stjerne i Østen, og er kommet for å tilbe ham." Da kong Herodes fikk høre det, ble han urolig, og hele Jerusalem med ham. Han kalte sammen alle overprestene og de skriftlærde i folket og spurte dem ut om hvor Messias skulle fødes. "I Betlehem i Judea," svarte de, "for slik står det skrevet hos profeten:*
>
> > *'Du Betlehem i Juda land,*
> > *du er slett ikke den minste av høvdingbyene i Juda!*
> > *Fra deg skal det gå ut en høvding*
> > *som skal være hyrde for Israel, mitt folk.'"*
>
> *Da kalte Herodes i all stillhet vismennene til seg og spurte dem nøye ut om tiden da stjernen hadde vist seg. Så sendte han dem av sted til Betlehem og sa: "Gå og få nøyaktig greie på dette barnet; og når dere har funnet det, så si fra til meg, forat jeg også kan komme og tilbe det!" Da de hadde hørt kongens ord, dro de av sted, og se: Stjernen som de hadde sett i Østen, gikk foran dem, helt til den ble stående stille over huset der hvor barnet var. Da de så stjernen, ble de over all måte glade; og de gikk inn i huset og fant barnet hos moren, Maria. Da kastet de seg ned og tilba det, og så åpnet de skrinene sine og bar fram gaver: gull, røkelse og myrra.*
>
> *Men Gud varslet dem i en drøm om at de ikke skulle dra tilbake til Herodes; derfor tok de en annen vei hjem til sitt eget land.*[1]

Epiphany is traditionally the end of the Christmas season in the United States. New Year's parties continue to occur and Christmas trees may still be spreading joy and light into our living rooms until the tree dries out too much. Then all is swept, vacuumed, dusted, and put away until the next year.

---

[1]Scripture quotation from *Det Nye Testamente*. Oslo: Det Norske Bibelselskaps Forlag, 1967. Pages 10–11.

# Saint Knut's Day
## The Twentieth Day of Christmas / *Tjuendedagen*

*Tjuendedagen*, January 13, is the twentieth day of Christmas and the last day of the holiday season in Norway. It is also known as St. Knut's Day for the Danish Duke of Slesvig, Knut Lavard. He was murdered by his political enemy and cousin, Magnus, on January 7, 1131, to prevent Knut from becoming King of Denmark. Several days later on January 14, Knut's son, Valdemar, was born and later became King of Denmark. Many years after Knut's death, his celebration day was moved from January 7 to January 13. At the place where Knut was killed, a spring came forth and a chapel was built.

It is believed January 13 was the *jul* feast of pre-Christian times as it was *midtvinter* or the middle of winter in Norway. January 7 was called *eldbjørgdag* then and was a day of fire worship. King Haakon the Good, King of Norway from AD 934?–961, was raised in England as the foster son of Athelstan, King of England from 925–940. There Haakon became a Christian. When he came to Norway, *"He made a law that Yule should be holden the same time as Christian men hold it, and that every man at that tide should brew a meal of malt or pay money else, and keep holy tide while Yule lasted. But aforetime was Yule holden on Hogmanay night, that is to say, mid-winter night, and Yule was holden for three nights."*[1] *Jul* was then moved to its current date in December with Christmas.

On *Tjuendedagen* a much loved phrase can be heard throughout the day is, *"Tjuende dag Knut danses jula ut."* "On the Twentieth day Knut dances Christmas out." By now all the Christmas food needs to be eaten and the Christmas beer must be drunk. The symbol on the calendar stick is a down-turned drinking horn. Christmas and all the spirits are swept out by cleaning the entire house. With all the windows and doors open, the family uses sticks to knock on the walls while saying, "Out goes the *jul*." A farewell song is sung to the Christmas tree as it goes outside. In the days long ago, people went from farm to farm to chase away all the unwelcome spirits which might still be lingering around home and help the neighbors finish the *juleøl*.

> *Tjuende dag Knut danses jula ut*
> On the Twentieth day Knut dances Christmas out

> *Hilsen fra Norge og Ballard*
> Greetings from Norway and Ballard

> *Gledelig jul og godt nyttår*
> Merry Christmas and Happy New Year

---

[1]Sturluson, Snorri. *The Stories of the Kings of Norway called the Round World (Heimskringla)*. Done into English out of the Icelandic by William Morris and Eiríkr Magnússon. London: Bernard Quaritch, 1893. Vol. 1, page 165.

# Index / *Indeks*

251